For Michael, who helps run all the things. This is truly the "family business" and I couldn't do it without you. And for the readers who have helped me live this magical life.

The Widow Wager

(THE NOTORIOUS FLYNNS BOOK 3)

By

Jess Michaels

THE WIDOW WAGER
The Notorious Flynns Book 3

Copyright © Jesse Petersen, 2015

ISBN-13: 978-1511418430
ISBN-10: 1511418435

All rights reserved. This book or any portion thereof may not be reproduced or used in any manner whatsoever without the express written permission of the publisher except for the use of brief quotations in a book review.

>For more information, contact Jess Michaels
>www.AuthorJessMichaels.com
>PO Box 814, Cortaro, AZ 85652-0814
>
>To contact the author:
>Email: Jess@AuthorJessMichaels.com
>Twitter www.twitter.com/JessMichaelsbks
>Facebook: www.facebook.com/JessMichaelsBks

Jess Michaels raffles a FREE Kindle or Amazon gift certificate EVERY month to members of her newsletter, so sign up on her website:
http://www.authorjessmichaels.com/join-the-jess-michaels-newsletter/

CHAPTER ONE

July 1814

Crispin Flynn came awake in throbbing, painful inches. His head burned like it was on fire and his stomach churned with bile and whatever God-awful spirits remained there from the previous night's revelry.

Or had it been revelry? In truth, he couldn't remember much after the moment where he got on his horse and rode out from his home, hell-bent on drink and women and gambling and…well, utter self-destruction. None of that sounded as fun as *revelry*, especially not in the cold light of morning, which he could feel burning against his still-shut eyelids.

He hesitated to open those eyes, firstly, so he could avoid that light a little longer, but, secondly, because he was never certain anymore where he would find himself after a night out. He had awoken in gutters, in his carriage, and once in the bed of an obliging duchess with whose husband he had only just avoided a duel.

And the third reason he avoided opening his eyes was that once he was alert all the troubles of his world came rushing back, crushing him and drowning him in their wake.

Yet he could not pretend he was dead forever, so he gingerly opened one bleary eye. He flinched at the burning light of the sun that pounded down on him from the window he faced.

He was not in a bed, but on his settee. He recognized the brocade fabric that his mother had chosen for the chaise what seemed like a lifetime ago. He let out a sigh of relief. At least if he had managed to stumble home, he could not have done too much damage.

He opened his other eye and swallowed back the rush of vomit that greeted him. His body would punish him for what he had done to it, but it was worth it to turn off his mind for a few blissful hours.

Slowly, he moved, inching his way onto his back. Every muscle in his body hurt, which meant he had probably danced on a table, fallen off a horse or gotten into a fistfight. On a bad night, it could be all three. Certainly he would hear about it though if he had truly done any damage. He always did. He also always paid the tab without argument or question and with whatever semblance of an apology he could muster for the sins he committed when he was out of his right mind.

He rolled a little further and froze. He could see his bed about ten feet away from the settee. And it was not unoccupied. A lump was under his covers. A woman-sized-and-shaped lump.

He groaned. Now he was going to have to kick some lightskirt out of his house. Always entirely awkward.

At the sound of his groan, the lump spun around to face him, and Crispin froze. The lady-shaped lump had the most beautiful face he had seen in years. She had bright gray eyes filled with intelligence and a slender face with full, pink lips. Her hair was red too. Damn, but it would be. He'd never been able to resist a redheaded woman who offered to perch herself on his knee.

He sat up. "Morning, love," he drawled, happy he didn't cast up his accounts or pass out thanks to the wildly spinning room.

She said nothing, but also sat bolt upright to reveal she was fully clothed in a wrinkled green gown. She pushed herself across the bed, as far away from him as she could get.

Crispin covered his forehead with one hand and tried to maintain some of his dignity at least. He attempted a smile.

"If I owe you blunt, you can collect it from the butler on your way out," he said.

Her eyes went wide at first, then narrowed to angry slits that barely revealed the sparking gray beneath.

"I am *not* a lightskirt, Mr. Flynn," she snapped.

Crispin was distracted for a moment by the musical quality of her voice, which even when angry was probably the prettiest thing he'd heard in an age. But then he realized what she'd said in that beautiful voice, and he stiffened.

"Aren't you?" he asked.

She folded her arms. "Certainly not."

He cleared his throat and managed to get to his feet without toppling over sideways. It seemed he had succeeded in getting himself into quite a pickle, indeed, last night. This one might be harder to extract himself from than the usual paying for a broken vase or returning a stolen phaeton.

"Damn. See here, miss, I was deep in my cups last night and I may have said or done things I don't recall."

She was watching him still, wary and seemingly ready to run. "You must think me very stupid," she all but growled.

He shook his head. "Honestly, miss, I do not remember a damn thing." He looked at her a little closer. "Seeing you, I wish I did, actually."

Her brow wrinkled and a fetching pink color filled her cheeks at the compliment. Then she tilted her head. "Are you being truthful, then? Do you really not remember last night?"

A sinking feeling worked its way through Crispin. A feeling that screamed he had really done it this time.

"No," he said softly.

She held his gaze for a moment, as if she were reading him. As if she were determining his honesty with just a sweep of her stare. He shifted beneath the intimate quality of the exercise and then watched as she rose to her feet. She had as pretty a figure as she did a face, with a lovely bosom and the hint of a flare of her hips as her wrinkled gown fluttered around her.

"Then I suppose I should start by saying good morning, Mr. Flynn," she said, but did not extend her hand. "My name is Gemma. I'm your wife."

Crispin's stomach churned higher and he slumped back onto the settee with a moan. "No." He shook his head. "No, that cannot be true."

She pursed her lips. "I'm afraid it is very much true. We married in the middle of the night. Despite my protests."

Crispin jerked his stare back to her. *Protests*? Had he forced this woman? She was dressed now, but that didn't mean he hadn't. Great God, he would never forgive himself.

"You are my wife," he said slowly.

She nodded, her jaw set with strength even as tears sparkled faintly in her eyes. "Yes," she said on a gasp.

He swallowed hard. "Gemma. Is that what you said your name was?"

"Yes," she whispered a second time.

He nodded. It was a pretty name to go with her pretty face. A pretty face that seemed to entirely hate him, which gave him even more pause about what he'd done in his stupor.

"Gemma, I need you to tell me exactly what happened last night." He shook his head. "I need to remember."

CHAPTER TWO

One Night Before

Crispin staggered as he retook his seat at the gaming table and set a full bottle of scotch beside him. There was a tiny voice inside of him that screamed at him to stop. But, as always, he ignored that voice. Lately it had gotten smaller and smaller, as if his conscience was finally being drowned in booze.

Good riddance to bad rubbish.

He looked around the room as the cards were dealt out by another player. It was a ragged place, indeed, not like the Donville Masquerade where he used to spend his time. But he didn't go there anymore. Not since his sister had married the proprietor just a few weeks before.

Annabelle had sacrificed herself for him. Yet another life he had destroyed. Yet another reason to take a long, burning swig from the bottle before him. He did so with relish and then shoved thoughts of his family from his mind. He already knew how much they disapproved and likely despised him. There was no use lingering on it.

He focused instead on the cards before him. He didn't have a good hand, in truth, but he examined his comrades, just three other men, before he placed a bet. He didn't know any of them well, just from gambling with them. Two were thugs, dangerous men from London's underground, but the third was a knight or some such thing. Sir...Oswald Quinn, he believed it was? The man was always loose with his cards and lost more than he won.

Which meant perhaps Crispin would stay a while, try his luck. He pushed some blunt into the center of the table and grinned at his companion.

An hour later, the other two men had faded away, but Quinn had stayed and the pile of money between them had traded back and forth several times, though at present it was all on the knight's side of the table. Crispin tried to lift his head and focus on his cards, but the empty bottle, which had now been joined by half of a second, made it harder to do so.

"I'll put it all in the center," Sir Oswald said with a thin smile as he shoved the blunt in front of Crispin.

He stared at the pile of money and back at his cards, which were spinning wildly in his hand.

"You know I can't call you," Crispin muttered. "I don't have enough."

Quinn leaned back in his chair, tucking his cards into his jacket pocket as he did so. He watched Crispin closely. "Yes," he finally said, "Your lack of blunt makes it a difficult hand, doesn't it?"

Crispin shrugged and the movement nearly put him out of his chair. "So what do you want? My phaeton? My horse?"

Sir Oswald laughed. "No, thank you. I'm certain they are both very fine, but they won't get me out of a particular bind I'm currently in."

"Which is?" Crispin said with a hiccup. He asked only because it seemed expected that he would, not because he was particularly interested. He was more interested in ending this hand and limping home.

"I have a daughter, Mr. Flynn," the other man said. "Two actually, but the elder is my current problem. She was married and she...well, her husband is dead, that is all. But she wasn't settled well and now she has become a drain on my household.

Not to mention that the circumstances of her husband's passing have made her less marriageable than she was the first time around."

"What do you want me to do about it?"

Sir Oswald leaned over the table. "If you lose, you marry her."

Crispin's eyes went wide. He had to be very drunk and misunderstanding. Or else this was a very strange dream. Certainly this man couldn't be serious.

"Marry your daughter?" Crispin repeated.

Sir Oswald nodded slowly. "Immediately." He leaned over and poured a drink from Crispin's bottle. He shoved the glass toward him. "What do you say?"

"And if I win?" Crispin asked.

"You get back everything you lost tonight, of course," Sir Oswald said as he motioned to the pile of blunt. "And then some."

Crispin downed the drink he'd been offered and tried to think. Thinking was so hard right now, but he had to do it. It was a lot of money on the table and if he was honest with himself, he could use it. The past few weeks since his sister's marriage had been a blur of guilt, wild bets and lost money.

But if he lost…

But he couldn't lose. He stared at his cards again. It was a winning hand, for certain.

"Fine," he said. "I'll take the bet."

Sir Oswald's face didn't move, but Crispin saw his eyes brighten enough that he questioned his decision. But it was too late now. He set his cards down so the other man could see.

And then Sir Oswald's face did change. He grinned as he set down his own hand.

With a grunt, Crispin turned his head and cast up his accounts in the nearest waste receptacle.

Gemma stared up at the cracked ceiling above her bed, just as she had every night for the past year since she'd been forced home after the death of her husband, the Earl of Laurelcross. Once upon a time, she had stared at that crack and imagined it was a slim opening to another world, a place where fairies danced and trolls made the tea.

Now she was older and knew the crack was really just a symptom of the nightmare that was her family circumstance. There would be no dancing fairies to come out and take her away.

"If only," she murmured as she yanked the pillow out from under her head and pressed it over her face. The dark warmth was comforting on some level, but she knew it wouldn't last. At some point, she would have to come out of this cocoon and back into a very uncertain real world.

"How did I get here?" she muttered into the pillow.

But she knew the answer to that question. She tugged the pillow away and gulped a breath of cooler air. She was here, back in her old childhood room, living under her father's roof and rules, because of what she'd done. She'd put herself here the moment she caused her husband's death.

She deserved this. This was her punishment. As were the sleepless nights, the loneliness, the anxiety that seemed to dog her every move.

She could have gone on, chasing her faults all over the room through the long night. Certainly, she had done just that many times, but she was interrupted in her reverie by a huge crash that echoed through the empty halls.

She jolted into an upright position and clutched her pillow against her chest. She could hear faint sounds from downstairs, muffled voices, but she didn't know the source. Were they being robbed?

"A foolish home to choose, since we have almost nothing," she muttered as she got up and began to search for something in the room that would make a good weapon. She could take it to Mary's room and wait to see if anyone would come for them when the intruders realized that there was nothing of value in the house. Her younger sister's innocence was likely the only thing anyone could barter with.

And Gemma would die defending that if she was forced to do so.

She sighed as she looked at the candlestick on the mantel. It was the best she would do, she feared. Without prying the half-melted candle loose, she swept it up. She began to move for the door but was stopped by a light knock from outside.

Did blackguards knock? They would be very polite if they did.

"Who is it?" she asked, hands shaking as she shifted the candlestick into a bludgeoning position.

"It's Kate, Lady Laurelcross."

Gemma relaxed. Kate was her maid, though she didn't know why the girl would come all the way through the house from the servants' quarters if someone was robbing them.

She opened the door and found her maid in her dressing gown, hair askew and eyes bleary with sleep.

"What is it?" she whispered, hearing the voices more clearly now. One sounded like…

Her father.

Kate shifted. "I'm sorry to wake you, my lady," her maid said. "But—but your father insisted."

Gemma pressed her lips together and lowered her candlestick. "In his cups, is he?"

Kate shook her head. "Not this time, my lady, no. But he…he wants to see you. He insists that you get dressed and join him and the other gentleman in the parlor."

Gemma stepped back and motioned her maid into the room. "My father wants to see me in the middle of the night?" she asked, shutting the door behind Kate and leaning against it. Suddenly the exhaustion that would not allow her to sleep hit her all at once at the thought of facing her father.

Kate nodded. "Come, I'll choose a dress."

Gemma shook her head. "I just don't understand. And you

say there is another gentleman? Who is he?"

Her maid took Gemma's candlestick and swiftly lit the wick. She set it aside and opened the dresser, where she found a gown.

"I didn't see," Kate said as she helped Gemma change with swift efficiency. "He sent Williams to fetch me, and you know the butler keeps his lips tight."

"So a mystery caller, loud voices, crashing sounds. I don't like it."

Kate shrugged as she motioned Gemma into a chair and swiftly pulled her hair away into a loose bun. "Neither do I, but there is little choice, isn't there? Your father will have his way."

"Always." Gemma squeezed her eyes shut. Kate had been with her a long time and she knew the truth as well as Gemma did, herself, though the servant would likely only ever say it when it was just the two of them.

As Kate stepped away, Gemma pushed to her feet and looked at herself in the mirror. She wasn't exactly ballroom ready, but this was as good as could be done under such strange circumstances. She could only hope that whatever awaited her, she could bear it with some semblance of dignity.

Sometimes that was all she had left.

CHAPTER THREE

Gemma stood outside the parlor, staring at the half-open door. Inside she heard her father talking incessantly, his voice rising and falling, and frowned. He only spoke like that when he was very nervous or very proud. Either one of those things, coupled with her being called here in the middle of the night, was not a good sign.

Especially since her father's guest hadn't spoken a word in the few moments she had stood composing herself in the hall.

With a gasp of breath, she pushed the door open and stepped into the parlor. Her father stood at the mantel, leaning there with a cat-in-the-birdcage grin that made her stomach turn. His eyes lit up as she entered and her knees almost buckled.

What had he been up to?

Immediately, she turned her gaze to the other man in the room. He sat half-slumped in a chaise, supporting his chin with a fist. The light from the fireplace hit him full on and she gasped.

She knew this man, at least by reputation. He was Crispin Flynn, the youngest son of one of the most notorious families in all of London. A family only very recently elevated by the elder brother's inheritance of a dukedom. But everyone knew that Crispin Flynn had not calmed with the boon as his brother had.

He was wilder than ever, if gossip was to be believed. Though she knew from personal experience that gossip was often very much *not* true.

She examined the man closer. He was just as handsome as others in her acquaintance had sometimes whispered about. At present, he was quite undone. His hair stuck up at odd angles, his eyes were bleary and his shirt was half-untucked.

"There she is," her father said, tearing her attention back to him and his smug tone. "My daughter."

"What is going on, Father?" she asked, tearing her gaze away from their guest. "It is the middle of the night. What could you possibly want from me?"

She was shocked her voice could sound so calm when she trembled with anxiety. It was a means of coping she had developed of late and was very happy to possess.

Her father flicked his head toward their visitor. "This is Crispin Flynn."

She glanced briefly at Flynn again. His eyes were unfocused, she doubted he was fully aware of anything happening at present.

"I—hello," she offered weakly. He only watched her without response.

"Mr. Flynn and I were gaming tonight, over at Rickman's."

Now Gemma's knees began to shake. "Oh, Father," she breathed. "That place is terrible. You are better than that."

His eyes narrowed at her admonishment. "You do not tell me what to do, girlie."

She pressed her lips together before she said, "What did you lose?"

There was so little left for her father to barter that she shuddered to think what the next humiliation would be. He had been out of control for years, but it had come to a head when Gemma had been forced to return to her family home without a settlement after her husband's death.

So this was all just one more punishment.

"You misunderstand," Sir Oswald drawled, that smug expression darkening his face once more. God, how she hated and feared it. "I didn't lose tonight, Gemma. I won."

Gemma blinked, confusion wiping her mind clean. "I—what do you mean? You won? Then why do you call me to you? You can gloat tomorrow at a decent hour."

She almost turned on her heel and left the room, but her father barked, "The wager was about you."

Gemma's jaw dropped open and her gaze darted between the two men. Flynn was sitting up straighter now, still merely watching her without comment.

"Me?" she repeated on the barest of breaths.

"You will go with Mr. Flynn tonight, Gemma. This moment. You are to be his bride."

Gemma couldn't breathe as she staggered away from her father, across the room, until her legs hit the edge of a table and she nearly toppled to the ground. She gripped the wooden surface, trying to think, trying to breathe, trying to wake up from this nightmare.

"What?"

"You heard me," her father said, his voice soft and impassive, as if he were telling her an order he'd made for the household.

"But—but you said you won the wager with Mr. Flynn," she stammered. "You—you said that he lost."

"And by losing, he is forced to take you from my hands," her father said, his voice dripping with the contempt he hadn't hidden from her since her return to his home months ago.

His words sunk in and Gemma choked on a sob that broke from her throat unbidden. Emotions bombarded her, nearly taking her to her knees. She felt shame for how low she had sunk, how low her family now was…she felt pain that this was to be her fate.

But mostly she felt anger. Anger that her father would betray her in this manner, anger that Crispin Flynn was such a cad that he would accept such a horrifying, ungentlemanly wager. They were two of a kind, bastards who only cared for themselves.

"No," she whispered.

Her father looked at her in surprise. "I beg your pardon?"

She moved toward him, hands clenched. "I said *no*! You sold me once, Father, but I will *never* be sold again. I will not marry this man."

She thought she saw Flynn's face light up a fraction at her words, the first expression that had come over him since her arrival in the room, but her father distracted her from that observation.

"You dare defy me?"

"Oh yes," she breathed. "I *will* defy you, consequences be damned."

Her father moved on her in that moment, face red and fisted hand raised. To her surprise, the sleepy form of their visitor flashed with movement and suddenly Crispin Flynn stood between them, his hand pressed firmly into her father's chest to keep him from whatever intent he had held in his angry heart.

Gemma stared up at her...what was he, anyway? Her protector in this moment, her tormentor hours before when he agree to her father's terms? Her intended, even against her will?

He was bloody handsome.

The door to the chamber opened behind them and all three pivoted to see the intruder. Gemma's stomach turned. There in the doorway stood her younger sister. Mary clutched her robe tightly around herself as she stared at the group in surprise.

"What is going on?" her sister asked, wide eyes finding Gemma behind the men.

Flynn's gaze flitted briefly to Mary, but then returned to Gemma. It was a surprise, really. Mary was so much prettier, with her delicate features and darker hair. Yet this man had dismissed her with a mere flick of his stare.

"Go back to bed, Mary," Gemma said, backing away from the distraction that was Crispin Flynn. "Everything is fine."

Her sister opened her mouth to argue, but before she could say something, their father moved on her. Gemma stared at his suddenly lit up eyes and the way he smiled.

"No, no, Mary. Come in. Join us." He slipped his arm around Mary's slender shoulders and dragged her forward to stand beside Gemma. Without a word, Mary reached out to take her sister's hand, trying to find comfort that Gemma wasn't certain she could offer in the face of the surprising and upsetting events of the night.

"I was just explaining to your ungrateful wretch of a sister how she is to wed this fine gentleman," her father continued.

Mary made a strangled sound in her throat and her grip on Gemma's hand became tighter. "Wed!" she repeated. "No, Papa, you cannot mean that."

"But I most definitely do," he drawled, his hard smile once again falling on Gemma. "It will happen, girl. Tonight. I have already arranged for a special license."

Gemma's lips parted. "A special license?" She shook her head. "That means…that means you have had this planned for some time."

His eyebrows lifted and he inclined his head slightly. "Someone had to make you worthwhile."

"So you intended to wager with any man…no, you would have had to know your mark." She spun on Flynn. "Did you know his intentions, Mr. Flynn?"

Flynn blinked a few times, but the bleariness in his stare didn't clear. "I didn't know anything." He hiccupped.

She squeezed her eyes shut. She tended to believe him. After all, aside from his intervention when he thought her father might commit violence, he wasn't interacting in this situation in the slightest. It seemed he was a victim, perhaps not as much as she was since he had made his own choices, but a victim nonetheless.

She returned her attention to her father, still piecing

together his repugnant plan bit by bit. "So does Mr. Flynn lose regularly? Fall deep into his cups like this?"

Her father shrugged and Mary let out another cry. "Oh, Papa!"

Gemma ignored her sister's outburst. Mary might be ashamed or saddened by this turn of events, but Gemma was far beyond that. She was enraged. She had never been so angry in her life.

She gritted her teeth, hoping to maintain some dignity rather than screech at her father. "You *planned* to get him drunk and make a bet with him where you knew he would lose. Where you knew he would be forced to take me as his bride." When her father said nothing, she shook her head. "Do you hate me so much?"

He folded his arms. "I don't think of you enough to hate you, Gemma."

She flinched despite all attempts to stay serene.

"You don't mean that," Mary whispered, gripping Gemma's hand with both of her own now. "You are both angry and—"

"There is no need to make peace," Gemma interrupted. She never took her eyes off her father. "We are beyond that now."

Mary shut her mouth.

"You had a chance to elevate us," her father growled. "And you failed. This is the only way to get rid of you, bring in an income to this household, and perhaps your sister will have better luck."

She felt Mary stiffen at her side and her stomach turned. Her father would barter with his youngest daughter just as he had with her.

"You cannot be serious," her sister cried. "Please Papa, reconsider. You cannot truly mean to sell Gemma off to this…this…drunken stranger."

Gemma watched as her father's lips thinned in anger. He stepped closer. "You will shut your mouth, Mary Elizabeth, or you will not be pleased with the results."

Gemma pulled her closer. "Don't threaten her."

"Please, we must all be calm," Mary pleaded. "This isn't happening."

Their father glared at them. "You two, thick as thieves. You want to save her, Mary?"

Mary nodded swiftly. "Yes. Stop this, I beg of you."

"Then perhaps you should be the one to take the bargain," their father snapped.

"No!" Gemma cried, drawing her sister behind her, as if she could protect her. That was a joke. There was no protecting herself, let alone anyone else. She had lived in terror of what Mary's future would hold for years.

"One of you will marry Mr. Flynn tonight," her father ground out through obviously clenched teeth. "The choice is up to you, Gemma."

Gemma bit the inside of her lip until she could taste blood. She stared at Crispin Flynn, still standing across the room, silent in the face of all that was happening around him. She stared over her shoulder at her sister. Mary was an innocent, still filled with the belief that things could work out, that she could marry happily and well, and live a joyful life.

And finally she allowed her gaze to settle on her father. "I hate you," she whispered, meaning every word.

"Gemma," Mary shook her hand away and moved to stand before her sister. She gripped Gemma's arms, her fingers digging into the cloth of her gown. "Please, no. No, don't do this."

"It's all right," Gemma said, even though they both knew that was wrong. A lie. She stiffened her spine. "I'll do it."

Her father's smirk made her want to slap him, but she ignored it instead and looked at Flynn again. His face was drawn, not with anger, but something else. He swayed slightly, his hand tightened on the chair nearby to settle himself.

"Please, Gemma," Mary whispered. "You have already given up so much."

Gemma squeezed her eyes shut for a moment before she cupped her sister's face. "And that is why I will do this. You have never...you don't know what a marriage would be like. I couldn't do that to you."

Tears began to stream down her sister's face and Mary wrapped her arms around her. Her slim body trembled as she wept into Gemma's shoulder.

"Hush," Gemma soothed her, stroking a hand over her hair. "It will not be as bad as all that."

Of course she didn't believe that. Flynn had a bit of a reputation, one of scandal and sin. She had to believe he was capable of using her body and soul. Her life could be one of fear and torment.

She could only hope his being drunk would save her rather than put her in even more danger.

"Mary, go to your room," her father said behind them, his voice sharp. "That is enough of this foolishness."

The sisters parted and Mary stared at their father. "I cannot leave her."

"You will," he snapped. "Go to your room."

Gemma squeezed her arm. "Just go, Mary."

Her sister shook her head and touched Gemma's face once more. "Send me word as soon as you can. Please. Please. I love you."

Gemma bit back a sob. She didn't want Mary's last look to be of Gemma hysterical, even though that was exactly how she felt at the moment. She was controlling herself for the sake of Mary, of not letting her father or her now-future husband see her terror...but inside she was swiftly unraveling.

Once her sister had departed the chamber, she gasped for breath, turning away from the men and leaning on the sideboard. "What will happen now?" she asked.

"Now we leave for your marriage," her father said, almost benignly.

She spun to face him. "Now? In the middle of the night?"

He nodded.

She covered her cheeks with her suddenly cold hands. "But my things, Kate—"

"It will all be handled."

"Word will spread," she continued. "People will know and it will—"

"We will leave *now*."

The harshness of her father's tone silenced her and she ground her teeth together before she exited the room, entering the foyer with as much dignity as she could muster.

Her fate was sealed. And there was nothing she could do but pray that she would wake up from this nightmare. Even though she knew she never would.

CHAPTER FOUR

Crispin lifted his throbbing head from his hands and stared at Gemma. She was sitting on the edge of one of the chairs beside his fire, her back straight and her face devoid of emotion. It was only the slight trembling of her lip as she told him what had happened the night before that gave away any of her fears.

"My God," he muttered, self-loathing rising in him.

Of course, hating himself was the normal place he lived—he was accustomed to it. This, though…this was magnified by the look of disdain on this woman's face. By the fact that he had no idea what he had done to her.

"And then what happened?" He watched her face for a flinch, for pain.

Instead, she glared at him. "We all drove in your carriage to the home of some fat, smelly vicar who married us in what must be the shortest and worst marriage ceremony in history. I cried and you…"

She trailed off and Crispin rose to his feet. "What did I do?"

"I cannot believe you truly don't remember what happened," she whispered.

He shook his head. Neither did he, honestly. Of course, huge stretches of blank time were becoming more usual for him. Now he was staring at the ultimate consequence of his bad behavior.

"You said nothing except what was expected of you. You said nothing at all. You could have protested, you could have stopped this...but you said *nothing*."

Her voice lifted on the last word and she sucked in a breath as she attempted to calm herself. He could hear her hatred and her rage with each ragged exhalation of her breath. And he deserved it all.

Crispin allowed her the effort a moment before he softly asked, "And after?"

"We came here and my father hustled us to this room." She stared at him, expression unreadable.

Crispin's stomach turned. "And?"

"And what?" she asked.

He squeezed his eyes shut. "You are a widow, yes? You must know what I'm asking. Did I touch you? Did I...did I *force* you to do something you didn't want to do?"

Surprise lit up in her dove gray eyes. "I—are you asking if we consummated the marriage?"

"I'm asking if I did something I cannot take back," he said. "I'm asking if I hurt you."

Her full lips parted a fraction, but then her face hardened back to the mask of disgust and anger. "You did hurt me," she said, "But to answer your question, you never touched me."

He sagged in relief back onto the settee. "Thank God."

Her nostrils flared. "Do you often take advantage of women while in your cups?"

He jerked his face toward her. Now her anger was joined by a deeper fear that stabbed him in the heart.

"Never," he reassured her. "I have never forced any woman to do anything, I promise you."

"Then why so much fear about me?" she asked.

He shook his head. "I have also never married a woman in the middle of the night. And with such contempt and loathing on your face, such fear when you rolled over and saw I was awake, I just...I wasn't certain that I hadn't gone too far at last."

She folded her arms. "You don't think that taking part in this scheme with my father to force our union is going too far?"

He cleared his throat. "You have a point there, Gemma."

"Lady Laurelcross," she corrected coldly.

He arched a brow. So her late husband had been titled. He hadn't known that. Of course, he didn't know anything about this woman before him. His wife, apparently.

"Not Lady Laurelcross anymore, I fear," he said gently.

Her face crumpled and tears welled up in her eyes. She struggled against them admirably, but her misery still clung to every frown, every tear that sparkled on her lashes but did not fall. Misery he had caused this lovely stranger by his wild, immature actions.

"However, since you do not feel I have earned the right to call you by your given name, a fact I do not refute," he said, "I am happy to address you more formally. My lady, I am sorry."

She drew back at the simple, yet heartfelt apology that came from his lips. She examined him closely.

"Are you, Mr. Flynn?"

Crispin got back to his feet and paced away from her. At this moment, she despised him and there was no getting around that. His words to her meant nothing, perhaps because in her account there had been so few of them so far.

Great God, how was this possible?

"Mr. Flynn?" she asked, and he realized he had been silent for far too long.

"I need to think," he said, scrubbing a hand over his face. His head still throbbed, but he did his best to ignore it. "This cannot be legal."

Behind him, she let out a rather unladylike snort and he found she had taken a seat beside his fire. She was watching him still, that strange focus burning into him when he turned to look at her.

"I'm certain it is not legal," she admitted, her voice as icy as a winter wind. "But does it truly matter?"

"What do you mean?" he asked, his chest beginning to tighten.

She shrugged. "I know my father. By now he has already begun spreading the word far and wide that we wed last night. I'm certain he used words like *whirlwind courtship* and waxed poetic about you sweeping me away with his happy blessing. No one will believe it, but the rumors will spread, nonetheless."

Bile rose in Crispin's throat, choking him once more. He swallowed hard. "Why? Why would he do this? Why would he create this grand plan to entrap me in a wager? He asked for nothing that I recall. So why would he give you away?"

She flinched at his question, and he wished he could snatch the words back. Damn, but he was a clod sometimes. Why could he not think before he spoke? Or acted? Or drank?

"I'm sorry, my lady," he began.

She held up a hand. "No need for apologies, Mr. Flynn. I know where I stand with my father. I have for years. I am an albatross to him, you see."

Crispin stared at her again, letting his gaze flit over her fine form before he settled on her lovely face. "Why?"

Her lips thinned. "I'm certain if you ask around, you will get some version of the truth."

"I would like to hear your version," he said, folding his arms.

She shook her head. "I would rather not discuss it, Mr. Flynn."

Crispin's first instinct was to push, but considering that this woman had already been pushed so far, perhaps that wasn't the best course of action in the end. Not if he wanted to work this situation out in some amicable way.

"Very well. Then do you know why your father chose me for his trap?"

She tilted her head. "Is that not obvious? Oh, that's right, you don't remember much about last night. Well, come back to my father's home when you are sober and you'll see how shabby it is." She blushed. "How shabby we are. You have money, everyone knows it."

Crispin bit out a sharp burst of laughter at that statement. Money? He'd had it, yes, but lately more of it had bled away than stayed in his coffers. He wasn't destitute, by any means, but he wasn't rich anymore.

Her eyes went wide. "Don't you?"

The panic was clear in her wavering voice and her wide eyes, and for the first time Crispin wondered if she had been more a part of this ruse than she let on. Had *she* wanted to land a rich troublemaker as much as her father did?

"Worried, my lady?"

Her spine stiffened at the obvious implications of that question. "I have been left penniless before, Mr. Flynn," she ground out. "I know what it is like. I'm also damn well aware of the consequences being poor can bring. Like this situation, for example. So excuse me if the idea of going from one empty household to another brings me no joy."

She turned away from him and paced angrily to the window behind his bed. She gripped the curtain edge and peeked outside toward his garden. For a fleeting moment, he wondered what she thought of the tangled mess there.

He shoved those thoughts aside. "My lady, you have no idea of my intentions, my character or my thoughts. Truly, I have no idea of the same when it comes to you. This is a marriage apparently thrust upon us both. But it is not something either of us wanted."

He paused for a moment. This brought him so much to mind of his brother, Rafe, and the marriage he had also been forced to enter. Only Rafe was happy now with his wife. Blissfully happy indeed.

But this was different. This wasn't a marriage contract that couldn't be broken and had to be accepted. This was a likely illegal ceremony performed when he was so drunk he couldn't see straight.

"We can break this," he said. "I'm certain of it."

She laughed bitterly, but didn't turn from the window. "Do what you will, Mr. Flynn. My reputation is already in tatters."

He hesitated at that statement. It was the second time she had made reference to her reputation, and he vaguely remembered her father doing the same in the haze of the previous night.

What exactly had she done that would make such a lovely creature a...how had she put it? An albatross?

There was a light knock at the door, and Gemma spun from the window with a furious blush. Crispin straightened up. "Enter."

The door opened to reveal his butler, Fletcher. The older man shifted uncomfortably as he nodded in acknowledgment to Gemma.

"I'm sorry to disturb, Mr. and Mrs. Flynn," he said. Gemma turned away, her hand gripped at her side. "But Mrs. Flynn's servant has arrived with her things. Where shall I send her?"

"Kate?" Gemma burst out, taking a step toward Fletcher. "Kate is here?"

Crispin was rendered speechless for a moment. For the first time, the woman who was now—if only temporarily—his wife smiled, and it changed her beautiful face entirely. She was lit up by the expression, her pale cheeks pinkening and her gray eyes brighter. If he had thought her beautiful before, that impression was now magnified tenfold.

"Yes," Fletcher said, and even the stern servant seemed to be enthralled by Gemma's light. He was...smiling. Crispin had never seen the old goat smile before. "She is just as anxious to see you, madam. Shall I send her to this chamber?"

Crispin looked down at himself. His clothing was wrinkled and smelled faintly of spirits. He felt sticky and unpleasant all around, and looking at Gemma with her tangled hair and equally wrinkled gown, he couldn't imagine she didn't feel the same.

"Send the girl here," he answered.

Fletcher nodded. "And I will have the staff begin to lay out breakfast. Will an hour suffice for timing?"

"That should be fine."

The servant tossed Gemma another brief nod and then left the room. The moment he was gone, she rushed toward Crispin.

"I've no intention of staying in your chamber, Mr. Flynn—" she began, her words running together as proof of how upset she obviously was.

Crispin raised a hand to stop her. "I will surrender my chamber to you, my lady, as it is the finest in the home. But I do not intend to force my presence upon you, I assure you. I will take another room until we can resolve this…" He sighed. "This utter mess I have created."

She stared at him, silent. Judging, he was fairly certain, though her expression was unreadable.

"Neither of us is at our best at present. It is a confusing and upsetting position for us both," he continued. "I will have a servant draw a bath for you here in the adjoining dressing room while you and your maid reunite. I will do the same in another room. Let us dress and meet for breakfast in the aforementioned hour my butler provided. I'm certain we will both be in a better mind frame then. Is that agreeable?"

Gemma opened and shut her mouth a few times, but finally she nodded. "As agreeable as any of this can be, yes."

"Good."

He moved toward the door and then hesitated. He turned back and found she was still staring at him, watching his every move just as she had been almost the entire time they had been together this morning. Her look of mistrust was quite the same as it had ever been.

"You asked me before if I was truly sorry," he said, choosing his words carefully. "And I want you to know I am. This is an untenable situation, but know that I will do everything in my power to rectify it. You may not put much stake in my promises at present, but I think you will come to see that I keep them."

Her lips parted and her tongue darted out to wet them, making his mind reach for very inappropriate images of her tongue licking other things. He pushed them away with violence.

"Thank you, Mr. Flynn. I hope you prove that to be true."

He nodded and slipped from the room, shutting the door behind himself. He leaned against the barrier for a moment, the events of the morning sinking in.

"What did you do?" he moaned softly. "What the hell did you do?"

Gemma took a long breath. When Crispin Flynn was in the room, awake or not, he seemed to take all the space, all the air, all the attention away from everything else. She wasn't certain if that was because she didn't trust him or if it was because he was so very, very handsome. Even more so when sober than when he had been drunk and silent the night before.

There was a light knock on the door, and she pushed those thoughts aside as Kate stepped inside. Her maid rushed on Gemma, dark hair flying back from her face as she wrapped her arms around her and hugged her hard and long.

"Oh miss," she cooed against Gemma's hair. "I was so afraid for you."

Gemma drew back, smiling to reassure her longtime servant that she was well even if it didn't feel entirely true at present. "I'm sorry."

"You shouldn't apologize, it isn't you who did this," Kate fumed as she paced away. The door behind them opened again to reveal two of Crispin's servants with her bags. They set them at the door as Kate ordered and left them.

Gemma stared at the four medium-sized portmanteaus and

sighed. "What a tiny little life I have left that it can be fit into four bags carried by two servants. Some women would take more than this to a weekend in the country."

"Some women are frivolous and empty," Kate said as she looked Gemma up and down. "Now would you like to tell me what that...*that man* did to you?"

Gemma smiled at the maid's motherhenning and relaxed for what felt like the first time in a very long time. Relaxed, that was, until she caught a glimpse of Crispin's cravat draped over a chair, caught a whiff of his scent as she picked up a pillow from the bed and held it to her chest.

"He didn't do anything," she reassured Kate softly. "Although he seemed to be just as afraid that he had done exactly what you imply."

"Rape you?" her maid said mildly.

Gemma flinched. "Yes, to put it bluntly. Or at least something close to it. But he didn't. We all went to a vicar's house, Mr. Howe—do you remember him from his visits to my father's home?"

Kate's lips pursed. "I do indeed. He pinched the bottoms of all the maids. Not a very godly man, for a vicar."

"Apparently not, since he was willing to take what I think amounted to a fairly substantial bribe to marry us. Once it was done, we were returned here by my father. And then he left and we were alone."

Kate leaned in. "And?" There was a knock on the door from the adjoining chamber and both women jumped. Kate scowled as she opened it, "Yes?"

A footman stood in the entryway. "Mrs. Flynn's bath."

For a moment, Gemma swayed at the idea of a bath to wash away the grime and pain of the previous night. As if cleansing her body would cleanse her soul of her father's betrayal, of her own impossible situation.

"Thank you," Kate said with a nod to dismiss the servant. Once he had departed through another door, her maid turned to her. With swift efficiency, the other woman stripped the buttons along the back of her gown open. "I'll lock all the doors while you undress."

Gemma did so and walked into the adjoining dressing room. The water steamed and something fragrant had been added to it. Oranges and vanilla swirled into her nostrils. Kate took her hand, steadying her as she stepped into the water with a hiccup of breath.

"A hot bath helps everything," her maid said with a smile as she handed over the soap.

"Not this," Gemma murmured, though in truth the warm water did ease her tight muscles and slow her tangled thoughts for a brief moment.

"You came back here and your father left you," Kate said. "What happened then?"

"He insisted on escorting us to this chamber. Servants were making a fuss, it was chaotic. He shut the door behind us and we stood there, staring at each other. Mr. Flynn was swaying on his feet. He moved toward me."

She squeezed her eyes shut as she pictured that moment. Gripped by both fear and anticipation, her heart had stuttered. She hadn't known if he would attack her or kiss her.

"He put his face very close to mine," she whispered. "And he said, 'You're too beautiful. This will not do.'"

Kate drew back. "What?"

Gemma shrugged. "It's what he said to me. And he hesitated a second more. Then he went to the settee and promptly passed out. I had little choice but to get into the bed—fully dressed, of course—and stare at the ceiling all night, listening to him mutter in his sleep."

Kate motioned her to lean forward and began to wash her back. The swirling motion made Gemma shiver with pleasure and released tension.

"What did he mutter about?" Kate asked.

"I don't know. It was gibberish." Gemma pursed her lips. That wasn't exactly true. She had been able to make out some words in Crispin's broken speech. Words like *sorry* and

29

betrayed you.

It seemed they both had their secrets.

Of course, hers could be rooted out very easily, as she had no doubt they would be soon. What would Crispin's reaction be?

"Let me brush your hair, my lady."

Gemma flinched. "*My lady.* He has been calling me that, but if this marriage sticks, you realize it will not be my title any longer. I will be Mrs. Crispin Flynn."

"*If* it sticks. I have a feeling Mr. Flynn is not the kind of man to get forced into anything."

Gemma rested back against the tub as Kate brushed her tangle locks gently. "I don't know what kind of man he is," she admitted. "When he was deep in his cups, he was silent, even sullen. His character was utterly unreadable. But he didn't take advantage of his claim for husbandly rights, when he could have very well done so. And this morning he is…"

When she trailed off, Kate filled in the space. "Is?"

"He is different, that's all. There's a light to him I didn't see last night. He said he was sorry. Perhaps he meant it."

Kate barked out a laugh. "Sorry doesn't help much now, does it?"

Gemma didn't respond to the question. In a way, the apology did help. No, it didn't fix what had already happened, or mitigate the scandal that would follow when the circumstances of their "marriage" came out and Crispin's drive to end it became public.

But the apology was certainly better than anything she'd ever get from her father, orchestrator of this madness.

She sighed. "What happened when my father returned? Is Mary all right?"

Kate's movements fumbled, giving Gemma the answer she needed even before she spoke. "Your father came back full of swagger, of course. And your sister was waiting for him. They had it out."

Any relaxation Gemma had found in the bath bled away at

that statement. She moaned. "Oh, Mary. I asked her not to do it. Father will punish her, especially if I'm not there."

"He railed at her quite cruelly," Kate confirmed. "And offered that she could be sold to someone far worse for a better price if she would like to continue to defy him."

Gemma sucked in her breath. There was her very deepest fear. She had hoped her first marriage would shield Mary, but that hadn't gone to plan at all. Her return home in disgrace and poverty had only heightened her father's drive to marry his younger daughter well.

But she knew from experience that the man wasn't below exactly what he threatened if Mary would not "do her duty" and find a husband of his liking.

"I will write to her as soon as I can today," Gemma whispered. "So she won't be afraid for me. And perhaps I will be able to see her."

That hadn't always been the case in her first marriage, but if Crispin was busy trying to dissolve their union, perhaps he wouldn't care if she had a visitor. Perhaps he would forget about her entirely.

"Until then, what is your plan?" Kate asked, offering her a towel. Gemma rose from the water, wrapping it around herself before she stepped out of the steaming heaven of the bath and back into reality.

She shrugged. "My plan is to have breakfast with the man as he has requested and see where it goes."

Kate pursed her lips. "The best solution, of course. I only wish everything weren't so out of your control."

Gemma laughed, though the sound was bitter and hollow. "It is the way of the world, Kate. The way of my world at any rate. We can only hope this man will prove to be a better protector of my needs than the last two."

CHAPTER FIVE

Crispin winced as he drank the rank brew in the tumbler he held. Fletcher and the cook had long ago concocted this...*poison* to aid him in getting over a night of over-imbibing. He had no idea what was in it, but it tasted like death. And yet it worked. By his second glass, his head was starting to feel a little better.

Which only meant he was more capable of thinking about the situation he was now in. *Married*. And to a woman who looked at him like she feared he might either jump on her or murder her at any moment. A woman he knew nothing about besides her name, the fact that she had a dreadful father and that she was absolutely beautiful.

"I suppose marriages have begun on worse," he muttered into his glass. He shook his head. What was he going on about? This would not be a marriage. It had been a wedding at best, and that was questionable under the circumstances. There was no reason, not in heaven nor on earth, to remain shackled in this way.

The door behind him opened, and he turned as Gemma walked into the room. All thoughts left his head as he stared at her. She was no longer in a wrinkled gown, her red hair mussed by lying in a bed all night. She wore a pretty gown of blue silk that clung to her breasts before it cascaded over the rest of her slim form. Her maid had fixed her hair into a simple but very flattering style, so that little curled auburn tendrils teased around her pale cheeks. Cheeks where he now noticed just a smattering of unfashionable but wholly endearing freckles.

She was stunning. And in that moment his body reacted the way his mind did not want, filling with desire and hot, heavy need. He wanted to touch her, to taste her, to feel her arch beneath him in that marital bed he had just been scheming to destroy.

"Good morning again," she said, her falsely bright voice mercifully breaking through his inappropriate thoughts and bringing him back to reality.

"Good morning," he managed to say, amazing since he could hardly breathe as he looked at her. "I-I hope the bath was restorative."

As soon as he said it, he wished he could take it back, for the word bath conjured images of her naked in the water, peering up at him with beckoning eyes, her legs spreading to reveal—

"Thank you, it was," she said, tilting her head to look at him. "You look different when you are shaved." He blinked at the comment and the way her cheeks darkened with color. "That was a foolish comment," she said as she turned her face. "I meant—"

He raised a hand. "This is awkward for us both, Gemma."

He waited for her to correct him, but she didn't.

"Yes, it is," she agreed softly.

He motioned to the sideboard, filled with all of the cook's best breakfast concoctions. She had outdone herself today, obviously striving to impress the new mistress, as temporary of a post as that would likely be.

"Would you like a plate?" he asked. "The food is wonderful. And I could pour you tea—or coffee if you would prefer?"

She looked at his glass before she took a plate and began to peruse the selections of meats and breads. "What do you have there?"

He cleared his throat. "I, er…it's something to help with the aftereffects of so much alcohol."

She hesitated in her selection of food from the sideboard and looked at him. "You have a drink to help you overcome too much drink?"

He looked at the glass. "It has no spirits in it. I don't think. To be honest, I have no idea what it is, but my servants started mixing it up years ago for me."

Her brow arched and she set her plate down. "You are very trusting, Mr. Flynn, to drink something that contains ingredients you don't know."

"Do we ever know what is in our food?" He laughed. "It isn't as if I'm in the kitchen when it's being cooked. Besides, if the servants wanted me dead, they have had plenty of opportunity to commit the crime over the years. They seem to like me well enough."

She moved toward him. "May I taste it?"

He drew back. The question was unexpected. It could even be considered sexual, though when he looked into her gray eyes, he could see no hint of flirtation there, only curiosity.

"Of course," he said, offering her the drink. "Though I warn you, it is vile."

She pressed her lips to the glass and he shifted slightly. There was something very intimate about that act, like a kiss they hadn't yet shared. Slowly, she tipped the glass back and took a sip of the brew.

Her face twisted comically as she handed it back to him.

"God, that *is* vile!" she said, half-laughing as she swallowed it with a look of horror. "How often do you drink it?"

He shrugged. "Too often, I fear."

"I would stop drinking before I drank that," she said, coughing.

He turned away, poured her a cup of tea, which he sweetened before he gave it to her. "This will help take the taste away. And perhaps you are right about the drinking. This potent concoction is only one of many unacceptable consequences of being too far into my cups."

Her gaze flitted to him as she swigged her tea in a very unladylike fashion. "Dire consequences, indeed," she agreed when she could speak again. But to his surprise, there was little heat to the statement.

"Will you eat?" she asked.

He nodded. "Yes, if only to get the taste out of my mouth."

They laughed together and Crispin tilted his head to look at her. It was actually surprisingly comfortable to be with Gemma. At least for the moment. Which was good. He didn't want every part of this odd circumstance to be filled with drama and emotion. There would certainly be enough of that later.

He filled a plate and joined her at the table where they ate in companionable silence for a few moments. Then Gemma took a sip of her tea, watching him as she did so.

"You realize I know very little about you aside from rumor and innuendo."

He couldn't help the way the corner of his lip lifted in a smile. Rumor and innuendo could have been his middle name. He was a Flynn, after all. He and his brother had once pilfered a very famous painting of a duchess and her dogs, and added...well, some very inappropriate cutouts to the image before they carefully rehung it in her halls. And that was the least of his sins.

"Why don't you tell me the rumor and innuendo and *I* will tell you if it is true?" he said.

"You will make me say some of these things out loud?" she asked.

He shrugged. "Sometimes the truth is painful, my lady."

She sighed. "Nearly had a duel with the prince."

"A terrible misunderstanding, but true." He shook his head. "The old fellow seems to like us well enough now. We aren't invited to the palace, of course, but he nods quite magnanimously if he sees us out and about."

Gemma was simply staring at him, forkful of eggs halfway to her lips. She blinked a few times. "I honestly thought that one was untrue."

He laughed. "Why?"

"Because it has been said that you avoid high society at all costs, Mr. Flynn."

He felt his smile fade. "Unfortunately, high society does not seem to avoid me or my family. Now what is your next rumor?"

She hesitated, as if she wished to pursue the subject further, but finally she let out a low sigh. "You danced on a table at a somewhat somber public event to celebrate the Treaty of Fontainebleau."

Crispin considered that. Had he done that? It was very recent, after all, and most of his bad behavior in the past six months had been fueled by large amounts of liquor. But wait...wait...there was an image of staid formality now. Speeches. And...

"Ah," he said. "Yes, there was something about that. But you know, why should a celebration of what we hope will be the end of a bloody war be staid? Should we not be dancing on tables? The folks around me thought so. I started a trend, I believe."

Once again, he saw more in her eyes, a curiosity that she seemed reluctant to explore. He wasn't certain whether to be happy or disappointed in that fact.

"And what about..." She trailed off, blushing suddenly. He braced himself for questions about the women. At least no one would ask about the *specific* woman, for no one knew about her.

"About?" he encouraged, rather enjoying the pink to her porcelain skin.

"I heard you ran naked in Hyde Park," she burst out, the words running together as her gaze flitted away from his and suddenly her food became very interesting to her.

He couldn't help but burst out laughing. "Damned Rafe, he always tells that story wrong to make himself look better. It was *he* who ran naked through the park, not me."

Her eyes were so wide now he thought they might roll from her head entirely. "So it is true? Why in the world would you...*he* do something so shocking?"

"A bet, of course," he said, laughing. "My brother lost a wager, fair and square, and he had to suffer the consequences accordingly, as is the way."

Suddenly she lowered her fork to the edge of her plate and her face drew down. "So you are accustomed to these kinds of wagers gone terribly wrong?"

Crispin flinched. He hadn't even been thinking about the wager that had brought them to this dining table this morning. He should have been, of course. Their unwanted marriage should have been the thing on the very top of his mind.

And yet talking to Gemma in this very comfortable way had erased those unpleasant thoughts. Odd, really.

"There is a vast difference between wagering that the loser of a bet would have to run through the park in only what God gave him and wagering a wedding," he said, as gently as he could. "I assure you I am not disregarding the seriousness of the former just because I can laugh at the latter."

"But you said you cannot escape the consequences," she whispered, her voice cracking. For the first time there was a break in her calm and he saw how devastated she truly was by this turn of events. He couldn't take it personally. What woman wanted to be forced into a union with a stranger?

Especially a stranger with a reputation such as his.

Slowly, he reached out across the table and placed his bare hand over hers. It was the first time he had touched her, and electricity all but crackled as he did so, jolting him and making him jerk his gaze to her face. She wasn't breathing now, just staring at his hand covering hers.

"Gemma," he whispered. "I'll fix this somehow."

She met his gaze slowly and shook her head. "You don't

understand. For me, it is either stay here as your very unwanted wife or go back to my father, who would sell me off to settle a debt. You *can't* fix it for me."

His lips parted in surprise. He hadn't thought of it from her point of view, only from his own. If he could manage to break this farce of a marriage, then he would be free. And she would still be in chains.

And suddenly he wanted to fix it for her so very badly.

He shook the feeling away, knowing where it led, and removed his hand from hers. "Well, we will figure something out, I assure you."

She watched him closely, too closely, and he wondered what she saw as she stared. What she thought. How she judged him. Did she know he itched for a drink? Did she know he itched to kiss her even though this was temporary? Did she know he often wished he could run away and never come back?

She blinked and the spell was broken.

"I have one more question about rumor and innuendo," she said, spearing the final remnants of her breakfast with her fork.

"That is?" he asked, doing the same.

She hesitated so long that he wondered if she'd lost track of what she was going to say. But just as he was about to press her, she looked him straight in the eye.

"I've heard you hate your brother."

The words hit Crispin one at a time, like stab wounds, burrowing into his chest and stopping his heart. Was that what people thought? Said?

Was that what Rafe thought?

Of course, when he considered his behavior over the last year, why wouldn't everyone believe exactly what Gemma had just asked? After all, no one understood the pain he had endured, the way his own loss had become entangled with Rafe's loss of freedom.

"I don't hate my brother," he said softly.

"But—" she began.

"And what of you?" he interrupted. He could hear how hard his tone was now, but he couldn't meter it sufficiently. "I don't even have rumor and innuendo to go by when it comes to you, my lady."

She shifted at the change of subject, that fetching blush returning to her cheeks. She took a few long breaths and looked at him. There was a hollowness to her expression that dug into his soul. He had seen that look on his own face in the mirror some days.

"I'm sure that will change, Mr. Flynn," she whispered, her voice broken and bitter. "I'm certain that as news of our marriage gets out there will be floods of people who will rush to you, more than eager to fill your head with gossip. And if you break this marriage, they will tell you even more about how you dodged the greatest mistake of your life."

He drew back at the angry words that fell from her lips. At the angrier expression on her face. Now he was utterly intrigued, for who could look at her loveliness and not desire it? Who couldn't see her as a fine match, even if there was not money to be exchanged?

But she seemed insistent that she was not a good fit for him...for anyone.

"Why?" he asked.

She shook her head. "Wait and see, Crispin. They will tell my story with much more entertainment value than I could ever do."

"Gemma," he began.

She pushed to her feet and walked away to the sideboard. With her back to him, she said, "I think it is foolish for us to explore the past when our future will not be shared. After all, you claim you can break this marriage. Perhaps you will tell me now how you intend to do that."

He hesitated. Should he press her on the past? He had an odd urge to do just that even though her words about them not sharing a future were very true.

Instead, he sighed. "I am going to be very honest with you,

Gemma. After all, you know about the naked racing incident now. We must be friends, yes?"

She turned slightly, her eyes wide and her lips twitching. He wasn't certain if she wanted to laugh or cry. Perhaps both.

"I appreciate honesty," she said slowly.

He nodded. "I am not entirely certain I can fashion an exit from this mess. But I know people who could help us and we will go right now to see them. It is late enough we won't be rousing them from sleep, I think."

She shook her head. "Who?"

He shifted his weight. "Well, you inquired about my feelings regarding my brother. Perhaps you would like to see them in action. We're going to see the Duke of Hartholm, Gemma. My brother, Raphael."

CHAPTER SIX

Gemma had lived in the company of the titled and landed gentry most of her life. She was...*had* been...a countess, for heaven's sake. And yet, as the carriage made its way through rambling streets toward the home of the Duke and Duchess of Hartholm, her heart pounded and her chest squeezed with anxiety. There were so many stories about the couple that she feared what she would find there.

"Do you know my brother?"

She jolted at the question and looked away from the window toward her companion. Crispin was slouched down in the carriage seat, as he had been the entire ride, his hand over his eyes.

"I thought you were asleep," she said.

"I was praying for death, not sleep," he said with a sigh as he straightened up and pulled himself together slightly. There was still a rakish dishevelment to him that was both frustrating and wildly attractive. He looked like a damned pirate. "Do you know him?"

She pursed her lips at his singular mindset. "I know *of* him. Everyone knows of him. But no, we never met."

"I thought your husband was a..." He shook his head and she could see he was searching for the information in the foggy catalogue of his mind. "A..."

"An earl," she provided for him with a frown. She tried not to think about Laurelcross when she didn't have to do so. It was too painful. "But he wasn't—he didn't—we weren't very active in Society. At any rate, he died close to the time your brother took over the dukedom, so we wouldn't have met regardless."

"Why?" Crispin straightened up even further now that he had a bone to nibble.

She stiffened. "Why did he die?" she squeaked out.

He shook his head. "Why weren't you active in Society?"

Relief flooded her. *That* was a topic she could discuss. It wasn't that she wanted to share her deep, personal issues with this man she didn't know, but being petulant and withdrawing wasn't going to help her.

"He was much older than I was," she began. "And he didn't care for that sort of thing. He was more interested in heirs."

The moment she said the words, heard them in the air around her, she clapped a hand over her mouth. She understood perfectly the implications of those words, and if Crispin's widening eyes were any indication, so did he. His gaze flitted over her and she saw desire light up in his stare.

A desire her body answered automatically, despite the tenuous situation they were in, despite the fact that she didn't know this person. Despite everything.

She felt blood heating her cheeks, felt her hands shaking with both humiliation and need. Felt everything in her want to shift toward Crispin Flynn and see if the rumors she had not dared discuss with him at breakfast were true.

Was he really the best lover in London?

The words rang in her head even though she hadn't spoken them out loud, and she turned her face. Thankfully, they were just pulling into the drive at the duke's home, and the moment a footman came to open the door, she hurtled herself from the vehicle as if the hounds of hell were behind her.

In a way, she felt they were. Crispin Flynn was the

embodiment of every sin she had ever committed. Perhaps he was her punishment.

The door to the house opened and a butler with a surprisingly tired appearance stepped out to greet them. His gaze passed her and fell on Crispin and his eyes widened.

"Mr. Crispin, you are…you are here!" he said.

Crispin grinned as he strode up the steps with every confidence and slapped the butler hard on the upper arm. "Latham, you old crow, you look well."

The butler's lips pursed, but Gemma thought his eyes also danced. It seemed there was a great amount of affection between Crispin and this household. "Thank you, sir."

"And my brother is in residence, I hope?" Crispin asked, and there Gemma heard just a hint of desperation in his voice.

Latham's eyes widened further. "Then you have not heard?"

"Heard?"

"Of course your brother is in residence, Mr. Flynn. He is upstairs at present with the duchess and…and the new baby."

Crispin took a step back and staggered as he slipped down several steps before he righted himself. His face was suddenly pale and his hands flexed at his sides.

"The—the baby?" he repeated, his voice as raw as his expression. There was pain and joy in every line of his face and it took everything in Gemma not to step up beside him to offer him some form of comfort.

Latham's expression softened slightly. "Yes, sir. The child was born just last night."

Crispin was nodding, but it seemed to be a reflexive motion, as was the way he swallowed very hard before he spoke. "I would very much like to see my brother, if…if he will see me."

"Come in," Latham urged, stepping back to allow them entry. But as Gemma passed him, he sucked in a breath. "I'm so sorry, Miss. I am so distracted, I admit I didn't notice you there."

Crispin stopped in the foyer, turning toward them but not looking at either her or the butler. "It is I who should be sorry, Latham. I should have said something sooner. This is—this is—er—this is my—my wife?"

Now it was Latham's turn to stagger a bit as his stare spun again to Gemma. She could read nothing on his expression, as was the way with the very best servants, but his voice shook slightly as he said, "Why don't you retire to your usual sitting room, Mr. Flynn? I will fetch the duke immediately."

Crispin nodded, motioning her toward a door down the long hall past the foyer. Her hands shook, but she said nothing until he had closed the door behind them. Immediately, he moved toward a line of liquor bottles on the sideboard across the room. She followed him toward them.

"Isn't it too early for that?" she asked as his hand touched one.

He looked toward her and his frown deepened. "Likely so."

"And I would think you'd want to have a clear head for this conversation," she continued.

He flinched. "Actually, I'd like to be drunk for this conversation so I won't remember it later."

She tilted her head at his candor, then gently slipped the bottle from his hands and put it back in its place. "Why did you tell Latham that I was your wife?"

He turned away slightly, but she could see his face and pain was written plainly on each and every line. "I don't know."

The broken quality of his voice erased any upset she felt for her own part. Slowly, she reached out, her hand moving toward his arm. She saw him watching it, too, from the corner of her eye, both of them seemingly mesmerized by the touch about to come.

When it did, she jolted a little, moved as she had been at breakfast by their bodies touching in any way. His arm was very strong, and as her fingers closed over it, the muscle flexed.

"It's all right," she whispered, making her tone soothing just as she sometimes did when Mary had nightmares. "It will be all right."

He shook his head. "I didn't know Serafina had the baby," he said, his voice almost imperceptibly soft.

"And now you do."

He turned his face so she could no longer see the emotion written there. "Yes. And now I get to tell him—"

"What?" she asked when he cut himself off.

He shook his head and pulled away from her. She watched him walk across the room and was filled with a desire to help him. A desire she needed to turn off right away because their situation was far from settled and she had to be ready to fight for herself.

Crispin could still feel the warmth of Gemma's fingers around his arm, as if she had branded or burned him with that touch. He stood at the fireplace, his back to her, trying to measure his breathing. He couldn't be wrapped up in her. Not when he was about to face—

He hadn't even finished the thought when the door behind him opened. He turned to watch his brother, Rafe, enter, followed by their friend Marcus Rivers, who had married their sister just a few months before.

Crispin was hit by so many feelings, seeing these men who he had been avoiding. The first feeling was joy, wild and unfettered. Rafe had always been his best friend, and despite the scandalous circumstances surrounding Marcus's marriage to Annabelle, Crispin liked him too. He hadn't been around people he loved and trusted for a very long time.

But the second and the more powerful reaction was shame. He had once again brought destruction and pain down around him. Just as he had so many times before. And he had to come here, like a dog with his tail tucked between his legs, and ask the great and glorious duke for help.

His brother stared at him for a brief second, then crossed the room. His arms were outstretched and to Crispin's surprise Rafe enveloped him in a hard, long hug.

"You're here," he whispered, close to Crispin's ear. "You came."

As Rafe pulled back, a wide smile on his face, Crispin forced his own. "Congratulations." He looked past his brother. "Hello, Rivers."

Rafe stepped back. "Did Mama tell you about the baby?"

Crispin blinked. "Latham didn't tell you?"

There was confusion on Rafe's face. "Tell me what? Latham just said you were here and wished to see me."

Shifting, Crispin said, "I didn't know about the child until I arrived this afternoon."

Rafe's smile fell. "No? Then why—" He cut himself off as his gaze shifted toward Gemma, who remained at the sideboard, allowing the scene between the brothers play out. She stiffened as the duke's exalted gaze swept over her, then back to his brother. "Crispin?"

"I'm in a bit of trouble, Rafe."

His brother's chin dropped and his eyes shut, but Crispin still saw his annoyance, his pain, his anger on his face. Those emotions stabbed Crispin through the heart and made him feel like the disappointment he was all the keener.

"Must we do this today, Crispin?" Rafe said, his tone soft. "My son was just born twelve hours ago."

"A son." Crispin shook his head.

"God help us," Marcus piped up from the door, tone dry as a brushfire wind.

Rafe ignored them both. "I must think of him now and Serafina, so I can't—"

"Your Grace, allow me to introduce myself."

They all turned at the interrupted and Crispin watched as

Gemma stepped forward, hand outstretched to his brother. She had a steady, cool look in her eyes as she reached him, and Rafe took her offering with a side glance toward Crispin. They shook, and as she released him, Gemma continued.

"I'm—" The veneer of her confidence slipped a little as she hesitated. "Up until recently, I was the Countess of Laurelcross. But last night, due to a set of unfortunate situations, I became Mrs. Flynn."

The statement had a consequence, though Crispin wasn't certain it was one Gemma had intended. Marcus and Rafe both straightened up, mouths dropped open and stunned into silence.

It took his brother a moment of opening and shutting his mouth before Rafe managed to squeak out, "Mrs. Flynn?"

"Yes." That fetching blush pinkened her cheeks again. "But as I said, this all happened under very bad circumstances, Your Grace. And we desperately need your help."

Rafe blinked. He just kept blinking, staring first at Gemma for a very long time, then slowly to Crispin. "Married?"

Crispin knew he was asking him, not her. Slowly, he nodded and managed to push one word past his suddenly very dry throat. "Yes."

Rafe nodded, then returned his attention to Gemma. He stepped closer and Crispin saw her tense, even though she didn't step back.

"Mrs. Flynn, may I present Marcus Rivers. He is our very old friend and recently married to our sister, Annabelle."

"Charmed," Marcus said, the word heavy as he looked Gemma up and down.

Of course, the humiliation of the moment would not have been complete until the door opened again and Annabelle and their mother came in, their faces tired but filled with joy at the news of Rafe's baby.

"His cheeks!" his mother was finishing, but she didn't say anything more as her eyes fell on him. "Crispin, my love."

He found himself enveloped in hugs from both her and Annabelle as Gemma stood by, watching with interest and he could see, a great deal of discomfort. It was rather overwhelming, he knew, all these Flynns in one room.

"Hello, hello," he said as the two women backed away.

"What is going on?" Annabelle asked as she stepped into the waiting arm of her new husband. Crispin flinched at the two of them standing there. Annabelle had fallen into disgrace while trying to help him, but he had to admit, she looked blissfully happy now.

"Your brother somehow ended up married to this lovely lady last night," Marcus explained. "Apparently it was under terrible circumstances."

"Rivers!" Crispin and Rafe burst out together.

Marcus shrugged. "I only thought it was better to cut through it to the core of the matter."

Gemma was staring at the floor now, her cheeks a vibrant red and her lip trembling with what he recognized were unshed tears of humiliation.

"Married?" his mother repeated.

Just as he had with his brother, Crispin nodded. "Yes, I'm afraid so, Mama."

Her lips parted but to his surprise, her eyes lit up with what he thought was relief and joy. She looked away from him, toward Gemma.

"Good afternoon, my dear," she said.

It must have been the gentle tone that spurred Gemma to look at her now (and what he hoped was *temporary*) mother-in-law. "Good afternoon," she whispered, her voice cracking.

Rafe's expression softened and he reached out to grasp her hands. He squeezed them gently and to Crispin's surprise, Gemma didn't pull away, but actually smiled up at his brother.

"Obviously, we all have a great deal to discuss, Miss…Lady…I'm sorry, what is your given name?"

"Gemma," she said.

"Gemma." He smiled at her. "I promise you, everything will be all right. We'll work this out. Stay here with my mother and my sister, who I promise will make you nothing but comfortable."

Crispin waited for her to show some of the anger, some of the frustration which she had vented on him earlier in the day. But no. She gifted his brother with another wavering smile. That was two Rafe had received, while none for Crispin.

"Very well."

Rafe released her and turned on him. "As for you, come with me."

There was no arguing with the order, so Crispin followed his brother and Marcus as they exited the parlor. At the door, he turned and took one last glance at Gemma. She had her chin lifted and she looked beautiful and brave. But she wasn't his. That was all a mistake.

CHAPTER SEVEN

Gemma leaned back against the comfortable settee with a sigh and took a long sip of tea. She had just told Mrs. Flynn and Mrs. Rivers the whole story of how she had ended up married to Crispin, and she had to admit there was relief in having said it all out loud to them. Relief and terror, since neither woman had reacted as of yet.

She dared a glance first at Mrs. Flynn. The older woman's lips were pursed together into a thin line. "That boy," she muttered.

"He isn't a boy, he's a grown man," her daughter corrected, eyes flashing fire. "Lost a *bet*? Damn it, Crispin."

Gemma jolted at the curse, but shook her head. "What you must think of me."

To her surprise, the women exchanged a brief glance before they dissolved into laughter. Although Gemma wasn't entirely certain they weren't making fun of her, she had to admit the sound was lovely. It felt like no one had laughed in her life for months.

"Are you mocking me?" she asked softly.

The women stopped laughing. "Absolutely not," Annabelle reassured her with a gentle squeeze of her hand. "It's only that Mama and I have seen far worse than this in our family. The idea that we would think less of you is absolutely ludicrous."

Mrs. Flynn smiled just as warmly. "My daughter is right. Though I *would* like to get to know you better. Tell us about yourself."

Gemma's brow wrinkled. She had met her husband's family a few times during their marriage, but no one had ever asked her about herself. It was all cold propriety in the Laurelcross line. Once Theodore was dead, well, she might as well have died too. They had only come to collect what was theirs and politely have her removed because he had not provided for her unless she bore him heirs.

Oh-so-politely.

"I don't know where to begin," she said.

Annabelle tilted her head. "Who is your family, Gemma?"

"My father is Sir Oswald Quinn. My mother was Regina Quinn, though she was born into the Briarwood legacy."

"Oh no, you misunderstand, I don't want to know about your pedigree," Annabelle said with another of those sweetly gentle squeezes of the hand. "I want to know about your family."

"My father is how I got into this mess," Gemma replied, trying and failing to keep the bitterness from her tone. "My mother passed when I was just seven."

Mrs. Flynn made a small sound in her throat. "I'm so sorry, my dear."

Gemma shrugged, though dismissal of that event was not as easy as perhaps she hoped to make it look. "It was a very long time ago. I do have a younger sister, Mary."

She turned her face so she wouldn't reveal her feelings on her sister. God, Mary was alone again with their father. The first time Gemma had left to marry, her sister had been too young to be manipulated for Sir Oswald's needs. Now that was not so. At twenty, Mary was ripe for the same kind of bartering that had landed Gemma an earl four years ago.

"You worry about her," Annabelle said. A statement, not a question.

Gemma found herself nodding. "It is humiliating to admit to strangers how low my father will stoop, but you can see it in this situation with Crispin—Mr. Flynn. I am afraid for her."

"There are advantages, my dear, to a marriage into this family, especially in its current state," Mrs. Flynn said.

Gemma dared to look at them again. "Advantages?"

Annabelle was the one who continued, "Yes. Although the duchess, Serafina, is of course abed recovering from the birth of her son, she *does* have some influence in Society, as does my brother. Despite the scandals that have surrounded my brothers or me or my new husband, we could help your sister, I think."

Gemma's heart leapt. Was that possible? It could very well be. After all, her father would never refuse the chaperone of a duke and duchess for Mary. And if the Flynns were as kind as they appeared to be thus far, that could mean Mary would get to choose her own path, her own life, her own husband, in a way Gemma never had.

She shook her head. Reality returned in an instant.

"I wish that were true, but it may all be a moot point."

The two women exchanged another glance. "I don't know what you mean, my dear," Mrs. Flynn said.

Gemma shifted. She felt like she was telling on Crispin behind his back to a nanny, but these women would find out the truth soon enough.

"Your offer of assistance to my sister would be greatly appreciated, of course. But it must be predicated on the fact that I am a member of your family." She cleared her throat. "And it remains to be seen whether or not that will continue to be true."

Annabelle's forehead wrinkled. "I don't understand. You said you and my brother were wed."

"We are...but Mr. Flynn does not wish that to continue. He is here to ask his brother's help in ending our union. And he very well could have the grounds to do exactly that."

Annabelle pushed off the settee and paced away, leaving a

trail of unexpectedly unladylike curses in her wake. Her mother watched her with a shake of her head.

"Darling, manners. You aren't in Marcus's club."

Annabelle turned back with a frown. "I'm sorry, Mama, Gemma. It is only that I cannot believe how ridiculous my brothers are."

"Both of them?" Gemma asked, trying to figure out why Annabelle would include the duke in her curse.

"Yes. You see, you may recall that my elder brother, Rafe, was in a somewhat similar situation with his own bride. And though they are deliriously, almost *shockingly* happy now, Rafe initially fought that union with all his might. And here is Crispin trailing behind his brother and imitating him as always."

"It may be more complicated than that," Mrs. Flynn offered, though Gemma felt her very focused stare on her. What did her new mother-in-law see? And did she approve, despite her kindness and welcoming spirit?

"Ridiculous!" Annabelle insisted. "There is nothing complicated about it. Crispin has been running around with no consequences for months and months, perhaps even longer. *This* consequence is really quite fine as far as I can see. And I'll be damned if we will stand by and allow him to avoid it just as he has avoided so much more in his life."

Gemma stood and moved toward her. "I don't think—"

Annabelle shook her head. "No. I have a good head for people, Gemma Flynn, and I like you. I swear to you in this moment, we will fix this. And once Serafina is recovered from the birth, I know she will help us too."

"Oh dear," Mrs. Flynn said, but she stood and slipped a very comforting arm around Gemma. "The Flynn women against the world again?"

Annabelle laughed. "No, Mama. Just against the Flynn men. As it was always meant to be."

Gemma stared at the two women. She had come here, resigned to censure and eventual ruin, but instead she had

53

found welcome and what felt like membership in an exclusive and wonderful club. And though she had no idea still what to think of her husband, she truly wanted in that moment to be a Flynn woman.

Marcus and Rafe were staring at him, and never before had Crispin wanted the liquor on the sideboard behind the billiard table more than he did in that moment. They were shocked by his confession of how he had acquired his "bride", but behind that shock was judgment. Frustration. Resignation that this was the kind of man he was. He could feel it oozing from his brother's pores as he just *stared*.

"By God," Marcus said, breaking the tension, or at least attempting to do so.

Rafe continued his silent observation until Crispin's skin felt like it didn't fit. He folded his arms and glared at his brother.

"Do you want to throw up in my face just how my drinking and gambling have come to get me? Do you want to tell me how right you always were that I should stop?"

Rafe's eyebrows lifted slightly. "No." The one word answer was so quiet that Crispin almost didn't hear it. But his brother's voice elevated as he continued. "You may see this as a punishment, Cris, but I see it as your greatest opportunity."

Crispin looked at his brother, then turned to Marcus in an effort to find support for how ridiculous those words were. But his friend was merely standing by, arms folded. He actually looked like he *agreed* with such a stupid thing to say.

"What the hell nonsense are you going on about?"

Rafe shrugged. "I think a marriage would be good for you. No, the circumstances of how this came to be are not ideal, I will grant you that. And people will talk, but then it is *us* and people always do. However, on first glance the lady seems to be of solid character."

Marcus laughed. "Indeed, when you were stammering and stuttering about telling us what had happened, she stepped in and saved you with her very forward introduction. There was a steel in her eyes in that moment that very much put me to mind of Annabelle."

Crispin turned away, his breath short. The two of them acted like this was fine. That there would be no help from them except in terms of acceptance of the inevitable. Panic bubbled up in him, but he covered it with anger. Anger was easier.

"You would lay your life on me, brother?" he snapped, the words harsh and cutting.

When he turned, he found Rafe had not reacted to the jab. He merely said, "Because I was forced to marry Serafina? You think I would allow the same for you as some kind of way to make myself feel better?"

"Would you?"

Rafe rolled his eyes. "The situations are entirely different for a start. I didn't drunkenly force some poor girl to marry me. If anyone should want out of the union, it should be Gemma. Does she?"

"I-I didn't ask her," he admitted after a hesitation while the question, and his shameful answer, sank in.

Rafe barked out a hard laugh. "Well, that's typical. I love you, Crispin, but you have traditionally been one of the most selfish people I have ever known. The last year of pouting over spilled milk is proof of it."

Crispin took a long step toward him. "It was far more than spilled milk, Raphael."

Rafe raised his hands. "I wouldn't know, you never told me. You just ran off, leaving Mama to worry and cry and age more than she has in a decade. You inspired Annabelle to run around in clubs trying to save you—apologies, Marcus, it did work out well."

Marcus smiled. "I agree she never should have been running around in clubs. But damn, I'm glad she did."

Rafe returned his attention to his brother. "And you left me to live with the fallout of my inheriting the dukedom and a bride and a life I didn't want. Thank God I had Serafina or I would have been entirely alone."

Crispin flinched. When laid out before him like this, his actions did seem utterly selfish. Perhaps this lost wager, this bride, was his punishment.

"Rafe—"

"No, I'm not quite finished," his brother said. "And when you say that I am allowing you to live with this consequence because of my situation with Serafina, that is absolutely correct. Because if you were lucky enough to marry a woman with half the spirit and character that my wife has, you would be vastly happy, indeed. Have a care what you say next, Crispin Flynn."

Crispin swallowed. He and Rafe had always gone wild together, caused trouble together, lived consequence free together. Yes, Rafe had saved him a few times, but mostly they were just two best friends doing whatever they wanted.

Now when he looked at his brother, he saw that Rafe had changed. He wanted to hate him for that, hate Serafina for it. But he feared that his brother had actually become a better man.

A better man who Crispin could never, ever live up to.

"I did not mean to insult Serafina," he said softly. "I like your wife, Rafe. I helped you with her, if you recall."

"You did," his brother agreed. "And I love you all the more for it." He reached out and touched Crispin's shoulder. "I would do anything for you, Crispin. But when it comes to this marriage, I will *not* save you. Nor do I believe you should make any effort to find a way out of this situation for yourself."

Crispin shut his eyes. The escape he had thought to find here was swiftly vanishing. He only had one more card to play.

"You say Gemma seems a good sort, and thus far I cannot deny it to be true."

He flashed to their breakfast that morning. He hadn't just

wanted her then. He had liked her. But something she'd said, something he vaguely recalled her father saying, stuck in his mind. To tell them was his final attempt at getting out of this with Rafe's help.

"She has secrets," he said. "Both she and her father said something about her late husband. I have no idea when he died, honestly." He winced at that admission. It was just more proof of how selfish he was. "But there are circumstances surrounding the death that are apparently untoward."

Rafe drew back in surprise. "I would not have expected that. Are you certain?"

"I'm not certain of anything, because I don't know anything except for a hint about a scandal."

"She said her husband's title was Laurelcross?" Rafe asked.

Crispin hesitated. Was it Laurelcross or Laurelvale? God, he really was a selfish bastard.

"Yes, yes, Laurelcross," he said. "An earl. She said he did not come into Society much, he was older than she was. When I asked if they had met you, she said no, so you likely wouldn't know him."

"Serafina would," Rafe said, glancing at the ceiling like heaven awaited him above stairs. "But I'm not about to go marching up there and disturb her rest to ask her about a dead earl and a rumor."

"Laurelcross." Marcus began to pace beside the billiard table. "Laurelcross—I thought it sounded familiar when she said it, but is it possible?"

Both brothers turned to their friend.

"Do you know something?" Crispin asked. It was completely reasonable that Marcus would. His club was very popular and he often knew the darker side of many of Society's elite.

"I'm not entirely certain," Marcus began.

"Well, we won't judge exclusively on what you say, then," Rafe reassured him. "What is it you recall?"

Marcus's lips pinched and he looked at the brothers with an almost apologetic expression. "What I recall was said only in passing. Laurelcross once held a membership in my club and came regularly to game and play in the back rooms with the ladies. He hadn't been around in a while, and when Abbot and I were talking about it, he mentioned the man had been married and was focusing all his...er...*seed* on making a legitimate heir."

Crispin found himself flinching. Gemma would be utterly humiliated if she knew they were discussing her life like this. He wasn't sure *he* liked it much himself.

"And?" Rafe pressed, clearly not as troubled by the fact.

"And then one day Abbot told me he was dead. But the rumor was..." Marcus hesitated and looked at Crispin carefully. "Some have said that Gemma *killed* her husband."

CHAPTER EIGHT

Crispin stared at his brother-in-law in shock as what Marcus had said sank in. When Gemma had begun her talk of secrets, he'd thought of a dozen potential scandals, but this...*this* had never even crossed his mind.

"I'm sorry, are you truly talking about *murder*?" Rafe said, his mouth dropped open and his eyes wide.

Crispin stepped forward. "Wait a moment, Marcus didn't say murdered. He said *killed,* and that means there could be much more to it."

Both men turned their heads toward him, as if astonished that he would argue semantics about a subject as shocking as this. He frowned.

"Don't look at me like that. I think we would all know, beyond mere rumor, if the woman ran screeching across the room and put a dagger in his back, yes? She likely would have been arrested if that were the case, I cannot picture that Laurelcross's family would stand for such a thing to go unpunished."

Rafe paced away, but he was nodding as he moved restlessly across the room. "I suppose you are correct. Were there any other details?"

Marcus shrugged. "You know me, since the woman wasn't a member in my club, I didn't have to worry about anything but removing her husband's name from the roster. I didn't press the issue and Abbot would never indulge in idle gossip—it isn't his way."

"And the entire thing may be idle gossip," Crispin offered. "After all, Rafe, you and I did a great many of the things that have made our family name so notorious, but many of the actions attributed to us were also lies. You cannot deny that we know from personal experience that a kernel of truth can be blown into something far larger."

His brother arched a brow and his tone was almost imperceptibly soft when he said, "We were never accused of being killers, Cris."

Running a hand through his hair, Crispin looked once more toward the liquor that almost winked in promise across the room. If anything was a reason to get obliterated, wasn't the idea that his forced bride was potentially a killer a good one?

"But you know her better than Marcus and I do, of course," Rafe said, his voice breaking into Crispin's longing. "What do you think?"

Crispin looked at him in sharp surprise. "You have heard my tale about last night—I don't know the woman."

"You spent a night and a morning with her. It is still better than the twenty minutes Marcus and I have in her acquaintance."

Crispin sighed. They were right, he supposed, but it seemed an odd exercise to sift through his thoughts about Gemma in that manner. Especially since they were increasingly confused now that this new information was joining his first impressions.

"I was either in a stupor that I cannot recall or asleep for the first portion of our time together," he began. "And entirely vulnerable. If the woman had ever wanted to kill anyone, I suppose it would have been me. She certainly seemed to be utterly terrified of me and despise me in the first few moments after I woke. And yet she didn't do anything at all."

"That is somewhat comforting, I suppose," Rafe agreed.

"Except that in the husband's case whatever was done could have easily been done in a moment of heated passion after months or even years of built up emotion."

Crispin found himself glaring at Marcus. "You are talking about a situation we have no idea about."

"You are utterly correct and I am wrong to speculate, except that in this case it is done out of worry, both for my wife and for you, a man I've considered my own brother since long before I swept your sister off to Gretna Green." Marcus's stare was suddenly very focused. "I suppose I take a more personal interest in what is truly happening here."

Crispin scrubbed a hand over his face. Part of him loved Marcus for both considering him a brother despite everything he had done and for giving a damn about him. Part of him felt uncommonly defensive of Gemma.

"Let us forget what she did or didn't do when I was unconscious," he ground out through clenched teeth. "When I awoke, Gemma seemed more like a dove with a broken wing, not a killer. Once we got past the idea that I would harm her, once she began to accept that I didn't recall what happened, well, she certainly didn't behave in a way that would make me suspicious as to her past. She was conversational at breakfast, even funny at times. And don't forget, she was the one who brought up that there would be rumors for me to deal with. She never tried to hide that fact."

Rafe folded his arms. "But she didn't tell you anything about the truth, either."

Crispin ducked his head. "I doubt I've earned her confidence to reveal something so utterly personal and I'm sure devastating, no matter the circumstances. After all, I am the blithering idiot who has forced her into a marriage right alongside the father she despises."

The room was quiet and Crispin watched as Rafe and Marcus exchanged a brief but meaningful look. He turned away from it in annoyance and chagrin. Probably they were shocked he was taking any responsibility in this situation at all. He hadn't done that for a very long time.

"So what will you do?" Rafe asked.

Crispin sighed. "I will speak to her about it. Not here, because it is between us and not a story I would force her to tell to a room full of people she doesn't know. But I *will* confront her with the rumors she herself admitted I would eventually hear and let her tell me her side of the tale. Only then will I be able to truly judge what happened and whether I am safe with her in my home."

Marcus nodded. "A fine way to handle it. But will you keep her in your home, assuming it turns out the girl is not a raving murderer?"

"You're asking if I will continue the marriage," Crispin said softly. "I-I don't know."

Rafe stepped forward. "You came here seeking my counsel and I am now going to give it to you. Should it turn out that the story of Gemma killing her late husband turns out to be exaggerated or untrue, I believe—"

His brother didn't get to finish the thought, because at that moment, the door to the billiards room opened without the preamble of a knock and all three men turned to watch Gemma enter the room, flanked on either side by Annabelle and their mother.

Crispin caught his breath at the sight of her. It was funny, he knew now that he was looking at a potential killer, someone he might not even be safe in the company of. But if she was not the most beautiful potential murderer he'd ever seen, he didn't know who was. He let out a long sigh.

Whatever was going to happen, the fact that he found Gemma so entirely attractive was going to be an issue. He already knew what beautiful women could do and it could be far worse than murder a man in body. She could capture a soul. She could take everything.

And whatever happened, he wasn't about to let this woman close enough to do any of that.

When Annabelle opened the door to the billiards room, the way the men brought their conversation to a screeching halt made every hair on Gemma's neck stand up. She stared at the three guilty faces, the three sets of eyes that wouldn't meet hers and her skin heated. She wanted to hide. She had come to be very aware of when others were discussing her in a less than positive light.

And even though she knew Crispin wanted out of their marriage, the fact still stung.

But then he did the unexpected. He turned his face back to hers, their eyes locked, and he just...*watched* her. Unflinching, unjudging. He just watched.

She finally looked away, just as Mrs. Flynn said, "Is it safe to assume that everyone in the room now knows the unfortunate details of Gemma and Crispin's marriage?"

Gemma suddenly found the design on the carpet fascinating, but even though she no longer looked at them she was well aware that everyone around her was nodding. The humiliation of all these strangers, kind as they had been so far, privy to what had been one of her worst nights cut deep. It took everything in her not to run from the room. After all, where would she go?

"Then I suggest this is something that would better be discussed all together, as a family."

To Gemma's surprise, Annabelle wrapped an arm around her shoulders in that moment and drew her forward, drew her into their circle. She felt her spine straighten and she let her gaze lift.

Part of their family? Could it be so easy?

"Gemma tells us that you wish to somehow annul the union on grounds of fraud, or at least drunkenness," Annabelle said, her tone cold. "Is that true, Crispin?"

"It *was* true." Crispin shifted. "Rafe pointed out to me a moment ago that I never actually asked Gemma's opinion on the matter. So I am asking you now, Gemma. What do *you* want to do?"

She stepped back in surprise. No one had asked her about her desires regarding her own future in years, decades perhaps. She wasn't even certain she had a reply.

"Gemma," he said, his voice softer as he took a step toward her. "I want to know your thoughts."

She cleared her throat. Her thoughts.

"Although being dragged into the night by you and my father, being forced to wed in the most unromantic and uncouth way would never have been my choice, the fact is that it *was* done. And I know my father. By this morning, he would have begun the announcing and the crowing to anyone who would spread the word quickest. If we then annul the union, I fear the repercussions will be devastating. Not to me. I already know a bit about scandal—"

She blushed at having to say those words, but forced herself to continue.

"It is for my sister I fear, you see. At this moment, Mary could still have some value if my father allows her to have a Season. He might even let her have a little bit of choice in husbands to save face. But if I fall, utterly fall, as I would with this broken, blasphemous marriage…well, my father might decide to barter with her innocence instead." She shook her head. "I realize I'm telling you something personal and horrible and trust me, I take no pleasure in it. But you asked me what I want, Crispin…Mr. Flynn, and what I want is to protect my sister from a future I have already survived."

His face softened, as if he were beginning to understand a little about her. He nodded.

"So you wish to keep the marriage intact and work something out for how we will proceed?"

"Wish is a strong word," she said with a shake of her head. "I believe that may be the best course."

To her surprise, he smiled. "It is something to consider."

"I think Gemma is correct," Mrs. Flynn said, breaking the moment between them without even trying. "Crispin, you could make an argument about fraud or duress and it would go to the courts and be dragged out for months, while you and especially Gemma are the topics of a kind of gossip that I promise you is nothing like the whispers about the playful antics of you and your brother over the years."

Annabelle nodded. "There would be censure for you both. It could very well be irretrievable."

Crispin's full lips were pinched. He continued to look at Gemma, holding her stare with his really very beautiful blue ones.

"Would censure pass to you, Annabelle? To Rafe and Serafina? To Mama?" he asked.

Rafe stepped forward now. "Yes. I believe this is the kind of scandal that might affect us all. Serafina would likely know best. But none of us would tell you to make this decision based upon what we would suffer."

Now Crispin turned and looked at his family. There was something different in the set of his jaw, as if he had changed in the brief time they'd been apart. Gemma found herself mesmerized by it.

"But I must consider it," Crispin said softly. "I must consider the consequences to my family and to Gemma. After all, it is I who did this with my foolish actions. *I* created this."

He looked at her again and reached for her. She let him take her hands, felt the warmth of him in his rough fingers. She couldn't withdraw and couldn't look away as he leaned in.

"I am truly, deeply sorry, Gemma."

She blinked at sudden tears that flooded her eyes. He had said those words before, but this was the first time his apology felt whole. It sank into her, washing away some of the anger she felt toward him. She nodded.

"I know you are," she whispered.

He nodded and pulled away. "I think Gemma and I need

some time to discuss this matter and others alone. But may we return for supper tomorrow night?"

"Of course," Rafe said. "Perhaps you can see Crispin as well and visit Serafina, though I think she will be abed still."

Crispin frowned. "See Crispin?"

"Yes. We named the baby that, you see. Crispin Reginald. After you and father."

The way Crispin staggered back, Gemma felt she had no choice but to reach out, steadying him with a hand against his arm. For a moment, tears brightened his eyes and he blinked to clear them.

"That is an honor to share a name with your son, Rafe. Perhaps I can do a better job moving forward in showing him how to behave."

"He's a Flynn," Marcus Rivers said with a laugh behind them. "You two have already blazed a spectacular trail for the boy."

The others laughed, but Crispin was still struggling with what were clearly extreme emotions. He nodded once more.

"So, tomorrow."

"Tomorrow." Rafe turned to Gemma, and she couldn't help but smile at his continually welcoming expression. Whatever they had discussed in this room about her, Crispin's brother did not seem to fully judge her. Yet. "I look forward to it, Gemma."

"As do I, Your Grace," she said with a slight incline of her head.

"Great God, woman—*Rafe*," he said with a laugh as he hugged first his brother and then gently embraced her. "You are my sister now. You can't 'Your Grace' me or I shall expire."

Gemma stood in stunned shock as the rest of the family repeated the embrace that Rafe had begun, each murmuring words of encouragement and support. Even Rivers pulled her closer for a moment.

"They're a family worth joining, my lady," he said. "But

we protect our own."

When she pulled back, she looked at him, but his face was unreadable. He merely smiled mildly and followed as the entire group escorted them to the carriage outside. But as they waved them off and they drove away, Gemma couldn't help thinking that whatever had happened in the billiards room was going to have broader reaching repercussions. And she wasn't certain she wanted to deal with those.

Not now. Not ever.

CHAPTER NINE

Crispin watched as Gemma picked at what was left of her supper, running the fork over the remnants of chicken and vegetables. When they had returned home in the late afternoon, she had retired to his chamber, but she clearly hadn't gotten any rest there. There were dark smudges beneath her gray eyes and a sad expression on her face that gave him an odd desire to take her hand or let her rest her cheek on his shoulder.

But there were distances to be kept and unanswered questions which required addressing. Of course, everything in him told him to follow his normal mode of behavior and ignore the unpleasant duty at hand, but he couldn't. This had to be dealt with.

He cleared his throat. "Why don't we retire to the parlor, Gemma, since neither of us seems especially hungry?"

She jolted, as if she had been daydreaming and forgotten he was there. He had to wonder if she had only been thinking about their situation, or if other thoughts plagued her.

She glanced down at her plate and frowned. "I hope your cook will not be offended. The food is delicious, I am just…"

He held up a hand. "I think everyone in my household is aware these are trying circumstances. I'm sure she will not be offended, especially since I will be certain we pass our apologies to her."

Gemma's face relaxed a little. As Crispin motioned to one of the footmen that they were finished, he shook his head slightly. Worrying about hurting the feelings of a cook didn't seem to match with the idea that this woman was some kind of killer.

They stood at the same time and he came around the table to offer her an arm, which she took with only a slight hesitation. When her fingers closed gently around his bicep, Crispin felt her touch all the way to his gut. It was odd how visceral a reaction he had when she laid her hands on him. The few times it had happened so far had lit his body on fire.

But he had no idea of their future, there was no reason to allow desire to confuse the issue. He led her to the parlor and closed the door behind them. She pulled away from his arm and walked to the settee beside the fire. He leaned against the door and watched her settle in, her frown still deep and troubled.

"Would you like a drink, my lady?"

She jerked her attention to his face before she slowly looked across the room toward the sideboard. "Do you think that is wise?"

He flinched. So she was already judging him a drunkard. Of course how could she not? She had seen what damage he could do when inebriated. Who else but a man with no control would go so far?

"One for you, Gemma and *one* for me to take the edge off. I promise."

She seemed to ponder the wisdom of this suggestion for long enough that Crispin began to salivate for the brandy that all but seemed to glow on the table.

"Very well," she finally capitulated, and he almost sagged with relief. He hadn't had a drink all day and his hands shook as he moved to remedy that. He poured them each a glass and returned to her.

"It's strong," he cautioned, uncertain if any such spirits had ever passed her lips.

She shrugged one shoulder delicately. "I've had brandy before. And perhaps we need strong right now. I certainly feel very weak at present."

Crispin knew the feeling. He had reached for spirits with the same desire to be buoyed up. In the end, that never worked.

He sat on the chair that faced hers and took a sip. "I don't think we can avoid continuing the conversation that was begun in my brother's house this afternoon."

She took a gulp of her brandy and set it aside as she coughed delicately into the back of her hand. When she had recaptured her breath, she said, "You mean about what they said? That they believe we should remain married to avoid the scandal and ruin that will follow if we break this union?"

He nodded once, watching every line of her face to try to determine her character at a much deeper level than he had before. Was she truly capable of hurting another person? It was so hard to believe that when she looked so delicate. So fragile. Like porcelain that was beautiful but too easily broken.

"You've had time to think about it, as have I. It would be foolish to pretend it has not been on both our minds for hours."

"I would never pretend it wasn't. I have thought of nothing else since we left the duke's home. I would like to say one thing, though, before we begin."

He cocked his head. "Please do."

"Earlier today you asked my opinion about what I wanted." She fiddled with a loose thread on her sleeve, refusing to meet his gaze. "I wanted to thank you for that courtesy. I have not been allowed to have an opinion on the subject of my own future for a very long time and you were so earnest in the question that I felt comfortable in speaking the truth. I appreciate that more than you could know."

Crispin drew back. That moment in Rafe's parlor had been meant to make up for what a clod he'd been, and yet she acted as though he had granted her a boon rather than a common courtesy.

"Whatever happens, Gemma, please know that I would

always like you to be able to voice your opinion, especially when it comes to those things which affect you personally."

"You say that now, but you'd come to not like it," she said, her mouth thinning into a line.

He shrugged. "I might not always like your opinion, but that doesn't mean you don't have every right to voice it."

"That is a very unpopular notion about a woman's mind, Mr. Flynn," she said, her tone hardened into a challenge.

He met her gave steadily. "You have met my mother and Annabelle," he said. "Do you think I was raised without a healthy respect for an intelligent woman's mind?"

She hesitated, the upset leaving her face to be replaced with surprise. "I-I suppose that must be true."

He finished his drink and, ignoring the desire that burned in him for another, folded his arms. He could get a second, a third, a tenth one later, after Gemma had gone to bed.

"Now, what do you think about what my family said today?"

"About us remaining married?" Her tone was suddenly breathless.

He nodded.

She sighed. "I told you already what was at stake for me and for my sister. If I think in terms of only myself, there is a greater benefit to me in remaining your wife and dealing with the fallout from our hasty, reckless, scandalous union than in facing the consequences of breaking it. Even though I don't want to do this, that is the best thing for me."

He watched her, increasingly fascinated not just by his questions about her past, but with how she held herself. There was both strength in her and also hesitation. Like a tightrope walker at a traveling circus, she balanced between the two.

"Is it the best thing for me?" he asked softly.

She blinked a few times, her gaze flitting to his face. "I-I don't understand. I couldn't know the answer to that, after all you have lived with scandal in the past and I have no idea how amenable you are to even more of it."

"That isn't what I meant," he said, leaning forward. He held her stare now evenly, reading every flicker of her lashes, every dart of her pupils. "You alluded to a secret earlier, Gemma. A rumor about your marriage that might make me hesitate. And I have now been told what that rumor is."

She swallowed hard, and he watched the color drain slowly from her face until she was so pale that he was glad she was seated for fear that she would have fallen if she had been standing. She drew a few ragged breaths, her hands shaking as she reached for her forgotten brandy. She didn't speak again until she had drained the glass.

"Were you?" she finally asked, her voice cracked and broken.

He felt desperately sorry for her in that moment. There was no denying her pain at the subject, her humiliation and even the fear that flickered deep within her stare. But he ignored any instinct he had to back off or comfort her. Those were dangerous urges considering the subject.

"There is only one thing I need to know right now Gemma," he said, enunciating each word carefully. "Did you kill your husband?"

Gemma's head spun and she gripped the armrest of the settee until her nails dug into the fine fabric. This subject always elicited the same reaction, and now her stomach turned, threatening to cast up what she had managed to eat of her supper and her head began to throb.

She'd known Crispin would eventually hear the whispers that followed her wherever she went. She'd known it would change whatever delicate dynamic they were slowly building between them. She'd somehow hoped for more time. That she would find a way to tell him that thing that she had never been able to discuss fully, even with Mary.

She didn't want to discuss it now. But she had no choice. She was trapped in this man's home, as this man's wife, held in place by his focused, deep blue stare. He would not allow her to avoid it. He would hold her there by one way or another. As her husband, he had every right to do it, even with violence.

Though she couldn't imagine him doing so. But then, she hadn't imagined a great many things in her life were possible.

"I need to know, Gemma," he said, his voice neutral. He offered no comfort, but there was no censure either.

She swallowed. "I realize I'm taking a long time to answer," she said softly. "And I know you need to know the truth. But it is very difficult to address this subject."

His gaze gentled ever so slightly. "Take your time. We have all night if need be."

She nodded. It could take all night if recounting the story was as painful as she feared it would be. If only she could escape the telling. But if she wished to save her sister, and perhaps herself, this was the only way.

God damn her father.

She exhaled a long breath and then let the first words croak from her dry lips. "My father wanted sons," she began. "He was obsessed with having them to further himself financially through their marital and working potential and to continue his name. He and my mother tried for decades to have them, but between the failed attempts that resulted in my sister and I and so many lost children that tiny caskets became commonplace in our home, he was thwarted at every turn. Even when my mother died birthing the last dead child, his first response was to rejoice that he might find a new wife who would better do her duty."

"But he is not married, is he?" Crispin asked.

She shook her head. "You've met him. He has little to offer to a lady, and his methods of courtship are as crude as his methods of parenting. Perhaps he will one day find a desperate young bride and his attention will return to siring sons, but for now he has other things on his mind."

"Such as?"

She pursed her lips. "When I came of age, I was finally of use to him. I could marry well, you see, link him to a better family and perhaps convince my rich and titled husband to provide him with an income of some kind. He allowed me two Seasons, and when I could not find a man of my own choosing, he somehow hurtled me into a union with the Earl of Laurelcross."

Crispin nodded. "Did you *want* that marriage?"

She hesitated. With everything that had happened between the first time she'd met Theodore and now it was sometimes hard to remember her thoughts at the beginning.

"He was older than I by twenty years," she explained slowly. "But he seemed kind enough and his courtship was friendly. I recognized I could do far worse with my father at the helm of my future. I suppose the word *want* might be too strong, but resigned sums it up better."

Crispin flinched. "I know such things are commonplace amongst those with title and rank, but I'm sorry."

"At first there was no reason to be," she said, her mind turning back to those first days and weeks. "Theodore was attentive and gentle. He thought of my needs both in our day to day life and…" She hesitated as heat flooded her cheeks. "I'm sorry, I must be very blunt, but I assure you it is only because the details I'm about to share are pertinent to the question you asked me about his death."

Crispin's brow knitted in confusion, but he nodded. "You may be direct. After all, I am a Flynn, I assure you it cannot be anything I haven't seen nor done myself."

She drew in a sharp breath. "My husband introduced me to the pleasures that could be found in a marital bed. And I-I liked it."

She stopped talking because her throat felt like it was going to close. She struggled for a moment, keenly aware that Crispin's eyes were now wide, and he leaned in closer at that shocking admission. She had no idea what he thought of her, but she knew what the world would say.

Harlot.

"You say that this fact pertains to your husband's death?" Crispin asked when she had been silent for too long.

"May I have some water?" she asked, handing him her empty brandy glass. He took it, quickly moved to the sideboard where he gave her what she needed and sat back down. He held the glass out to her.

She took it, dragging in deep gulps of the water. It still tasted of spirits, but at least she felt she could breathe again.

"We went on that way for a few months and I found myself becoming content." She shook her head at the foolishness of that sentence now, with hindsight as her guide. "I *thought* we could have a life together."

"But?" Crispin asked.

"My husband began to change. *Then* I realized I had married a man with the same desires as my father had. The earl had children from his first marriage. But they were daughters who were grown and close to my own age. He never had a son, and soon he made it clear that my failure to breed was an issue."

Crispin frowned. "I see."

She shivered. "At first it was just looks in the hall when my courses would come. Glares that could cut like a knife, and icy silences. After months, he began with angry statements about how he had paid for a product he hadn't received. Then he progressed to screeching at me. He seemed to be morally affronted that he had offered me pleasure in our bed and in return I had not granted him the child he required."

"One has nothing to do with the other," Crispin muttered.

She shrugged. "Perhaps he figured that out too, because after a year and a half of our marriage, he took away whatever remaining pleasure he gave."

"How?"

"He would not touch me. He started using an oil to ease the joining when once he used to…" She blushed again, the humiliation of this story almost overwhelming. "Must I say it?"

"No." His lips pursed. "I understand, please continue."

She somehow gathered her remaining composure. "And then he even stopped doing that. He told me if I wanted to keep from feeling pain, I would ready myself with my own dirty hands."

"He said that to you?" Crispin asked.

"That and worse. He felt, I think, that he had been given a bad trade. He'd paid for a biddable young bride who would give him an heir and a spare to continue his line. I was a lame horse."

"His words again?" Crispin asked, and now he sounded angry.

"Perhaps," she whispered, trying not to remember every awful exchange. In the months since Theodore's death, the nasty things he'd said to her had faded somewhat, becoming softer in her mind. This brought the truth of them rushing back.

"This is a very sorry tale," Crispin said, and it sounded like he was speaking through clenched teeth. "With the villain in the piece a bastard who did not deserve you."

"He wasn't a villain," Gemma said, but the words were weak.

"He was," Crispin said, tone utterly firm and certain. "However, I still don't understand how he died. Did he drive you too far with his attitude? Did he turn to violence and you defended yourself against his attack?"

"No!" Gemma recoiled and thrust herself from the chair. She paced away from him. The entire room seemed to spin and she gripped the surface of a tabletop to center herself.

"Then explain it, Gemma." He stood up too but made no move toward her. "I have not judged you thus far, I swear to you that I will not judge you later. Just explain why people think you killed the man."

"I did kill him," Gemma murmured, and she watched Crispin stiffen. "Just not the way you think."

"Tell me," he insisted again.

Her breath came out as a sob and Gemma bent her head. She swiped at the tears that suddenly filled her eyes as she braced herself for what came next.

"One night he told me that he was coming to me for…for…"

"Sex," Crispin said gently.

She nodded. "Yes. I prepared myself."

Crispin's eyes fluttered shut for a brief second and his face drew tight. Was he disgusted by the fact that she touched herself? If so, he would be even more horrified to know she still did, finding that pleasure she liked so much even though it had caused so much pain.

"And?" he said, his voice strained.

"When Theodore entered my room, I was frustrated, I was ready. I wanted more than a few perfunctory thrusts from him. So when he got into the bed, I-I took charge."

Crispin's eyebrows lifted.

"I touched him. He was protesting, but I saw how he reacted, how he liked what I was doing even if he was far beyond the point of liking *me*. So I continued, and finally I straddled him and we began to make love." She stopped, placing her hands on her stomach as she tried not to think back, tried not to have those images mob her. "Just as I reached my peak, his face contorted. I thought he was finding his pleasure for a moment, but then it became clear it was something else. I flew for a maid, utterly naked, everyone came running, a doctor came…but it was too late."

"He died."

The words were said so flatly, a two-word summation of the most altering moment of her life. Gemma looked down at the floor and nodded slowly.

"An apoplexy, the doctor told me, after he shouted at me to put some clothes on and called me some variation on a whore."

"You were the man's wife," Crispin snapped.

She glanced up at his sharp tone and found he was red

with anger. At her or at the situation, she did not know.

"He was friendly with my husband and he blamed me for the death. The whispers started with him, with the servants. They spread out into Society and suddenly the salacious nature of his death wasn't good enough. The story twisted from that he had died between my legs to that I had killed him."

Crispin rolled his eyes. "But you *didn't* kill him, even if the old goat might have deserved a good smothering with a pillow for the way he treated you."

"And as a Flynn, you should know better than anyone that the truth isn't what matters. The rumor rules the day when it comes to reputation." She sighed. "That is my story. I hope you believe it."

"Considering you looked like you wanted to vomit the entire time you were telling it, considering there was nothing but truth in your blunt words, I will tell you I entirely believe what you say," Crispin said with a wave of his hand. "But I have a question."

She tensed and he shook his head at her reaction.

"It's not about the night of Laurelcross's death, Gemma. You've told me enough details about that."

Relief coursed through her. She'd been ready for censure and interrogation, but that didn't seem to the future.

"I'll try my best to tell you everything you want to know."

"How long were you married?"

"Three years," she said softly. It felt so much longer when she looked back.

"So you were married to the man for three years, he was an earl, and I assume he had a reasonable fortune."

She nodded. "He was not without means."

He laughed. "A formal way to say he was rich as Midas?"

She was shocked to find herself smiling at his quip. Here in the middle of talking about Theodore and all his ugly qualities, Crispin made her *smile*. Was that wrong? She wasn't certain, but she found herself liking it more than she should.

"Not quite Midas, but no pauper."

"And yet you have been his widow for…" He looked to her to fill the space.

"Almost a year to the day my father tricked you into marrying me," she said bitterly.

His lips pursed. "Why are you back in Sir Oswald's house, under his thumb? You should have had a good settlement from whatever wasn't tied up in the entail, perhaps been left a home to stay in. Laurelcross's death should have been a boon to you. It shouldn't have sent you back into the control of your father."

"Yes, that," she murmured, and the bitterness grew stronger in her mouth. "Theodore's will was clear. If I had produced a son, I would have received a massive settlement and all you say. I never would have had to marry again and my father couldn't have touched me. I likely would have even been able to save Mary."

"But?"

She shifted. "If I didn't produce an heir, then my husband left it up to his grown daughters to decide how I was settled. And they stripped me of everything. I was left without money, without property. They took any jewelry I had been given, including my wedding ring. They even took clothing and gifts I had received after the marriage."

"Did they return the dowry if they were going to set you back to your original state?" She lifted her brows and held his stare long enough that he shook his head. "Of course not."

"And now you know every humiliating detail, Mr. Flynn, of my past and of my husband's untimely death, as well as the reasons why I was damaged socially and financially by it. I believe I no longer have any secrets from you."

"That shall make our marriage quite boring, I think," he said, once again smiling at her and once again eliciting the same from her when she should have been weeping in humiliation.

She tilted her head and forced herself to meet his all-too-beautiful blue eyes. "But that statement leads us back to the original subject. *Will* we remain married or will you pursue your desire to somehow see the thing annulled?"

CHAPTER TEN

Crispin heard the tone of Gemma's voice when she said the word *annulled*. It was like it was a curse word to her, even though she had wanted this arrangement no more than he had. But his spinning mind kept reviewing the consequences his family had laid at his feet. Consequences for them. For him. But mostly, for her.

And he knew exactly why she wanted to avoid them. Hearing her story, he could well imagine what she wanted now was a very proper life where no one would dare whisper one thing.

He sighed. "Being my wife won't be easy. You are tired of the rumors, I know, but my name and how I have behaved will only create more of that for you."

"True whether we stay married or not," she pointed out with a laugh that he could see held no humor. "We've already established that if you petition to have the marriage dissolved it will cause more trouble for me. But this isn't just about me. You are involved as well. Since you don't care what anyone thinks—"

He raised a hand to cut her off. He had already spent the day having his selfishness thrown in his face, there was no need to rehash.

"I don't care what anyone thinks about *me*. So if this was

about a stolen phaeton or a torn gown or a thwarted duel, you are correct, I wouldn't give a damn. I would let it play out and perhaps even relish it."

Her cheeks turned pink again and she dropped her chin. "I see."

"But it isn't," he continued. "For the first time in a long time, what I have done isn't all about me. I have the potential to damage my family and to destroy you and your sister. So what can I do?"

"You could walk away," she said with a brief glance at him. "You have every opportunity to do so."

"And become a monster in every sense," he mused. He felt close enough to that edge as it was when he considered...

Well, everything he didn't want to consider. That he *couldn't* consider when faced with this decision.

"What do you propose, then?" she asked.

He cleared his mind of all the tangled thoughts that troubled him, took a deep breath and merely looked at the woman in front of him. She was undeniably one of the most beautiful creatures he had ever had the pleasure to look at. Beyond her beauty, though, there was something else. A quality that drew him in. Perhaps it was strength or resiliency or something else that he could not name.

He was drawn to her. And that draw had turned into full-blown desire when she talked about sex and her enjoyment of the acts in the bedroom. Though she had been embarrassed to reveal those telling secrets, he had seen the glimmer in her eyes. The need that had obviously gone unfulfilled for far longer than her husband had been dead.

It was a need he could very easily satisfy now. Every night. For a very long time before he bored of her. Having a willing—dare he say wanton?—wife would go far in making up for the shackles a marriage meant to him.

And it would save her from ruin. Save his family from despair. Since there was no other good choice at present, he knew what he *had* to do.

"We are stuck, my lady." He smiled as he corrected himself. "*Gemma*. I think you know that as well as I do."

She nodded. "I do, Mr. Flynn."

"Crispin," he said softly. "It's time you started calling me Crispin."

She squeezed her eyes shut as if she knew what crossing the line into that familiarity meant. "Crispin," she finally repeated on a rough whisper.

God, he wanted to make her say his name like that out of pleasure instead of pain and resignation.

"But it does not have to be horrible," he continued, moving toward her. "I am not like your husband."

She caught her breath. "I hope you will not be."

"I won't. I guarantee it. I have no care in the world if you provide me with heirs and I would not think to punish you if you didn't."

She nodded slowly, but he could see she didn't truly understand his meaning.

"But that isn't what I'm saying. Your husband was apparently of a delicate nature. Giving you pleasure was a chore he completed, I suppose. And when you demanded it, he wasn't able to oblige." Now he reached out and dragged his hand against her cheek. Her skin was impossibly soft and he almost growled as he stroked it. "I am able. And I would not see making you quake and moan and beg as a chore."

Her breasts lifted up and down at a wild pace thanks to her short breath, and Crispin smiled as her pupils dilated. She wanted him. And that desire only increased his own.

"We can be as strenuous as you like," he continued, sliding his fingers into her hair and gripping the base of her skull firmly but gently. He tilted her face up, molding her against him so that he knew she felt his erection against her belly. "In fact, I would insist on it. I will make you come, Gemma. I will make you scream. I will enjoy every damn moment of it."

He expected her to agree or disagree to these things, to say something at all. But to his surprise, she instead launched herself against him, crushing her mouth to his in a heated, desperate kiss.

He caught her seeking tongue in his mouth and sucked hard as he tightened his embrace and took back over in his seduction. She moaned into his mouth, arching her hips as she tangled her tongue with his. He couldn't help but respond to her ardor, even though he was surprised by it. Despite her confessions about wanting to be pleasured, most ladies did not act with such abandon.

He counted himself lucky, in that moment, that he had found one who did. It was intoxicating. So intoxicating that he backed her across the room until he lowered her onto the settee. She relaxed back, her arms still around him so he could not escape and continued kissing him with passion.

"Slow down," he murmured as he pulled back a fraction to look into her eyes. The dove gray was filled with panic and desperation. Not what he wanted. "I'm not going anywhere."

She swallowed hard. "I must seem quite foolish to you."

He shook his head as he found the buttons on her gown along the front. One by one he freed them without breaking eye contact with her. "On the contrary, you are incredible. But I don't want to rut with you like a dog. Not at this moment. I want to make this last."

She stared at him like she didn't understand, and he frowned. Her damned husband, who acted like pleasure was something she should grovel for...even when Laurelcross was thinking about her needs in the beginning, had sex been a perfunctory act? Just enough to give her a flutter of pleasure and then out the door with hopes that his seed had been planted?

If that was true, this woman was about to get a very different experience. Crispin shifted his weight from her and got up. She watched him go, and he smiled to reassure her while he approached the parlor door and turned the key. He didn't want interruptions of any kind, that was for certain.

"Stand up," he ordered.

She clutched her open gown around herself and did as she had been told, but when her fingers went to close the dress, he shook his head.

"I'm not having you stand so you can fix yourself," he clarified. "I'm having you stand so I can do this."

He moved on her and slowly slid his hands beneath the shoulders of her gown. He slid the fabric from her body, letting his hands glide down her goosebumped arms, her trim waist, her perfect hips until the entire contraption fell at her feet. She stood in what looked to be a very cheap chemise, one that was well worn enough that it was nearly see-through. His heart stuttered, for he could see the lines of her body with almost perfect clarity.

"God help me," he muttered before he cupped the back of her neck and drew her in for another kiss. She whimpered against his lips, the needy sound coursing through his veins and settling heavy in his already hard and ready cock.

"I don't think it's fair that I'm the only one in my undergarments," she whispered as he broke their kiss to drag his lips down her throat.

He chuckled. "You may divest me of whatever you like, Gemma, but be warned…I do not wear undergarments."

Her eyes went wide. "You mean beneath your clothes you are…are…naked? Entirely naked?"

"Entirely," he said, holding his arms out as if in offering. "Do you still wish to undress me?"

She nodded swiftly and unhooked his jacket first. She shoved it from his body and tossed it aside without seeming to care where it landed. He smiled as she went to work on his shirt, pulling and tugging at his cravat and eventually the buttons that kept her from bare skin. When she managed to wrestle the garment free of his trousers and open it, she gasped and stared at his chest beneath.

"What?" he asked, enjoying how her hands trembled as she reached out to smooth her fingers across his flesh. The touch was like electric heat and his cock throbbed with it.

"When you slept last night...was it only last night?" She shook her head. "I-I watched you and I wondered, I wondered what you looked like under your clothes."

His mouth dropped open at her unexpected admission. "You did? I thought you hated me."

"I did, a little," she whispered, her voice shaking. "But I also couldn't help but be fully aware of how handsome you were. How...desirable."

He frowned. "When I woke, I feared I might have done something to you...forced you."

She met his gaze. "If you had climbed into bed with me, I don't think you would have had to force anything. I think I would have been as wanton then as I am being now, despite my hesitations and misgivings."

"You are not being wanton," he murmured as he pushed his shirt away and gave her a full view of his chest and bare arms. "You are being wicked and wonderful. I hope you will never be anything less when it comes to me and my bed."

She didn't respond, but pressed her hand flat against his chest. "So beautiful," she whispered, more to herself than to him. She moved closer, dragging her fingers against him. "I want more."

He nodded, barely able to maintain his composure with her looking at him like he was a cake she wanted to devour.

"You'll get it, but once we remove these trousers, I shall be naked and I will have a very hard time not plunging inside of you right away, so why don't we focus on you for a moment?"

She let her gaze hold his again. "Should I remove my chemise?"

He held back a strangled moan and managed to squeak out, "Yes, I think that would be best."

Slowly, she grasped the edge of the last scrap of her clothing and tugged it up, up, over her thighs, over her hips, over her breasts and finally up and over her head to toss away.

She stood before him, naked, blushing slightly but not making a move to cover herself.

Of that fact, he was eternally grateful because all he wanted to do was stare at her. She was perfection, utterly beautiful in every way. Her breasts were full with dusky, hard nipples. They swelled over a trim waist and slightly flared hips. It was the kind of body men had been sketching and waxing poetic about for all time. The kind of body men dreamed of when they pleasured themselves. The kind of body men had killed for.

His hands shook as he reached for her. He caught her hips and moved her closer, close enough that he could explore without effort. Then he began to touch her, sliding his hands over her hips, cupping her backside until she hissed out a surprised gasp of pleasure. He kneaded the soft flesh there, exploring her reaction of bliss and filing it away for later use.

He slid his hands upward now, across the smooth line of her spine, around her ribcage, and finally he cupped each breast. Her head tilted back in surrender. When she did so, her back arched and the unintended offering she made was just too much. He leaned down and sucked one tight nipple between his lips. She moaned as he swirled his tongue around her, over and over.

She quaked in his arms, her soft moans growing louder with every suckle, every hot sweep.

"Oh God, Crispin," she finally managed on a strangled gasp. "I can't—I want—"

He pulled back reluctantly to look up at her. She still had that desperation on her face and perhaps he was beginning to realize why. She was a sensual creature, one who liked sex even if the world told her that was wrong. And she had been without for a very long time.

He gently steadied her, then released her. "Lay down," he said softly.

She blinked as if coming back to reality, then nodded, taking her spot lying across the settee a second time. She stared up at him, watching every movement as he found the waist of his trousers and freed what seemed like far too many buttons. Finally, he pushed them away and stood before her, erection curling against his belly.

She sat up on her elbows, and he was nearly undone when she licked her pink lips.

"That is…impressive," she murmured.

He couldn't help it—he tilted his head back and laughed at her compliment and the shaky way she delivered it. How long had it been since he laughed like that with a woman…hell, with anyone? It seemed like forever. But his humor didn't stop him from bracing an arm on either side of her head and lowering himself against her.

"It's what a man does with what he has, my dear," he said softly, his mouth a fraction of an inch from hers. "But I thank you for the compliment."

"You're welcome," she choked out, her voice trembling.

He smiled. "Are you ready?"

She nodded, but he still snaked his hand between them and found the soft outer folds of her pussy. He opened her delicately, never tearing his eyes away from hers, and stroked his index finger across her entrance. She was not lying when she said she was ready. She was wet and hot and as he touched her, she arched for more with another of those beautifully needy moans that seemed to directly tug his cock.

"Good," he panted. "Because I'm more than ready to be inside of you."

"Please," she whimpered, her arms coming around his shoulders. "Please hurry."

It was all she needed to say. He pressed the head of his cock to her slit and pushed. There was no resistance as he glided inside, except for the inner muscles of her body, made tight by months of being unused. They relaxed swiftly enough, though, when he flexed his hips against her and she welcomed him inside fully with a sigh of pleasure.

"My God, you are perfect," he grunted, trying very hard to

control himself so he wouldn't just fuck her like an animal. It hadn't been *that* long since he had a woman, but he felt as if it had been forever when he was inside of her.

"Then take me," she pleaded, lifting to force his movement. "Please take me. I need you to."

That was all. Those words stole all his control, all his good intentions to take his time. His hips began to move, almost without his permission, and he took her with long, hard strokes. She gasped, arching with every one, meeting him and squeezing him both as he entered and withdrew. She mewled with pleasure, her fingernails digging into his shoulders, her cheeks darkening with a blush and finally she let out a keening cry and her body spasmed around his in one of the most powerful orgasms he had ever seen a woman experience.

He pounded harder through her crisis, hoping to drag out her pleasure longer, but all the while her body milked his release to the surface. As she thrashed beneath him, he had little choice—with a roar he came deep within her. The pleasure was so intense that his vision went dark and his arms shook as he lowered himself on top of her to allow for a moment of respite.

CHAPTER ELEVEN

"I think our argument is over," Gemma said from beneath him, her voice slightly muffled by his shoulder.

Crispin shifted to look down at her. "Was that an argument? Because if it was, I shall pick fights with you twice a day."

He smiled as she blushed, her eyes bright with her recent release. She seemed much more at ease in that moment, and how could she not be? The tension she'd been carrying for a year must have been heavy indeed.

"Perhaps an argument is not the best word," she conceded. "The *discussion*, about whether we would stay married."

"It is over," he admitted, a bit of solemnity returning to the situation as he slid from her body with a soft groan of displeasure. "We have consummated the union, which would negate any argument I would have thought to make about the fraud that brought us here."

She watched as he stood and searched around for his trousers on the floor. Propping herself up on one elbow, seemingly unaffected by her state of nudity, she said, "And are you sorry, then? That you took away your out?"

He looked down at her, beautiful and tousled by lovemaking. Normally he was bored of a woman the moment he found release, but Gemma did not bore him. Not yet. He wanted to explore her a bit more, not just her lush body...but everything else.

"I'm not sorry."

She shifted and for the first time doubt returned to her face. "And you...you didn't find it difficult to want me?"

His brow knitted with confusion. "You couldn't tell by my ardor?" he laughed. She didn't join him with even a smile, so he perched himself on the edge of the settee and looked down into her face. "Gemma, there is no difficulty whatsoever for me in wanting you. There may be difficulty in stopping so that we can do mundane things like eat and drink and get dressed."

Her lips parted slightly in surprise, but then she turned her face with a bashful smile. "Good, I'm glad that at least for now this is not a...a chore for you."

He frowned, for he wasn't certain that it wouldn't someday become a chore. There had only been one woman in his life he had pictured spending more than a few nights with. That had not worked out. The others...well, they were in and out of his mind and his bed swiftly.

But then, Gemma didn't want him beyond sex any more than he did. They could work this out.

"I think we need to discuss the parameters of this marriage," he said.

She sat up, the relaxation that had been on her face now fading and returning to anxiety. He hated to do that to her, but there was little other choice now.

"Very well," she said, grabbing for her chemise. She didn't put it on, but laid it over herself like a blanket. He was almost happy for it—her naked body was a fair distraction when discussing something so serious.

"What do you expect from a husband, Gemma?"

She bit her lip. "I don't think anyone has ever asked me that before."

"Well, you've never had a choice in seemingly anything before," he replied with a shrug.

"Including this, to be fair to both of us," she said with a

faint laugh.

"Yes, but with us the difference is that we were both forced into this circumstance, but now we can decide our fate together." He smiled to reassure her. "So be honest. What would you like from a husband?"

She shifted. "When I was a girl, I would have said a man who loved me."

Crispin tensed. Great God, she couldn't ask him for that. He couldn't give it to her. He wasn't certain he was even capable of such a thing ever again.

"But," she continued, "I think I am more practical now, with time and experience. And in this situation, I think it would be expecting too much from both of us. So instead, I think I would like respect from my husband."

"And what does respect mean to you?" he asked, tilting his head.

"Exactly what you are doing right now, Crispin," she admitted. "You ask me my opinion and it seems you care about it."

"I do," he said softly.

She smiled. "I would like a little freedom, since I have been in what amounts to a gilded…and sometimes far less gilded…cage for the past five years."

"Freedom to do…" he began, wondering if she meant she wanted to go off and pursue other lovers. His stomach began to knot.

"Not to look at every penny spent of my pin money, should I receive any," she said with a frown that told him that was exactly what her so-called husband had done. "The freedom to spend time with my sister or my friends. The freedom to run some elements of the household without being watched and judged."

"Great God, you *were* in a prison," Crispin muttered.

She shrugged. "But can you do those things?"

"You will have pin money, of course," he said, trying not to think about his depleted resources. He would have to talk to

Rafe about that, he supposed, his brother was doing very well now, as was Marcus. "And you may spend it as you please, because it is yours. I want you to spend time with your friends and your family and hopefully my family. I would never count your hours. As for running the household, take it all. I care very little for such things and I know poor Fletcher is often frustrated by my unwillingness to participate in conversations about silver or menus."

"And you will introduce me to the household, then?" she asked.

He jolted. "Damn, I suppose I should have done that today."

"Well, we weren't certain of our future, were we? But now that we are to remain married, it would be a courtesy to them to do so." She tried to smile, but it wavered. "And hopefully it will reduce a bit of the humiliation I feel when they enter a room and look at me."

"Gemma, God, I'm a clod," he said, reaching for her hands. "I was not raised under particularly normal circumstances, though I think you can see that my mother is the picture of gentility. But I sometimes don't think beyond myself. You will have to bear with me and perhaps gently point out when I am being an idiot of the highest order."

She laughed. "Will it happen often?"

He grinned. "Likely every damned day. But let me further assure you that my servants have seen and dealt with some...well, we will just say circumstances that have likely scandalized them more than this one."

Her mouth twisted. "Worse than a bride you had to marry after you lost a bet?"

"This would be the first time I did that, of course," he said. "I think." He expected her to laugh again, but when she didn't, he rushed to continue, "But all I'm trying to say is that I think they'll be relieved to have a lady in the house. A true lady who will put things in order. You will have no trouble or judgment from anyone in my employ. If you do, they will no longer *be* in my employ."

She drew back. "Truly?"

"Truly."

She slid her hands from his. "Crispin, do you often drink so much that you don't recall what you've done?"

He was accustomed to seeing her blush by now, but he was taken aback when he felt his own cheeks begin to fill with embarrassed heat. "I—many men drink, Gemma. All the men in my acquaintance."

She held his gaze. "That wasn't the question."

He sighed. "I didn't always do this, if that is what you want to know. But in the last year, yes, I have likely been too deep in my cups and far too often."

"Why in the last year?" she pressed.

He scowled as he turned his face. "I think that is enough confession for this evening."

He knew she was watching him as he stood up and walked away. He knew she wanted to question him further, but the subject she had just broached was not one he discussed with anyone *ever*. No one knew the answer to her question and he wasn't about to start giving over his soul to her about something that was none of her damned business.

He moved away and found himself stopping at the sideboard. He had only had that one drink all night and despite what he had just said about imbibing too much, his body ached for the bottle. Any bottle.

But before he could do anything about it, he felt a gentle touch on his still bare elbow. He turned to find Gemma behind him. Utterly naked Gemma, her delicate hand sliding up his biceps as she held his gaze evenly.

"We are all entitled to some secrets, Crispin," she whispered. "Please don't think I will pursue yours like a bulldog. I have no interest in making your life difficult, especially since you seem to be willing to extend the same courtesy to me."

He found himself nodding, though he couldn't have

formed a word to respond in that moment. Not when she eased closer and let her breasts flatten against his chest. Now when she tilted her lips up in clear offering. Offering he couldn't deny. Offering that made him forget everything and anything else.

He ducked his head and kissed her, breathing her in, drinking her in like he would have done brandy in the hopes it would empty his head. She did it, oh so much more pleasurably. And as he backed her toward the settee a second time, he pushed away all thoughts of anything but this woman and how much he wanted to be inside her.

Gemma didn't think her body had ever been so satisfied, even as her mind raced. She lay in Crispin's bed...well, *their* bed, at least for the time being, staring up at the ceiling. They had made love twice in the parlor and once here before he drifted off to sleep. She hadn't thought that was possible. Certainly Laurelcross had never made the barest attempt at such a thing. If she had asked to be touched more than once in a night, he probably would have looked at her in utter disgust.

But Crispin...Crispin seemed to like bringing her pleasure. He was aroused by it, that much was clear from how his body reacted.

And yet despite all that, she could not sleep. All she could think about was their talk in the parlor about the design of their marriage going forward. Crispin had said the right things when it came to her requests in a husband. But he was hiding something. Something dark. Something deep. It was a secret she found herself wanting to know even though she'd told him she didn't care.

"You shouldn't care," she whispered out loud.

Beside her Crispin stirred, and she froze. Was he so light a sleeper that her quiet admonishment to herself had woken him?

Would he confront her? Could she pretend he had dreamed what he heard?

He moaned a little and she relaxed. He was moving in his sleep due to a dream. He wasn't awake. She held still and waited for him to fall back into deeper slumber, but he didn't. He moved more, his legs and arms reaching for something that wasn't there as incoherent sounds of distress left his lips.

"I'm sorry," he murmured, his tone broken and shaking. "I'm so sorry."

She reached out, unable to resist when he was in such obvious distress. She touched his bare arm and found a thin sheen of sweat on his body. "Crispin," she said gently. "Crispin, wake up."

He did just that in a burst, sitting bolt upright with a heartbreaking cry of, "No!" He sat there, panting for a moment, his fists clenching at the bedclothes. Then he turned toward her. "I-I'm sorry."

"There's no need," she reassured him, wanting so desperately to touch his face but resisting. He still looked rocked by whatever horror had entered his sleep. "You were dreaming. It was just a dream."

"That's what they say," he breathed, flopping back on the bed and covering his face with his forearm.

She frowned. What did he mean by that? Was his dream about something that had truly happened? Perhaps that dark secret that had been troubling her in the moments before he woke?

She lay down on her side and finally allowed herself to touch him. She smoothed a hand over his bare chest. He tensed at first, but then he exhaled slowly.

"Do you want to tell me what it was about?" she asked softly.

Any tension that had left his body with her touch returned as he stiffened beside her. He was quiet for a long moment, then he grunted, "Don't remember."

He was lying. She was certain of it, but if he didn't wish to tell her, she had no right to demand more. But it hurt her to see him so upset. Hurt her to know that he needed comfort that she couldn't provide.

She glanced down at his body, half-hidden beneath the sheets. Unless she could provide that comfort somehow.

She let her hand at his chest glide lower, caressing the defined muscles of his belly. He stiffened again, but this time it wasn't in displeasure. Slowly, he lowered his arm from his face and stared at her.

"What are you doing?" he asked.

She smiled. "If I cannot talk to you about your dream, I'm simply hoping I can help in some other way." His eyes went wide and suddenly she felt very awkward indeed. "Unless…unless you don't want me to do so."

He shifted closer to her on the bed. "Trust me, Gemma, I very much want you to do so, if you can take more tonight. You must be sore."

She slid her hand further under the sheet and found his cock already half-hard. She smoothed her hand over it, loving how it came to life with her touch.

"Sore from wanting more, perhaps," she whispered, watching his face as she began to work her hand over him again and again. His neck strained and he let out a groan of pleasure. He was entirely at her mercy. And she liked it.

She leaned in to kiss him, and he lifted his mouth to her greedily. She sank into his lips, tasting him, teasing him. He was allowing her control, whether by design or not, and it both thrilled and terrified her. The last time she had taken control, it had not ended well.

But she shoved that out of her mind and instead focused on Crispin's pleasure. Her working hand around his cock was obviously what he needed, for he arched his back and thrust up into her with moans that vanished into her mouth.

"I want you around me," he murmured, his groggy voice heavy with desire. She hesitated long enough that he met her gaze. "What is it?"

"I'm worried that—"

He smiled and the softness of it silenced her. "You can't break me, Gemma. Only please me."

She swallowed hard and straddled him. She leaned down, prolonging the wait for taking him, and kissed him again. His fingers came up to tangle in her hair and he sucked her tongue gently. Her body twitched in response and the wetness that had already begun from touching him increased tenfold. She wanted him. She needed him.

Those desires overcame her fear and she slid into position above his seeking cock. He gripped her hips and met her gaze as she slowly lowered over him, taking him in inch by heavenly inch until he was fully seated in her.

It was so different to be the one in control of lovemaking. It felt so different to hold him inside of her this way. She reveled in it for a moment until he gasped, "Please!"

His begging dragged her from her spell and she began to move over him. Slowly and first, but then faster. She rolled her hips over him, hitting the sweet spot of her clitoris each time. Her pleasure mounted higher and she squeezed his sides with her thighs as she rocked against him, seeking, reaching and finally exploding with a cry that ripped from her throat.

She continued to jerk over him, even as her orgasm made her movements erratic. He gripped her hips and guided her, lifting to meet her. With a deep, throaty groan, he arched her almost off the bed and she felt the hot burst of his seed deep within her.

They collapsed together, her body half on his, their breathing broken. He leaned down to press a kiss to her brow, then his arms closed around her and she felt him start to slip back into the sleep his nightmare had interrupted. She glanced up at him. His eyes drooped, his face relaxed and comfortable as if making love to her had at least cleared his mind from whatever he'd dreamed about.

She had never known anything like this physical connection with this man. But they shared it. And if it was all they ever shared, at least it was something.

CHAPTER TWELVE

Thanks to her aching body, Gemma was more than aware of every rock and bump of the carriage the next morning. As they rattled over cobblestones, she gripped the seat edge and tried to suppress a moan of both pleasure and pain. When she looked across to her husband, she found Crispin with an arched brow and a very smug grin.

"Sore?" he asked with laughter in his voice.

"Well-used," she teased, and saw desire light in his eyes at the term. Good, let him ache a little like she did, since she doubted the bumps made his body so very aware of what they had done last night.

"I'm pleased to use you well," he drawled. "But since our preparations were rushed this morning, I would suggest perhaps we have a long, hot bath drawn for you when we return. It will help with your soreness."

She smiled at the thoughtfulness of the suggestion, but she was struggling to feel anything but anxiety, even as they teased. "After an afternoon with my father, I think a relaxing soak would be just the thing." She shook her head. "Though I'm not certain it will be able to perform magic and make me entirely forget whatever is about to happen."

The smug grin faded. "I can well imagine the worry you feel when you are forced to face your father. But there is one thing to keep in mind."

"Yes?"

He reached out and briefly caressed her hand. Even through her thin glove, it was like a brand being pressed to her skin. He lit her on fire. "You are not alone in it."

She blinked away her desire and stared at him. "You are under no obligation to face off with my father—"

He cut her off with a laugh. "Indeed, I am. Isn't that in the marital vows? Thou shalt endure your wife's family and protect her from them always."

She couldn't help but join him in his laughter. "I don't know. I don't recall it, but my first marriage was long ago and my last one was very late at night."

"Then we shall assume that in my stupor I did recall that one thing correctly," he said, folding his arms as if that were the last word on it. "And even if it wasn't, I actually look forward to facing off with him."

"You do?" She shuddered. "I don't know how. He can be horrible."

"Yes, but you look at it all wrong, my dear. When he swipes at you, you cower from the attack, and of course you would. What choice did you ever have but to do so? Me, on the other hand..."

She leaned toward him. "Crispin, what are you going to do?"

He gave her a thin-lipped smile she did not trust in the slightest. "Your father wanted me, did he not? He chose me as his mark for his marriage trap? Well, he's about to find out exactly what winning me means to him. Hell, by the time I'm done with him, *he* may ask that our union be dissolved."

Her laughter faded at that quip and she felt the color drain from her face at the implication. "But you...you already told me you had set that idea aside, yes?"

He jolted at the question and met her eyes. "Gemma, you know the answer to that question. You and I came to an accord last night, completely separate from any arrangement your father made. He cannot break that and he no longer controls you. So do your best to enjoy your time with Mary and leave your father to me."

"But I—"

"Gemma..." he said, tone filled with playful warning.

She shook her head. He was teasing her, of course, but there was more to his expression. He truly did seem to want to be her champion of some kind. Or at least be the one to put her father in his place.

She rather looked forward to it. At least she did until their carriage slowed to a stop at her father's home. Then the churning in her stomach returned. It must have shown on her face, as well, for Crispin frowned before he stepped out of the carriage. When he turned back to retrieve her, his smile was gentle.

"Trust me," he murmured.

She smiled, but had no reply. What reply was there? They had known each other but two days, and for half that time she had believed him to be a villain. Now it was different, of course. Yesterday had changed things.

Last night had changed things.

But she certainly wasn't ready to put her trust in this man who she knew so little about. In the foyer Williams greeted them and led them to the same shabby little parlor where Gemma had first met Crispin. Again it seemed like years ago rather than days, and she sighed as she looked around the rundown room.

"You look tired, Williams," she said, turning to face her father's longtime butler.

The other man's lips pinched. "I'm sorry, my lady—er, Mrs. Flynn."

She tilted her head. "You needn't be sorry. I understand the conditions here. Has it been very difficult since my departure?"

The butler looked over his shoulder as if to confirm his master wasn't within hearing. "Miss Quinn has been agitated since your departure, and she and Sir Oswald have been in several rows."

"Oh dear." Gemma covered her face with her hand. "I had hoped but not believed they wouldn't continue to fight."

She felt Crispin's hand move to the small of her back, and though he said nothing, the comfort he offered was certainly there. It took everything in her not to lean back into him and vanish into his presence.

"Does Mary know of my arrival?" she asked.

"Yes, she was told that—"

Before he could finish there was a rush of feet in the hallway and Mary herself all but skidded into the room. When she saw Gemma, she let out a sharp cry and launched herself forward. Gemma caught her, nearly tumbling backward as she held Mary tight.

Williams arched a telling brow, then bowed from the room with some muttered words about fetching her father.

"Oh Gemma, I was so afraid for you," Mary whispered against her ear before she drew back and looked her up and down. "Why didn't you write?"

Gemma shifted. "I should have penned a short note, I'm sorry. Mr. Flynn and I have been somewhat busy trying to figure out what to do with this strange circumstance we have been thrust into."

Mary pivoted away from her, and her dark eyes locked on Crispin now instead. "You…" she said, her voice low. "What did you do to her? How could you?"

Crispin said nothing at the accusations, but stood impassive, with only the slightest look at Gemma.

"Mary!" Gemma cried, placing a hand in front of her sister to keep her from making movement toward Crispin. "Stop."

"Still he is silent," Mary snapped. "Is he mute?"

"*He* is not mute," Crispin said softly. "But is there anything I could say to make you think better of me, Miss Quinn? After all, I swept into your home, drunk as anything, and left here with your sister as my…captive, I suppose, at least in your eyes. Why *would* you think well of me?"

Mary's mouth snapped shut at his quiet words and she stared at him for a moment, then back to Gemma. Gemma could see the questions on her sister's face, and she took both her hands.

"It isn't as you think. Both Mr. Flynn and I were taken advantage of by Father and—"

"Taken advantage?" her father tsked as he entered the room with the widest of smug grins. "I would say given you advantage, Gemma. And do you thank me?"

Gemma turned on him, her eyes narrowing as she looked him up and down. He had a new waistcoat, and an expensive one by the look of it. It must have been his reward to himself for managing to pull off the coup of Crispin's entrapment. And yet around him, their house crumbled.

"Thank you?" Gemma repeated, rage bubbling.

She said nothing more, for Crispin stepped between her and her father. "Sir Oswald, we have much to discuss, don't we? Why don't we retire together to your billiards room or your office and let the sisters reunite in private?"

Her father's eyes darted to Gemma and Mary, and he nodded once. "I'm sure neither one of us want to be involved with the hens, yes. Come, I have a good whisky that just arrived today."

Gemma tensed as Crispin's eyes lit up. He had not had much to drink since the morning he realized they were wed, but she'd seen him eyeing the liquor multiple times. And judging from the mistakes he made when drunk, she didn't relish the moment when the draw became too powerful for him to resist.

The men left the room, with only a brief glance over Crispin's shoulder for her. As soon as they were gone, Mary rushed to the door and slammed it, leaning against it as if she would keep them from ever returning.

Gemma examined her sister's face. Mary had dark circles beneath her eyes, and her frown was deep and filled with sadness and fear and anger.

"I'm so sorry you were left to worry," Gemma said softly as she advanced on Mary. She took her hand and led her to the settee where Mary all but collapsed. "But you can see now that I am unharmed and I hope that gives you some relief."

Mary stared at her. "How could I have relief? Yes, I am pleased to see you were not beaten, at least not where I can see it, but I can only imagine what other tortures you were subjected to."

Mary's deep blush made Gemma gasp. "Well, first off, no one has beaten me, not where you can or cannot see. And if you are implying that perhaps I was"—she dropped her voice—"raped, that is not the case, either."

Mary sagged a bit. "Thank God."

"Darling, you must listen. Father arranged this travesty. Crispin had nothing to do with it. Yes, he was foolish and drunk and those things kept him from protecting himself or me, but he is not the ogre you somehow think he is."

"How could he not be?" Mary sighed. "He stole you."

"No, Father sold me," Gemma replied, putting her sister's hand in her lap where she stroked it gently. "But Williams implies that the past two days have likely been harder on you than on me. What has happened here since my departure?"

Mary shook her head. "Oh, just Father being himself, you know. He was crowing when he returned from forcing you to wed. *Crowing*! I could not help it, Gemma, I-I shouted at him."

Gemma sucked in her breath. It had always been she who had faced off with her father, not her sister. That had been her only way to shield Mary.

"What did he do?" she asked.

Mary fisted her hand. "What do you think? He threatened me, of course. First with a beating I would not soon forget and then with being sold to the highest and worst bidder he could find."

"Did he touch you?" Gemma whispered.

Mary shook her head. "You know he only blusters. I'd heard him threaten you with violence without following through for so long that I hardly registered it. But the other thing…the other threat…"

"He is very capable of that, yes," Gemma said. "As we have seen twice with me, now."

Although she was beginning to feel she might have made a much better bargain the second time. Though she wouldn't admit that to her father, for certain.

"I have been allowed two Seasons…well, I'm halfway through my second, at any rate." Mary's voice shook. "Do you think he would do this?"

Gemma shook her head. "I don't know. Right now he is riding high off of landing Crispin. Despite his bad reputation, it is said my new husband has a great deal of money."

She hesitated as she thought of Crispin's face when she had said as much to him. He acted as if his coffers were not quite as high as was believed. She shook her head and continued, "Mary, you must be careful with Father. Don't fight with him and don't give him a reason to punish you with a future you will have no control over."

Mary put her head in her hands. "I'm not even close to finding someone to offer for me, Gemma. I cannot imagine he'll allow me my freedom for much longer one way or another."

"I'm sorry about that, Mary. I'm afraid the whispers about Laurelcross's death have likely damaged your chances in the marriage mart."

Mary laughed bitterly. "Or perhaps it is the common knowledge that Father gambles away his living or that he is willing to barter with his daughters or that he acts a fool regularly."

"Well, yes, I suppose those facts may have also played a part." She squeezed her sister's hand. "We'll work something out."

"What is there to work out?" Mary asked.

Gemma was taken aback by both the question and the tone in which it was asked. Mary had always been the lighter spirit of the two, looking for the bright side in all situations. But now Gemma saw defeat lining her sister's face, despair. It broke her heart.

"Mary—"

"No, we must be reasonable. If I do not find a husband of my own choosing within a few months, it is likely Father will take control in my third Season. He will decide and we all know what his criteria are." She sighed. "In the meantime, I will also suffer knowing you are shackled to a drunk and a scoundrel."

Gemma stood. "You can at least ease your mind about me, Mary. Honestly, I am not lying when I say that Crispin did not force me in any way. In fact, when he is not in his cups, he can be rather charming."

"Yes, bastards often are," Mary said, her tone dry as a fall leaf.

Gemma pursed her lips. "He has actually asked me what *I* want, Mary."

Her sister stared at her, and she could see that the concept was as foreign to Mary as it was to her. Mary let out a long sigh. "Well, that is a good sign, I suppose. But I also have to add that just because he asked you your desires does not mean he'll make any effort to grant them."

Briefly, Gemma flashed to Crispin's mouth on her, his hands on her, his body inside of her. With a jolt, she pushed those wicked memories away. That wasn't what Mary meant. Mary would be horrified if she ever knew about those things.

"You are right," she admitted. "He may not fulfill any promises made or implied. After all, Theodore behaved one way at the beginning of our union and eventually changed his colors significantly." She shivered. "And I confess that I do fear Crispin may do the same thing in time. But I can't live in that foggy future that does not exist. I must hold on to the time I am in and I tell you that for now, at least, Crispin is not a monster."

Her sister shook her head slowly and Gemma could see

she didn't believe her. With a sigh, she clasped Mary's hand.

"Come. Father has had the poor man under his sway long enough. Why don't we join them and you can see for yourself?"

Crispin had spent his life avoiding grasping bastards like Sir Oswald Quinn. They were the antithesis of all his family was and all he wanted to be. But here he was, standing in the man's run down billiards room, watching the knight of the realm pour him a drink.

He tried not to salivate as he tracked the amber liquid make its way to him, and he prayed his hands wouldn't shake as he took it.

"Thank you," he managed, subtly sniffing the liquid. God, it was like heaven. A very cheap version, yes, but heaven nonetheless. He would have to sip slowly so he wouldn't lose control. He didn't want to do that with Sir Oswald, but more than that, he didn't want Gemma to see.

"So did you get my minx of a daughter to come in line?" Sir Oswald asked with the most annoying laugh in all the empire bubbling from his lips. "Sometimes it takes a bit of muscle."

Crispin paused with his glass halfway to his lips and stared at his wife's father. "Are you implying that you have raised a hand to Gemma?"

The very idea of it made his vision blur and his stomach turn. Certainly Gemma had described a rotten life with this man, but she had not expressed that she had been abused.

Sir Oswald shrugged. "She might have deserved it, but I always spared the rod. The threat is often enough I've found, haven't you?"

"I don't threaten women," Crispin ground out. "Only a weakling does that."

"Hmph," Sir Oswald replied, seemingly unoffended by Crispin's accusation. "What brings you here?"

Crispin knitted his brow as he took a slow sip of the alcohol and let it burn its way down his throat. "My wife wanted to see her sister. And I wanted to discuss this marriage with you."

Sir Oswald shrugged. "What about it?"

"You realize I was too drunk to approve anything that night," Crispin said slowly. "And there is some proof that you intended to trap me from the beginning."

The other man chuckled. "And?"

"Well, part of the reason you chose me, I assume, is because of my money. You don't think I would use it to end this farce?"

The smile fell from Sir Oswald's face. "You would have no grounds."

"Fraud could be considered grounds," he said mildly. Of course he knew his own bluff, he simply enjoyed making Gemma's father squirm. As he was doing now.

"You would not."

"I assume the other part of why you chose me was my penchant for scandal," he said, taking another burning sip of whisky. "You created one thinking I would have no choice but to allow it. And yet, you don't believe I would be more than willing to create an even bigger one to escape?"

Sir Oswald's face was impassive enough, but Crispin saw the terror in his eyes. The desperation. It should have made him happy to know he had struck the man down with his threats. Instead it made him…

Nervous.

A man in such a state could easily hurt someone. Gemma was protected thanks to him, but what about Mary? Gemma obviously loved her sister, and if Mary's hatred of him was any indication, she felt the same way. If this man used her to try to further himself it would destroy the girl.

Not to mention what it would put Gemma through.

He shouldn't have cared about those things, but he did. Who wouldn't, knowing what Gemma had already endured?

"You wouldn't dare," Sir Oswald blustered, his face reddening and voice elevating.

"Test me," Crispin snapped back as he finished his drink in one long slug. As he slammed it down against the closest table the door to the billiards room opened and Gemma stepped inside, followed closely by her sister. Mary glared first at him, then at her father.

"We heard shouting," Gemma said, her voice remarkably calm. "I hope you two are not behaving badly."

Crispin stared at her. He could see her shifting into what was obviously a comfortable role. Peacekeeper. Apologist for her father. How long had she had to do this? Her whole life?

"Your husband was just talking to me about reneging on bets," Sir Oswald hissed.

Crispin squeezed his eyes shut. He'd been goading Gemma's father, but when he dared to look at her, he saw that that sentence terrified her. She didn't fully trust in him and his promises.

And why would she?

"Crispin," she said softly, staring at him.

He looked past her to Mary, who folded her arms and looked at him like he was yesterday's trash.

"Let Mary go riding with us this afternoon," he said suddenly, shifting his attention back to Sir Oswald.

Everyone in the room drew back at the shift of topic and he smiled. At least he was still capable of the element of surprise. A few more drinks and he would shock them all.

But Gemma's gaze kept him from taking one.

Sir Oswald looked at him, his eyes narrowed and filled with lingering anger over Crispin's suggestion that he would end the marriage with Gemma. He folded his arms.

"What is it worth to you, Mr. Flynn, to allow your wife to spend time with her sister?"

CHAPTER THIRTEEN

Gemma recoiled at her father's question and the ugliness to his tone as he asked it. Crispin clearly did not yet understand. If one challenged her father, one would be met with fire, not meekness.

Crispin's eyes narrowed and then he darted his gaze toward her. Their eyes met and she saw that he recognized the truth as well as she did. Her sister was in danger.

"What is the shared time worth?" Crispin mused, pacing the room. "An interesting question. What about the help of a duke?"

She sucked in her breath. Crispin's relationship with his brother was already strained one would have to be deaf and blind not to recognize that. And yet he offered her father access to the man?

What would his family think of her when they found out? Or worse yet, after they encountered her father? Her heart sank at the thought.

Her father merely gaped at Crispin, apparently struck dumb by the offer. Crispin smiled, but she could see there was no real warmth to the expression. No friendliness. He seemed disgusted by her father. Was he equally hardened to her now?

"We have already discussed some reasons why you chose me as your mark for this forced marriage, Quinn, but I would think my connection to the Duke of Hartholm is not the least of them."

"Everyone knows you two are estranged," her father spat, even though his eyes were lit up with interest.

"Estranged or not, my brother has already offered to help Mary with a Season," Crispin said softly. "With his help and the help of the duchess, your daughter could marry far better than you would ever dream. You could have access to more influence and wealth than you ever could have had with your precious potential sons."

As Mary let out a gasp from behind her, Gemma stared at her husband. She had never heard the duke make such an offer. He had said he might be able to help, yes, but this? This was far beyond the bounds of mere kindness.

"If this is true," her father said, "that would be a boon for Mary, indeed. What do you say, daughter?"

Mary's hands were clenched at her sides. She whispered, "A boon, yes. But at what cost?"

Crispin now looked at her sister and his expression softened. "A good point, Miss Quinn. After all, nothing in the world is ever free, is it? This offer *does* come at a cost."

Whatever headway Crispin had made with Mary now faded and Gemma saw the hatred for the man flash back into her eyes.

"What is the cost?" she asked.

He turned his attention to her father. "Mary will come to stay with Gemma and I for the remainder of this Season and all of the next."

As her father made a sound of utter outrage, Gemma's knees actually went weak at that statement and a flash of utter joy nearly swept away her control. Mary stay with them? It would mean her sister would be protected!

But they had never spoken of such a thing. Crispin could not truly want this.

"Crispin," she whispered.

He moved toward her and took one hand. "It is the only

way to keep Mary safe, yes?" he said softly.

She held his gaze as she nodded. "Y-yes."

"You will not interfere in her movements about Society and if you even think of arranging some kind of marriage without speaking to me or to my brother, I promise you it will go very badly for you." Crispin glared at her father. "In exchange, occasionally you will be allowed to chaperone the girl into the best Society parties and balls, and I'm certain my brother will introduce you to some of his new…" Crispin wrinkled his nose. "…*friends*."

Gemma watched her father closely and saw how much he wanted this, how much he ached for the acceptance Crispin now dangled before him like a bone before a pathetic dog. And still he had not yet answered.

"What do you think, Father?" she asked.

He looked at her, and the steel reentered his stare. "How dare you try to remove my only remaining daughter from my control," he sputtered.

"Please don't pretend as if you give a damn about Mary and her future beyond what it can grant *you*. Crispin is making a fair offer. More than fair, I would say."

"That is, assuming Miss Quinn would want to live with us," Crispin said, turning on her sister.

Mary folded her arms, her chin jutting out as she stared at Crispin, measuring the man who was her new and very much unwanted brother-in-law. Gemma held her breath. To protect her, she rather believed Mary would cut down the man before her, even if it meant her own ruin.

"You know I have no say in this," Mary said.

Crispin shrugged. "In my mind, you do. I wouldn't want you to be forced into any future that wasn't of your choosing."

Gemma shook her head. He was picking his words very wisely, making Mary think about what she had to lose. And by the way the color drained from her sister's cheeks, Gemma thought the message had been received perfectly clearly.

"I would be very happy in my sister's home," she choked

out. "And perhaps I could be a help to her as well. After all, she has a great deal to adjust to, doesn't she?"

Crispin smiled. "Doesn't she." He turned back to their father. "So, it is down to you, Sir Oswald, as the rest of us are in perfect accord. Will you allow the youngest to join the oldest in her new home, with all the advantages it will bring to you?"

Her father shifted from foot to foot, and then he sniffed. "I will consider it."

Crispin's face twisted into a sneer and he took a long step toward her father. With a cry, Gemma hurtled herself between them, pressing a hand against her husband's muscular chest to keep him from doing something that would destroy any chance at the agreement they both wanted.

She continued to hold him back as she said, "Fine, Father. Think on it." She faced Crispin again. "We will leave you."

Her husband glared down at her, his face a stormy sea of unfulfilled anger. But then he shook his head, as if resigned to let her lead the way when it came to her father. She took his arm and motioned to her sister to follow them out as they walked from the billiards room. But at the door, Crispin stopped and turned back once more.

"Think fast, Sir Oswald," he growled. "Because the hospitality you have been offered may fade with every passing day you wait to cash in on it. Good afternoon, *sir*."

With that, he all but dragged Gemma from the room. In the foyer, she allowed herself the first breath in what felt like ages as Crispin waved for their carriage to be brought. She ignored him and all his bubbling masculinity and instead looked at her sister.

"Don't poke at him, Mary, if you can," she said softly. "Let him stew on what Crispin has offered. Don't give him a reason to punish you despite his desire to take a chance at creating a bond with a duke."

Mary pursed her lips. "I'll do my best to avoid him all together," she promised. Her sister took a long breath and then turned toward Crispin. "I should thank you, I know, for your offer, Mr. Flynn."

"You're wel—"

"But you must know that I still don't trust you, especially when it comes to my sister. And if you think I am willing to overlook any pain she is caused just to protect myself from my father's machinations, you are very wrong."

Crispin arched a brow as their carriage rumbled to a stop before the house. "Your point has been taken, Miss. I certainly look forward to seeing you again. Good day."

He released Gemma and left without another word. Gemma let out a long, heavy sigh as she watched his retreating back. No one in her family was going to make it easy on the man, that was certain. He might renege on their agreement to remain wed after all.

She turned on her sister. "He is trying to help you," she whispered.

"What is he trying to do to you?" Mary replied. "I see him watching you and I wonder."

Gemma waved her off. "Stop. And just hope that his plan comes to fruition because I would wager your future in Crispin Flynn's home will be happier than here."

Mary looked as though she wanted to say more, but then she simply caught Gemma's arm and dragged her into a tight embrace. "Be careful. I love you."

Gemma squeezed her back. "You too." Then she turned on her heel and headed out to the carriage where Crispin waited to help her in. As he did so, she wondered at what kind of conversation they would have on what seemed like the very long drive home.

Crispin settled back against the carriage seat and shut his eyes. His head pounded and he very much wished he'd taken not one but two drinks from Sir Oswald.

"I think we should discuss this plan of yours," Gemma said softly from across from him.

Crispin barely suppressed a sigh. He hadn't truly expected a quiet drive home. He opened one eye and found his wife wringing her hands in her lap, staring at the floor of the carriage in distraction.

He straightened up. "You already said this is likely the only way to protect Mary from your father," he said. "You cannot be upset by it."

She shook her head. "I'm not. If he allows it, oh, how it would remove so much fear from me to have her under my roof and know that we were controlling her destiny, *she* was controlling it, rather than him."

"Then why are you worrying your very pretty lower lip?" he asked, watching her perform that very action with interest. Her mouth was utterly distracting, indeed.

"It is only that your brother did, of course, offer to help me, but he didn't say he would host my sister for a Season, Crispin. So we are predicating our plan on something that might not even be done. And I assure you, if my father feels double-crossed, he'll snatch Mary back and likely marry her off to some toothless old villain who wants nothing more than her virginity as his prize."

Crispin lifted both eyebrows at the earnestness with which she said those words. "That is very dramatic. Was your late husband *your* toothless old villain or am I?"

She stopped for a moment and stared at him, then she smiled. "Well, neither of you was toothless, that I can admit. And as for which of you was more villainous..."

"Oh, please let it be me," he teased. "I don't think I could concede even a quarter to that milquetoast former husband of yours."

"You want to be the villain?"

"No, I want to be more *villainous*," he corrected, leaning toward her. "That could be fun."

She shook her head. "You play with me and I admit it does

lighten my mood, Crispin, but this is serious. My sister's future is in the balance and no matter how dramatic you think my fears are, they're sadly based in fact and personal experience."

He nodded. "I know and I hope you realize from my offer today that I *do* take them seriously. As for my brother, I know him."

He stopped. He'd spent a very long time telling himself he didn't know Rafe anymore, not since he inherited the title and his bride. But being with him the day before...well, there were moments it had felt like old times. Like nothing had changed.

"You know him and...?" she asked, but her voice was soft, as if she could see how much he struggled with his relationship with Rafe.

He blinked and tried to clear whatever emotions were too obvious on his face. "I know him and I know that he will not refuse to help your sister."

She went back to worrying her hands. "But Crispin, won't he think I'm trying to take advantage of his title? Won't he and his wife think I'm a grasping social climber?"

"My brother doesn't give a damn about that. And you haven't met Serafina yet. She is the last person who would ever see you as that. She's too kind. She'll see you as a loving sister, bent on saving Mary."

She didn't look convinced even though she jerked out an uneven nod.

He shook his head. "We'll discuss it with them tonight when we go to supper. If you feel they're resistant, we'll find another way to help Mary. I promise you."

The words sounded so odd coming from his mouth. He was no hero. He didn't want to be. And yet here he was, making promises to a woman who he hadn't even known three days before. Strangely enough, they were promises he hoped to keep.

"You are kind to help her, especially considering her attitude toward you," Gemma said with a darting glance at him.

He laughed. "Your sister *does* seem to see me as an ogre."

Gemma let out a long sigh. "I am sorry about that. Normally she is very reserved, very quiet."

He shrugged. "Well, in this case she believes she is coming to the rescue of her obviously beloved sister. I can't fault her for doubting me or my intentions, considering what state she saw me in last."

Gemma blinked in surprise. "Truly, you do not blame her for her directness with you?"

"No." Crispin shook his head. "I have certainly been treated and called worse than anything she said. Perhaps someday she will come to like me, if she sees I mean you no harm."

"I suppose in a way, it doesn't matter if she likes you or understands whatever agreement we have come to," Gemma said softly before she slowly moved to his side of the carriage.

Suddenly he was very aware of her, of her warmth, of the sweet smell of her hair. Of the fact that her lips were slightly wet as she looked up at him.

"What is between you and me is between you and me," she whispered.

"That is certainly true," he murmured in response, lowering his mouth as she lifted hers.

They met in the middle, first with a rather chaste kiss, which swiftly spiraled into more. Her mouth opened and she brushed his lips with her tongue, eliciting a moan from him that allowed her access. Their tongues tangled, dueling in a battle for pleasure. One he realized they would both win when she eased herself into his lap.

"Mrs. Flynn," he teased. "You are shocking."

"I am, I think," she agreed. "Do you disapprove?"

He pushed a hand under her skirt, hissing out pleasure as he stroked his fingers up her smooth thigh until he found the sweet wetness of her pussy. She gasped as he began to stroke his fingers over her.

"I don't disapprove at all," he murmured before he claimed her mouth again.

He continued to tease her, tracing her outer lips, reveling in her warmth and heat until she groaned low in her throat.

"How much time until we're back at your home?" she whispered.

"Enough, but do you really want this? I know you ache."

She looked up at him, her eyes wide and filled with desire. "I ache for you."

He almost came undone right then and there. He'd never known a woman with such passion before. Even the widows and courtesans who had thrown themselves at him over the years had not been so exuberant in their desires.

And he found he met her need beat for beat. His cock was rock-hard and his headache long gone as he wrestled to free himself from his trousers. When he had, she let out a sigh and took him in hand right away.

He let his eyes flutter shut as she stroked over him. God, she was good at that. She held him just right, just perfectly for pleasure, and he could have easily found release with just her hand.

But he wanted to make her come. He wanted to fill the carriage with the steamy heat of their joining. He wanted her to always think of that when she rode in it.

He caught her hips and maneuvered her to straddle over him. They both hurried to shove her skirts aside, bundling them between them as she laughed at the ridiculousness of it. But her laughter abruptly stopped when he lifted her and his cock naturally found her slit. She slipped down over him, her body pulsing as she let out a strangled moan.

She wrapped her arms around his neck and kissed him as she immediately began to jerk over him. At first her rhythm was clumsy as the carriage rumbled and turned, but soon she found the way to use the movements to their advantage. She stroked over him and he lifted into her, lost in her heat, lost in her kiss, lost until the moment that she tilted her head back and let out a long, low moan of release.

Her body pulsed wildly around him and he grasped her

hips to force her continued movement. Her orgasm milked him, her sighs and moans urged him on, his pleasure mounted rapidly, like an out of control stallion and finally, with a roar he feared anyone on the street could have heard, he exploded inside of her.

She smiled as she dropped her forehead to rest on his, her arms tightening around him a little. He sucked in a breath. This felt so natural, so normal, so right.

And it also felt like a betrayal of the deepest kind.

Gently he helped her move away from him and moved to sit on the other side of the carriage. As he fixed himself, she watched him, her smile fading with every passing moment.

"Did I do something wrong?" she asked.

He forced a smile. "Not in the least, I think that was exactly what we both needed after the unpleasantness at your father's. But we'll be home soon, so I thought I should fix myself so we don't end up in an embarrassing situation."

She watched him for a moment more, then slowly began to do the same, smoothing her skirts over herself, fixing her hair. He watched her do it all, mesmerized by her movements and wishing, for a fleeting moment, that he could launch himself at her and undo all her work.

But he didn't. He stayed on his side of the carriage as they turned down the drive and stopped in front of his home. He felt the footman coming down from the back, heard voices as they prepared to open the door and he reached for her, wanting to offer her comfort so she didn't think he judged her for her passion as her first husband had.

He drew her across the gap and kissed her once, gently, on the lips. He wanted more but refrained as he whispered, "Now, how about that bath, Mrs. Flynn?"

Some of the tension bled away from her face and she nodded. "Together, Mr. Flynn?"

That hadn't been what he meant, but as he stared into her face, so open, so filled with desire and passion, he found himself nodding.

"I would like nothing better."

CHAPTER FOURTEEN

Gemma hoped her emotions were not clear on her face as she stared across the Duke of Hartholm's parlor and watched her husband pour them each a glass of wine. If they were, the entire family would see how confused she was by Crispin.

He was never anything but kind, so far. Yes, he could be selfish, but when he recognized that, he always did his best to remedy it. But there was still the matter of how he withdrew from her. He made love to her in the carriage with abandon, only to set her aside like he had done something wrong.

And just when she'd started to feel despair, he took her up to their chamber and they shared a bath where he brought her pleasure over and over again until the water went cold.

But tonight, he had once again been withdrawn, never touching her, hardly looking at her as they shared dinner with his family.

Not that it hadn't been a nice evening. Once again, the Flynn clan had welcomed her with open arms. Annabelle and Serafina—who had come down to join them despite what was obvious discomfort after the birth of her baby—had dragged her in like an old friend. His mother was sweet and treated Gemma no differently than she did Serafina. Even Rafe and Marcus had made her feel she belonged as they shared supper.

She just feared all that would change once Crispin

broached the subject of the promise he had made regarding Mary's Season.

"You are pale, my dear."

Gemma jolted at Serafina's voice and the touch of her new sister-in-law's hand on her own. She glanced over and smiled. It was difficult not to smile when one looked at the Duchess of Hartholm. Serafina was as beautiful as any gossip had ever said. She was the kind of woman men stopped to stare at as she walked by, that other women watched and copied in the hopes they might obtain just a fraction of her luster.

And yet, despite that outward physical beauty, what shone from within her was the warmth of kindness, the depth of love. Gemma could see why Rafe was so in love with her, why the entire family adored her.

"I suppose it is been a difficult few days," she admitted.

Serafina's face gentled. "The beginning is always difficult," she said. "You must recall that Rafe and I were also forced into a marriage, though certainly under very different circumstances. I know how you must feel as though you have been spun around a dozen times, then flipped onto your head."

Gemma laughed. "You know, that is exactly right. I cannot seem to find my footing."

Serafina glanced across the room and Gemma followed her gaze. She was looking at Crispin, who stood now with his brother, sister, their mother and Marcus. He was holding two glasses of wine, but had obviously been waylaid by whatever discussion they were having.

When Crispin's eyes darted to her, Gemma stiffened. Were they talking about her?

"My advice is to try to find your footing together if you can," Serafina said. "Rafe and I were uncertain at the beginning, but even with all my misgivings I recognized the good qualities in him. Qualities I could live with for the rest of my life. It helped me accept what was happening. Those are qualities his brother is also capable of displaying."

Gemma stared at Crispin. Yes, she had also seen his good

qualities on display. His kindness. His willingness to help her sister merely because she had asked him to do so. His gentleness when she confessed her past with her husband.

She looked at Serafina. "You seem very content now."

Serafina's face lit up. "More than so. Rafe and I fell deeply, passionately in love, despite our rocky beginning. I am happy every day for the odd circumstances that brought us here. I hope one day you and Crispin will feel the same way."

Gemma turned her face to hide her blush. She could not imagine a time when she and Crispin would say they were deeply in love. Yes, when he touched her, she felt more alive than ever. She wanted him, seemingly every moment of the day now. But that was not love. And perhaps it was for the best.

Serafina seemed unaware of her thoughts. She sighed. "I see our love grow even more now that our son has arrived."

"Will we meet him tonight?" Gemma asked, happy for the change of subject.

Serafina nodded. "In a short while, it will be time for him to be fed. I've insisted on doing it myself—I don't want a wet nurse. So they'll bring him to me and everyone can coo and aww over him."

"Are you two plotting?" Rafe asked as he broke away from the rest of his family and moved toward where they sat on the settee. He placed a hand on Serafina's shoulder and she looked up at him with what could only be described as adoring eyes.

Gemma glanced away from it, feeling as though she was interrupting something far too intimate to be viewed by a relative stranger.

"You know me, my love. Aren't I always plotting?" Serafina teased.

His laughter was light and his smile bright as he turned it on Gemma. "Stick with my wife, Gemma—she will always lead you into some kind of mischief."

Annabelle and Marcus came to sit on the settee opposite them and Annabelle laughed. "That is true, isn't it, love?"

There was a moment where a world of unspoken but highly passionate conversation went between the Riverses, and once again Gemma found herself blushing as she glanced at her lap. Every marriage in this family was a love match. She and Crispin were the only odd ones to the group.

"Actually, this is a very good transition," Crispin said as he led his mother to a chair and helped her into it. He smiled down at her, then looked at the group as a whole. "You see, we *do* actually need your help."

Rafe straightened up and suddenly he was all seriousness. "You know I've always been there to offer it."

To her surprise, Crispin flinched slightly before he continued, "We visited today with Gemma's father and her sister, Mary. You all know that her father is the one who created this marriage with his machinations, but he also did the same with Gemma's first marriage."

Serafina jerked her gaze to Gemma and their eyes met. All the kindness that was in her stare was almost too much, but Serafina didn't allow her to look away. She took her hand once more and squeezed it.

"I know exactly how you feel and I am sorry," she whispered.

Gemma blushed and tried not to cry as she nodded. "Thank you."

"We will compare war stories someday, I think," her sister-in-law said. "And take solace in where our lives have taken us."

"Yes, Gemma is safe now from whatever he plans," Crispin continued, though his voice was gentler now, softer. "But Mary is not."

Rafe nodded. "We discussed her yesterday. We would be happy to help."

"Good, because I've already offered the man two Seasons hosted by the celebrated Duke and Duchess of Hartholm." Crispin folded his arms, as if daring the two to deny him.

Gemma covered her face briefly. God, he could be a clod

sometimes, utterly unaware of himself. He was supposed to be politely asking his brother and sister-in-law for assistance, not declaring the deed to be done and expected.

"I am so very, very sorry," she moaned, forcing herself to lift her head and look at the duke. Rafe stood impassive behind the couch where she sat.

His brow wrinkled and he exchanged a brief look with his wife. "Why?" they asked in unison.

Gemma struggled for words. "Because we were put in a terrible position with my father today and Crispin claimed an offer that didn't truly exist. We should have talked to you about it first, we should have verified that it was all right with you, we should have—"

Rafe held up a hand with a laugh. "Great God, woman, stop before you hurt yourself. We are happy to help your sister. Of course, at this moment, I speak for my wife, since she will likely be far more help than I could be."

Serafina shook her head, but she was smiling. "You may speak for me on this subject, my love, for you know my mind exactly." She turned her attention to Gemma. "I am very, very happy to chaperone and host your sister. For you and for Crispin, but also because I do know what it is like to have all your choices torn away. If we can grant Mary a few, I will be exceedingly happy to help."

"Truly?" Gemma breathed, all her anxiety fading for a moment.

"Of course," Serafina reassured her. "I will need a few weeks before I can return to the ballroom, but I could pass that time by talking to your sister, we can work out a few strategies, we can discuss gowns and potential good mates. And if your father insists, Rafe could easily step out as chaperone."

Annabelle smiled. "Serafina is a wonderful help. She and my brother helped me greatly."

At her side, Marcus snorted. "You helped *yourself* right into a scandalous marriage with a club owner. Please don't terrify poor Gemma with your story."

Gemma found herself laughing as Annabelle playfully swatted her husband. "From all I've seen, I think she made a good match, with Serafina's help or not."

Annabelle sighed. "Indeed, I would agree. If your sister ever has to choose between a titled fop and true love, I will strongly advise her to choose true love. I think Serafina will agree to that, too, despite having her own fop."

Rafe clutched his heart. "You wound me," he growled, but it was all in jest.

Their mother rolled her eyes and looked at Gemma. "Do you see what you have married into?"

Gemma nodded, playing along, but her heart had been swelling more and more with every exchange. Yes, this was what she'd married into. This loud, funny, exuberant, and very loving family. And they accepted her, at least so far.

She glanced at Crispin. He was also watching it all, but his wry smile held caution that made her happiness fade.

"I knew you would all help willingly," he said, interrupting the reverie. "However, the point may be moot. Gemma's father may not allow Mary to do any of this. He has not yet accepted the offer."

The jovial tone in the room vanished and Gemma clenched her hands in her lap. It was so easy to feel light with this family, that she had forgotten that one dark point. Her father was petty enough he very well might deny them their plan.

"Well, if that is true than we must urge him along," Rafe said. "I could—"

Serafina glanced up at him. "You will do nothing," she interrupted. "In this case, I think it will be better if I make the contact." She rubbed her hands together, as if plotting a delicious coup. "I shall use my very best Duchess of Hartholm signature."

"You have a Duchess of Hartholm signature?" Marcus asked.

Serafina nodded. "Oh yes, of course. It's very fancy and fine and conveys the importance of my role. Especially to those who may need reminding. I think I shall say, 'The Duke of Hartholm and I very much look forward to escorting your daughter Mary through the remainder of this Season and all of the next.'"

"But he hasn't agreed," Gemma sputtered.

"No, Serafina is brilliant," Crispin said. "She will address it as if it is already resolved. It pressures him to acquiesce so he won't look like an idiot."

Serafina smiled at him. "Thank you, Crispin."

Crispin stared at his sister-in-law for a moment, then he slowly came around the settee and knelt before her. "No, thank you, Serafina. Thank you."

Gemma watched the exchange and she saw that there was far more to it. Crispin was apologizing to her as much as thanking her. And from Serafina's gentle expression, she knew it too.

"We're so happy to have you back," she whispered.

He nodded, but there was a flicker of pain in his stare.

At that moment, there was a light knock and a maid stepped into the room, a bundle of blanket in her arms. "I'm sorry to interrupt, but you asked me to bring Young Crispin when it was time for his feeding, Your Grace."

Crispin got up and helped Serafina do the same. She did so slowly, but her face lit up as she held out her arms for her baby.

"Thank you, Bridget."

The maid smiled warmly at her mistress and then the rest of the room before she left the family alone.

"Ah, the little man is hungry," Serafina cooed. "And I'll take him out the room to do that, but before I do." Her lashes fluttered up. "Do you think you'd like to hold him, Uncle Crispin?"

Crispin tensed at the question. Had he ever held a baby

before? Not in his recollection, though perhaps he had held Annabelle as a baby.

Still, that wasn't exactly his style. He stammered, looking for an answer, but Serafina didn't wait. She moved a step closer.

"Hold your arms like I am," she encouraged him, and he copied her stance as best he could. "I'll lay him in the crook there and all you must do is hold his head steady."

Crispin hesitated. "Serafina, I—"

She smiled. "You won't break him, Crispin, I assure you." With that, she set the warm armful of blanket into his arms and, once her hands were free, pulled the edge away to reveal a tiny pink face.

Crispin froze at the sight of it, the sight of this little life in his arms, created by his brother and the sister-in-law Crispin had been avoiding for months. This baby was a Flynn. This baby shared his blood. And his name. He couldn't forget that this baby shared his name.

An intense, powerful and very sudden swell of love filled him as he stared into the blue eyes that looked very much like his own. He would protect this child. He would love this child. He would do everything he could to make this child happy.

"Powerful, isn't it?" Rafe asked, and Crispin jerked his head up. All he could manage was a nod, for he feared his voice would crack if he said anything at present.

The baby squirmed ever so slightly and let out a plaintive cry. Crispin stared at Serafina in horror. "What did I do?"

"Nothing, he just wants his supper." Serafina laughed. She motioned to Gemma. "Give him to your wife, and the ladies and I will retire so I can grant him his wish while you men talk seriously over port."

She walked away, and Crispin met Gemma's eyes as she slowly stood. She looked as nervous as he had as she held out her arms for the baby, but as soon as the child was in her arms, she relaxed with a happy sigh.

"Oh, it's the smell of them, isn't it?" she whispered.

It was Crispin's mother who laughed. "They should bottle it."

"Come, ladies," Serafina said as she opened the door. "Our parlor awaits."

Crispin watched as his new wife carried his brother's child from the room, her beautiful face focused entirely on the little bundle in her arms. Relaxed as she was, her expression was readable in every way. He saw that it wasn't only her late husband who had wanted a child. The flicker of joy and pain in Gemma's eyes told him she had wanted that just as desperately.

The door closed behind the four women and Crispin sucked in a long breath, the first he had taken in what felt like an eternity.

"So that is your namesake," Rafe said, coming around the settee to clap him on the shoulder. "What do you think of him?"

"He's a handsome boy," Crispin said, still almost feeling the weight of the baby in his arms.

"Which will make it easier for him to Flynn his way through whatever Society he chooses to keep." Marcus laughed as he made his way to the sideboard to peruse the choices of port. Neither man stopped him. As the owner of an infamous club, he certainly knew more about spirits than either of them.

"Do you think he will be wild, with you a duke instead of a free gentleman?" Crispin asked, musing briefly about his carefree youthful days with his brother, causing trouble in every corner.

Rafe's mouth pinched. "You act as though everything has changed. But damn it, man, do I seem so different to you?"

Crispin hesitated. When his brother had been forced to wed, it had been difficult for him. At the very same time, he had been faced with his own decision about the future. Decisions that had ultimately been ripped from his hands in the worst way possible. Rafe's being trapped into being a duke had seemed to represent every loss of freedom, choice and life that

Crispin had ever imagined.

Perhaps he had not handled it well at the time. Afterward, he had run. Far and fast and hard and never thinking about the consequences until Annabelle got herself twisted up with Marcus in the hopes of helping him.

"There are some things that are different," he said softly. "With everyone since last summer."

"Of course there are," Rafe said with a shake of his head. "I am happily married and now a father. Annabelle gave up her ridiculous notion that respectability would make her happy and eloped as scandalously as can be with Marcus. Mama is a grandmother, Serafina is a mother. She also took up some new form of needlepoint and Annabelle learned a piece on the pianoforte. If you leave a family for long enough, Crispin, they will change. That is just the way time works."

Crispin flinched at his brother's words, even though there was little heat behind them. It reminded him of how he had failed those he loved. How he had let his own tangled emotions trump everything else.

Which is how he had ended up here.

"But you can't go back," Rafe continued. "So all I can say is that I'm glad you're here now. Are you?"

Crispin nodded and there was no hesitation to it. "Yes. Very glad I'm here. Very grateful for your help with Gemma's sister. It will take a great deal of pain and pressure from her shoulders."

Marcus cleared his throat as he finally brought over a glass of port for both Rafe and Crispin. Crispin eyed it greedily. It wouldn't make the world soft like harder spirits, but it would help the itch in the back of his throat that kept reminding him of his thirst.

"I assume you must have discovered the true story about the accusations around her and that it was not as bad as rumor made it sound," Marcus said.

Crispin took a sip of his drink. "I did. I won't get into the details, but she didn't kill anyone. He died of natural causes.

And he was a bit of an ass." His eyes narrowed. "Wait, why did you assume I uncovered the story and it was in her favor?"

"Because it seems her happiness is already important to you," Marcus said, grasping his own glass and tipping it toward Crispin as if toast to this ridiculous notion.

He had been about to take another drink, but now Crispin paused. "What?"

"Well, I assume there is no ulterior motive for you to save this girl from her father," Marcus said with a shrug.

Crispin tensed. His friend had hit upon a fact that made him very uncomfortable. He *was* very interested in Gemma's happiness and well-being. But that was because of guilt. Yes, only guilt drove him to this. After all, if he hadn't been so drunk, she wouldn't be in this awkward position.

"It's all right if you like her," Rafe said softly. "There is nothing about her not to like."

"And she's certainly easy on the eyes," Marcus added.

Crispin glared at his very handsome brother-in-law. "I think the only woman whose looks you should be commenting on is my sister."

Marcus chuckled. "Trust me, I only have eyes for Annabelle. But it would be a blind man who didn't recognize how pretty she was. And red hair. Exactly your type."

Now Crispin set the glass down. "Wait, I don't have a type."

Rafe snorted. "Oh, yes you do! I've never seen you pass a redheaded lass that you didn't turn around to take a second glimpse. It's been that way since you were in short pants. Annabelle and I have had a running bet about how red the hair of the girl who tamed you would be."

"Who won?"

"I said carrots," Rafe admitted with a sigh. "And Annabelle waxed poetic about auburn locks. So I paid her ten pounds after you and Gemma left yesterday."

"Well, take it back," Crispin snapped. This ridiculous conversation was putting him out of sorts.

"Why?" Marcus asked. "I would say Annabelle was spot on."

"No one has bloody well tamed me," Crispin said, downing the rest of his wine in one swig. "And I assure you that as lovely as Gemma is, as desirable as she may be, she will *not* tame me. We will only find a way to survive."

The room was quiet for a moment and Crispin set his empty glass down with the realization that he had been shouting. Both his brother and Marcus were now staring at him, but slowly their gazes slipped to each other. Marcus grinned.

"It's already starting."

Rafe nodded. "I recognize the signs. Anger is the first one. Denial is usually combined with it, and here we are with both."

Marcus chuckled. "Do you want to place a wager with *me* about when he'll come here wailing and confessing he loves the girl?"

"I'll think about my timeline, but we *should* wager. Let's include Annabelle on the action. And why not Serafina and Mama as well?"

Crispin turned his back. "You two are idiots. And I'm not listening to you anymore."

With that, he stormed out of the room with their laughter echoing behind them. But as he walked away, his chest began to hurt. What the two men in that room didn't understand—*couldn't* understand, because he'd kept his heart a secret—was that he had no room to love anyone ever again. And if Rafe or Marcus or God forbid Gemma thought he would, that would be a wager none of them would win.

CHAPTER FIFTEEN

Gemma stood outside her husband's office door, staring at the barrier that separated them and trying to summon her nerve. It wasn't that she was afraid of him. The past few days since their supper with his family had all but erased any lingering worries she might have had about a penchant for violence. It was more that she never knew what she would find when she intruded upon him.

He could be warm and welcoming, sensual, and they had made love several times since that night. But he could also be distant, cool, and she had found him drinking once where his eyes had looked so...*sad*.

He was a man with his secrets and she was beginning to think they were secrets she would never ferret out after all. And since they had agreed this would not be a marriage of the heart, but of acceptance of the facts, she had to let that go and also accept what Crispin Flynn was.

An enigma.

With another long sigh, she pushed the door open and breezed in with what she hoped was a bright smile. "Good afternoon."

She broke off when she realized her husband was not alone. He stood at the picture window looking off into the distance while a man she didn't know rose from the desk at her entry.

"I'm sorry, I didn't realize you had a guest," she said, her cheeks flushing.

Crispin turned and smiled, but the expression was brittle, indeed. "No need to apologize. Mrs. Flynn, may I present Mr. Paul Abbot."

The tall, wiry blond man held out a hand to her. "Mrs. Flynn, a pleasure to make your acquaintance at last. I've heard a great deal about you."

Gemma blinked as she shook his hand and looked to Crispin for an explanation.

"Mr. Abbot is Marcus's man of affairs. He helps manage my brother-in-law's club and he kindly agreed to come here to look at the mess I call my books," Crispin explained.

Gemma nodded as Mr. Abbot released her hand. "Very nice to meet you. Any friend of Marcus is a friend of ours, I know."

Abbot shot Crispin a look. "A very good friend." His tone was dry as he gathered up ledgers and receipts in a box. "I shall continue going over these and come back to you in a few days, Flynn. I'm certain we'll work it all out. I already have a few ideas about investments."

Crispin nodded, but his gaze flickered toward the liquor along the wall behind his desk.

"I'll show myself out," Abbot said with another nod toward her. "Good day, Mrs. Flynn."

"Mr. Abbot," she said, still watching Crispin. Once the door had closed behind their unexpected guest, she moved forward. "I am very sorry to intrude."

Crispin shrugged. "You didn't. Abbot was almost finished anyway. And honestly, I could only take so much of his clucking tongue."

Gemma wrinkled her brow. "Why would he cluck his tongue at you?"

Crispin cleared his throat and took the few long steps toward the liquor he had been ogling since her entry. He splashed one of the amber liquids into a tumbler and took a sip. She saw the bliss on his face, the utter surrender, but once that passed, she also saw the guilt. The shame.

He needed to drink, but in some way he didn't want to. He didn't like the loss of control that had seemingly defined his life, at least lately...and she thought perhaps even longer.

He didn't meet her eyes as he said, "Your father hurtled you into a marriage with me for a great many reasons, I think. The fact that I was...*am* out of control enough that I made a good mark for the fraud was likely firstmost. But there was also my connection with the Duke of Hartholm and my...my purported wealth."

Gemma stiffened. They had touched on this subject before, with Crispin growing angry with her when she questioned if he had money. Now she chose to tread carefully.

"Yes, my father had his reasons, I suppose."

Crispin took another drink, nearly downing the entire glass in one swig. "Well, in this, at least, I have deceived him. Gotten the upper hand, I suppose."

She took a long breath. "How?"

He shook his head. "If you are to run this household, you will find out. Gemma, I have lost over half my fortune in the last year. Perhaps even closer to sixty-five percent of it. It amounts to tens of thousands of pounds down the drain in bets, pay-offs and other foolishness."

Gemma staggered. Tens of thousands of pounds lost? She had never thought of living with a man who had tens of thousands of pounds all together at all. She had, however, lived with a man who knew how to gamble away his life without thought to anyone else. Her father had been excellent at it, and seeing Crispin this way, hearing his confession...

It was slightly terrifying.

"Crispin," she said softly.

He turned his face away, the embarrassment clear on every line. "I knew it was bad," he mused and she thought it was almost more to himself. "But I didn't know it was this bad."

She straightened her shoulders. "Crispin, I don't know what my father's intentions were, but I can tell you I don't give a damn about the money. I can live on far less than tens of thousands of pounds, that is for certain. I don't need new gowns or fancy things."

His lips pursed. "You'll have your allowance, Gemma. And you do need gowns—I saw that sad little case that carried all you had in the world."

She smiled at the gentle teasing in his tone, his attempt to console her. "Well, I appreciate your looking out for my fashionable well-being. I suppose what worries me more is that you would allow yourself to be in a mindset where you lost so much in the first place."

He turned his back to pour another drink and she let her breath out in frustration. Slowly, she came around the desk and placed her hand over his, lowering the now-full glass back to the table.

"Perhaps I could be of some help, Crispin. I could be a partner in your troubles. *Our* troubles."

He released the glass and stared down at her. She saw a world of struggle in his dark blue eyes, and for a moment she thought he might tell her what he kept bottled inside. But then he put a false smile on his face.

"You never told me why you came to see me this afternoon."

She held his gaze for a moment, then stepped back, removing her hands from his. He didn't want her comfort. As seductive as he could be, as warm as he could be, he would always put a wall between her and anything real in his soul.

But then, why wouldn't he? She had been forced into confession by circumstance but that didn't mean he would practice a quid pro quo. She could never forget this wasn't a marriage either of them had wanted and it would never be a union of two people who cared for each other. The best they could hope for was some kind of mutual respect.

Perhaps his reticence was best.

"Gemma?" he asked, his tone gentler.

She stepped away and returned to the other side of the desk. "I received a letter from my sister just after lunch," she began, digging the folded missive from her pelisse pocket. "Mary says that our father was thrilled to get a message from the Duchess of Hartholm."

Now Crispin's smile became true. "Serafina is good to her word. Not that I ever expected differently."

Gemma nodded. "Yes, and apparently it was quite a note, because she says he told her he will be coming here to meet with us tomorrow on the subject of her future. Of course, he hasn't sent any indication of that himself, but my father was never much for being polite when it came to me. He will likely simply show up unannounced and demand our time."

"And we will certainly make it available to him," Crispin said. "I'll be certain my calendar is clear all day for just that purpose."

She had been trying to harden herself to the man across from her, but those words ruined the attempt. He was so very confusing, locking her out of his secrets but then doing everything in his power to save her sister, merely because it meant something to *her*.

She inched to the edge of his desk and leaned in. "Thank you for your kindness toward her. Toward me."

He shrugged, but there was a tinge of color in his cheeks at her acknowledgment of what he'd done. "It's nothing. I'm simply trying to ensure her future. I think she deserves that and you deserve not to have to live in terror about her."

"The future is wide open," she said softly. "Unlike the past, which you cannot change."

He stiffened, and it was clear they were both aware they were no longer talking about Mary. "I suppose that is true."

"The future is *yours*," she continued, watching every reaction he was trying so hard to hide. "You can be...*one* could be...whatever one liked. Notorious or respectable. Rich or poor. Drunk or sober. It's all in your hands."

His face twisted a fraction, and for a moment she thought he might throw her out of his office for overstepping the boundary he had so purposefully put between them. He straightened up and slowly stepped around the desk. His expression was unreadable as he stopped in front of her, close enough that she could feel his heat, close enough that she could smell his skin.

He said nothing, but slid his fingers into her hair and tilted her head. His mouth captured hers in an unexpected and utterly passionate kiss. She melted immediately, despite her lingering misgivings about this man and where she stood with him.

He drove his tongue into her mouth with a deep, guttural moan, and she found herself being pushed back until her backside hit the edge of his desk. He trapped her there, leaning in against her so that she could feel the rigid length of his erection teasing her belly.

"Crispin," she sighed against his mouth, her arms coming around his neck so she could accept him, accept what he offered. Even if it wasn't everything, in this moment it was enough.

To her surprise, he leaned away from her, his blue eyes darkening with wicked need and equally wicked plans.

"I want to kiss you," he whispered. His voice was rough and raw.

"You are kissing me," she said, tilting her head toward him.

He shook his head, dodging her lips. "Oh no, Gemma. Not on your mouth."

She wrinkled her brow. Where in the world could he kiss her besides her mouth? As she stared at him in questioning, his eyes went wide.

"He never did this," he said—a statement, not a question.

"Did what?" she asked. "I don't understand."

His smile widened. "Good. Then this will be mine. Only mine."

"Crispin—" she began, but he cut her off by lifting her

further on the edge of the desk. He dragged up one of the chairs behind him and sat down in it, inching himself forward so that he pushed between her legs, tightening her skirts around her thighs.

"What are you doing?"

He looked up at her. "You'll like it, Gemma," he promised as he slid a hand beneath her skirt and caressing her stocking-clad thigh beneath. "Oh, you're going to like it."

The feel of his hand on her leg made her gasp and she held her breath, watching as he did the same with his other hand. He massaged up her body slowly, giving every inch of her legs attention as he stroked higher and higher, closer and closer to her core. Her skirts lifted as he touched her, bundling around her thighs, then he shoved them higher so they tangled around her hips and stomach.

She was revealed to him, spread open, the only thing keeping her from flashing herself to the room was a flimsy pair of drawers. When his hands reached the edge of them, he stopped.

"Where do you think I want to kiss you?" he asked, his tone as hypnotic as the way he glided his fingers back and forth, back and forth over her thighs, teasing under her drawers, setting her on fire.

"I don't know," she gasped, gripping the desk edge.

He looked up at her, meeting her eyes with a dark and dangerous one of his own. "Guess."

She swallowed. If her drawers weren't there or if he parted their opening, he could easily lean in and place his mouth against her—

She felt her eyes go so wide it almost hurt. "Crispin?"

He chuckled, a very male and possessive sound, and reached up to find the waist of her drawers. He loosened the thin thread that held them in place and then glided them down, down, and tossed them away.

She squirmed. He had seen her naked. Naked didn't bother her. She looked forward to naked because he could do so many wonderful things with his hands and cock.

But she had never been spread out in front of another person before, splayed and on display for his pleasure. She felt compelled both to watch him as he examined her and also to look away in embarrassment.

"You are so beautiful," he whispered, pushing her thighs apart even further and reaching out to trace the trembling outer lips of her pussy. "So beautiful and tempting." He glanced up at her, holding her captive with his stare. "And I want to taste you, Gemma. I want to lick you until you scream in pleasure. Until you beg me to stop, to never stop. Until you are weak with it."

She couldn't help it. Her breath was coming in little pants now, her heart was pounding. "Will you like tasting me?" she asked.

He nodded. "So very, very much. And so will you."

He said nothing more, but his dark head descended and she tensed as his mouth met her entrance in a closed-mouth kiss. She dug against the desk edge, searching for purchase as he parted his lips and blew steamy, hot air against her already wet and trembling body.

"Crispin," she whispered, a question, a plea, a prayer.

He glanced up at her with only his eyes, and then his tongue darted out and he licked her from top to bottom in one luscious, unexpected caress.

She jolted at the intimacy of the action, but also at the pleasure it elicited. Her entire body tensed and tingles shot through her that were reminiscent of those glorious moments of orgasm.

The spasm of her body seemed enough encouragement for him. He began to lick her in earnest, pressing a hand against her hip to hold her steady while his other hand held her body open so that he could taste and lick every single inch of her entrance.

She collapsed back against her elbows on the desk as the swirling pleasure grew. It began where his tongue pressed her, teased her, and spiraled out through her belly, her blood, her limbs. She found herself lifting into his mouth, seeking more, moaning even though it was possible someone in the hallway would hear her.

She was beyond caring. She wanted the release his mouth promised.

"Please, please," she panted, her hips jolting again as he circled his tongue over her.

"Please what?" he asked, removing his mouth and eliciting a long, wailing groan from her. "Tell me."

"I want to...to..."

"To come," he finished for her.

"I want to come," she begged. "Please let me."

He didn't respond with words, but by dropping his head back to between her legs. This time, though, he didn't taste or tease. No, now he focused in earnest on her clitoris, sucking the little bud between his lips and pressing his tongue against it.

Her back arched and she screamed as the orgasm that had been eluding her hit her with full force. But it wasn't like the others. No, this was never-ending waves of exquisite pleasure, sharp bursts that made her hips jolt and her fingers dig at the wooden desk top.

He dragged her through them all, continuing to play with his tongue even when she went limp, even when it was too much and she was spent with pleasure. He sucked and sucked, tasted and pleased until she let out one final moan and collapsed all the way back across his papers.

Only then did he stand up. She managed to look down at him and smiled. His eyes were wild with desire, his cock bloomed against his trousers, pressing for release. So tasting her *had* pleased him.

She parted her legs a bit further in invitation. "I think we need to solve that, Mr. Flynn."

"I agree," he growled, tearing open the flap of his trousers in a few swift motions and allowing his cock to burst free. He took himself in hand and she stared as he stroked himself, once, twice. Then he pulled her further down the desk by her hips and speared her in one smooth, wet stroke.

She arched again at the invasion, at the slide of his cock against exquisitely sensitive nerve endings. To her shock, she was already on the edge of orgasm once more—a fact he seemed aware of, if his grin was any indication.

He loomed over her, trapping her against the desk in the cage of his arms. As he began to stroke into her, he leaned down and kissed her.

She melted into him. He tasted of earthy sweetness. *Her* taste, and she was surprised by how arousing she found it. She lifted into his strokes as she greedily sucked her flavor from his tongue, and her body burst a second time. He pounded through her orgasm and just as her moans subsided, he made a guttural cry and spurted his seed deep into her body before he collapsed over her on the desk.

She wrapped her arms around him, holding him close as his panting breaths faded back to normal. Slowly, he eased up and their bodies parted. She found herself sorry for that moment and for the removal of his warmth as he stood up.

"Did I hurt you?" he asked, reaching out to tuck a tangled curl behind her ear.

She laughed. "Those were not sounds of pain, Crispin."

He grinned. "No. But the desk is very hard."

She stood up and stretched before she began smoothing her skirts back down over herself. "Not as hard as the man, and I enjoyed it very much." When she stood up, she found him staring at her, his eyes wide. She bit her lip. "Was I too crass?"

"No," he sputtered, reaching for her hand. "I was just musing to myself how lucky I am to have been forced into marriage with a lady who knows what she wants. A lady as heated in the bedroom as I myself can be."

She smiled in relief. "We are well-matched in that, yes."

"The things I'm going to teach you, Mrs. Flynn," he murmured as he dragged her closer and kissed her once more.

But even as she enjoyed the press of his mouth to hers, the

need in his every touch, there was a small part of her that niggled, that wondered even though it shouldn't...

Was this all they would ever share?

CHAPTER SIXTEEN

Kate made a hissing sound as she turned Gemma around to fasten her gown in preparation for a new day. "Is that a bruise?"

Gemma jolted from her memories of her and Crispin in his office the afternoon before, in their bed the night before, and shot her maid a glance over her shoulder. "Likely so."

Kate stepped back and folded her arms. "Is there something I should know, my lady?"

"No more *my ladies*, Kate," Gemma scolded. "New husband, no title. And there is nothing that you should know except that I am vastly satisfied by the physical affections of Crispin Flynn. The bruises are not from him bringing me harm, but pleasure, I assure you."

Kate blushed and ducked her head as she began to fasten the dress. "Well, I am happy for you, my lad—Mrs. Flynn."

Gemma nodded, but her serene smile was false. Her maid was happy for her. A strange notion considering that less than a week earlier she'd had no idea where she would be now. She still felt dizzy, a fact multiplied by Crispin's passions toward her.

As Kate fastened her last button, there was a light rap on the door that led from the bedchamber to her dressing one.

"Yes?" she called out, smiling as Kate smoothed her gown

here and there, making it perfect. It was not an easy task considering the dress was rather old. She had been looking forward to getting a few new things, but after hearing about Crispin's financial troubles the day before…

"Good morning, wife," Crispin said as he pushed the door to her dressing area open and leaned against the wall beside it most casually. "And…Kate, isn't it?"

Her maid was blushing furiously as she bobbed out a nod. "Yes, sir."

Crispin shot Gemma look and grinned. "Well, would you mind if I had a moment alone with Gemma, Kate?"

Kate picked up Gemma's wrinkled nightdress—the one that had resided on the floor of their bedchamber until she hastily shoved it on before Kate came to help her—and said, "Of course, sir. Good day."

Gemma clenched her teeth as Kate refused to look at Crispin when she rushed past him into the main room. He chuckled as he reached behind him and closed the door, trapping them in to the smaller room together. Suddenly the space that had seemed perfectly fine felt confined. Why did he have to smell so good all the time?

"Have you been whispering naughty secrets to Kate?" he drawled as he took a few steps toward her.

She took one backward and nearly tripped over a bench. "No."

"Then why does she look like she knows what *you* did last night, my saucy little wanton?"

Gemma's cheeks flamed at his words, but she was anything but offended. She actually wanted to laugh, but somehow refrained. She cleared her throat. "Actually, Kate saw a…a mark on me. And she was worried I might be being…er, harmed. So I had to explain that—"

The teasing left his eyes. "A mark."

She nodded. "Just a little bruise."

"A bruise. Let me see it." He reached for her, but she batted his hands away. "No, Kate just fixed me."

"And when I have seen what she saw, *I* will fix you," he said. "Gemma, let me look."

She let out a huff of irritated breath and turned her back so that he could unhook her gown. He did it quickly, efficiently, but she was shocked that she grew very aware of him as he did it. Of his fingers brushing her spine through her chemise, of his breath on the nape of her neck. Damn him for having so much power over her.

"Show me," he said as he finished unfastening her.

She shrugged the gown off her arms and around her waist. She pulled the chemise edge free of her dress and lifted it just enough that he could see the round, fist-sized bruise on the backside of her ribs.

"Goddamn it," he muttered as he reached his fingers out to gently trace the mark. "I did that?"

She turned around, dropping her chemise. "No. The desk did that. I must have been leaning on something. I assure you, at the time I didn't even realize it. I was a bit focused on other things."

She expected him to smile, but he stared at her ribcage, his face troubled. "And then last night I wasn't exactly gentle. I must have hurt you when I—"

"Oh for God's sake," Gemma muttered, then cupped his cheeks with both her hands and pulled him down to kiss him. He was stiff with surprise for a fraction of a moment, then his lips parted and he let her in. After she felt he was sufficiently silenced, she drew back. "I *liked* what we did on the desk, Crispin. And I *liked* what we did last night. So please don't waste time torturing yourself about it. It seems to be you have enough to torture yourself about while you brood without adding me to the mix."

She stepped back and pushed her chemise back into her waist, and then pulled her gown up. "Now fasten me," she ordered.

He chuckled as he turned her back to him and curled his body around hers, perhaps a bit more gently than he would have fifteen minutes before.

"I like you unfastened," he whispered, close to her ear.

A shiver she could not control worked through her. "Do you now?"

"I could…" He trailed off and she peeked at him over her shoulder. He was suddenly frowning.

"You could?"

He shook his head. "I got distracted, I forgot something. Here, step forward a bit and I'll fasten you."

Her heart sank. He'd wanted her, that much was clear from everything about his touch, including the bump of his erection against her backside. But something had stopped him and she was a little afraid of what.

He hooked her gown slowly. "Have you made an appointment with the dressmaker?"

She squeezed her eyes shut. "No. But considering our conversation yesterday about the current state of our finances, perhaps I should wait to—"

"Gemma!" He turned her to face him. "You don't have to fix things with me like you did with your father. I told you yesterday, I want you to get new gowns. It will please me to see you in pretty things, things that make you feel good. Buy a Season's worth."

She examined his face, lined with worry and embarrassment in that moment. She reached up reflexively and smoothed his cheek, as if she could stroke the pain away even though she knew she couldn't. He wouldn't let her help at all.

"I will," she promised, "if it would make you happy."

He seemed startled by her response and he stepped away from her, granting her space for the first time since he entered the room. He shifted as if uncomfortable and then said, "I have something to tell you."

She clenched her hands in front of her and nodded. "Yes?"

His pinched expression made her heart leap a little. What was wrong?

"Your father is here," he said.

She let out a little cry and rushed toward the door. "Why didn't you tell me? We should have gone done straight away to—"

He held out a hand, blocking her from exiting the dressing room and gathered her into his arms. "Gemma, take a breath."

She struggled. "I don't want to take a breath, I need to go down before he—"

"Before he what, angel?" Crispin soothed gently. "He no longer has power over you, Gemma. You don't have to jump for him. You don't have to run for him. He has been sitting in our parlor for half an hour, I hope cooling himself off. He will be fine waiting a moment longer."

She stared up at him. "You don't understand," she whispered, hating how broken her voice sounded. "He has power over Mary. And if I don't jump, he'll punish *her* for it."

Crispin shook his head. "The moment we have her safe, I swear I'm going to—"

"To do nothing," Gemma said, grasping one of his hands. "You will do nothing because his good graces and boons are always removable."

Crispin's face was suddenly and quite shockingly *sad*. "You deserve so much better than him. Than me." Her lips parted, but before she could reply, he took her arm. "Come. Let us not bargain with his good graces again, shall we?"

She followed his lead, but could not help feeling that this conversation had been one of the most unsatisfying she'd ever had. In every way.

When they entered the parlor Crispin found Sir Oswald exactly where he had expected him to be, standing at the sideboard, guzzling Crispin's best liquor. And despite the early hour of the day, Crispin desperately wanted to join him. But given that Mary was not with her father, he refrained.

He'd known Gemma's sister had not come with Sir Oswald, and he didn't have to look at his new bride to recognize she was as concerned by that fact as he was.

"Father," Gemma said, her tone icy even as she moved to press a brief kiss on his cheek. "How nice to see you."

Crispin smothered a smile. His Gemma was not hard to read. She didn't seem capable of hiding her emotions.

His Gemma. What a foolish thought. She wasn't his except by law. He had to recall that whenever his mind took him to stupid places. Betraying places.

"Quinn," he said, his voice as cold as hers. "To what do we owe this surprise?"

"You kept me waiting half an hour," he snapped, addressing Gemma with a glare.

She shifted. "You did not send word ahead, Father. We had no idea you were coming, and we were still preparing for our day."

He sniffed. "Taking to the life of leisure already, I can see."

Crispin stepped forward. "The blame is mine, Sir Oswald. I interrupted your daughter's toilette and—"

Sir Oswald's face twisted in what appeared to be disgust. "Well, don't think you're going to get her with child," he snapped with a glare in her direction. "She's barren. Might not have been entirely honest with that fact, but the deed is done now, isn't it?" He chuckled.

It was the laugh that made a red veil of anger fall over Crispin's eyes. The way Gemma flinched didn't help, the way her father seemed to enjoy the flinch.

"You bast—" he began, lunging for him.

Gemma caught his arm, holding him back as she elevated her voice and talked over him. "To what do we owe the pleasure of your arrival, Father?"

He grinned once more at Crispin, a look that made Crispin want to knock each and every one of his teeth from his skull, before he said, "I've been thinking of the offer made by

Hartholm and his duchess."

Gemma released his arm and stepped forward, her hope too clear on her face. Crispin wished he could freeze her father in his spot and whisper to her not to reveal too much. It was obvious the bastard who had raised her would take advantage of her love for Mary, of Gemma's desire to save her.

"Have you?" he said, keeping his own tone bland even as he reached for her hand and pulled her back a fraction. When she looked at him, he met her eyes and prayed she could see the message there. It seemed she did, for she also suddenly took on an affected air of disinterest.

"Yes," Sir Oswald said. "It seems as though my beloved youngest would be in good hands if I agreed to allow them to sponsor her. And the offer of compensation for being deprived of her company that the duke made is more than adequate."

Crispin froze. "Compensation?"

"The duke offered you money?" Gemma breathed.

Crispin turned his head. Rafe, damn him. Sweeping in on a white horse and doing what he had not. Perhaps could not, considering his conversation with Abbot the previous day. And he hated that Gemma's expression of gratitude was now about his brother rather than him.

"He did," her father said with a grin. "So you can have Mary for the two Seasons, though I will require the aforementioned access and invitations. But it will all be worked out. She and her things are in the carriage on the drive."

Gemma let out a gasp as she staggered toward her father. "You've left her in the carriage in our drive for nearly an hour?"

Sir Oswald shrugged. "You made me wait, Gemma. You've only yourself to blame."

She let out a cry of pain and rushed from the room to collect her sister. Crispin watched her go, anger burning within him not just for her father's callousness, but for the fact that he himself had done so little to get Gemma what she wanted more than anything.

He spun on Sir Oswald. "You bastard. Your beloved daughter my ass, if you left her outside for so long."

Sir Oswald's smile remained unchanged in the face of Crispin's wrath. He shrugged. "She will get me what I want one way or another, unlike her ungrateful sister, so Mary is most beloved to me. As long as your brother and sister-in-law keep up their end of the bargain and see her married well."

Crispin moved on him. "When she is settled, I swear to you, old man, you are going to pay for what you put Gemma through. And her sister."

Sir Oswald's eyes flickered with fear for one satisfying moment, but then he shrugged. "Have a care, *boy*. If my daughter hasn't already told you, I will say that my mood should not be tested."

"I am not those young women," Crispin said, pointing in the direction of the door where Gemma had departed a few moments ago. "Not only am I not afraid of you and your petty threats, I have far more power than you do thanks to my name, thanks to my brother's name. So if you hurt them, either of them, even in the tiniest way, you must know that every bit of my person, every bit of my influence, every bit of the rest of my life will then be dedicated to destroying you. Body, soul and finances."

Sir Oswald's smirk faded. "You have her now. Don't foul it up as you apparently have done everything else in your life."

Without another word, he turned and left. And even though Crispin knew he shouldn't care what Sir Oswald thought or said, his parting shot rang in his ears.

CHAPTER SEVENTEEN

Without a word, Gemma and Mary's father hustled past them through the doorway of the parlor and out to the carriage. As soon as the footmen removed the final piece of luggage from the top, the vehicle all but screeched away.

"Is he truly allowing this?" Mary asked.

Gemma nodded, but her attention was through the door just a few steps in front of them. She had heard a little of the last part of Crispin's confrontation with her father. Including her husband's defense her and her sister.

And her father's nasty last words.

She slipped her arm through Mary's. "It seems he is," she said. "Now let us come and greet your savior."

Mary arched a brow. "Oh, is the duke here?"

Gemma shot her sister a glare and guided her into the parlor. She was disappointed to find Crispin at the sideboard, pouring himself a drink. He turned as they entered and smiled, but she could see the expression didn't meet his eyes.

"Miss Quinn," he drawled. "I'm so very happy to have you here at last."

Mary nodded. "I am very happy to be here." She said nothing else, and Gemma nudged her. "What?" her sister asked in a theatrical whisper.

"Don't you want to thank Crispin for his assistance with

Father?" she asked, glaring at her sister.

Mary sighed and stepped forward. "I-I do want to thank you, Mr. Flynn."

"Crispin," he said as a soft interruption.

She hesitated. "Crispin. I do appreciate all you have done and all the influence your brother has exerted on my behalf. I will do my best to take advantage of the opportunity granted me."

Gemma watched Crispin's face carefully as her sister spoke. He had been smiling at her until she mentioned Rafe's part in the bargain. Then his expression had hardened and now he took a sip of that blasted drink.

"Well, I was happy to help." He glanced at Gemma. "I will leave you two alone to celebrate."

She stepped forward, arm outstretched. "No, Crispin, we would welcome your presence. This is all because of you, after all."

His lips thinned. "We both know that isn't true. At any rate, I would not want to interrupt whatever giddy ladies talk there is to be had. No, you two have your time together. You don't need my interference."

Gemma frowned as he nodded to Mary and then slipped from the room. Everything in her wanted to pursue him, to comfort him in whatever pain or disappointment he felt in himself. To thank him more properly. Or improperly. That desire almost drove her to follow him, despite the fact that Mary had only just arrived.

The realization struck her in that moment. Normally her focus in this situation would only be on her sister. But right now it was not.

"I'm so glad he left," Mary sighed as she flopped into the closest settee. "Now you and I can truly be ourselves."

Gemma shoved her desire to pursue Crispin aside and went to the door to pull the bell and have some tea brought. As she waited, she frowned at her sister.

"Honestly, Mary, you should be more open to the man."

"Why?" Mary asked. "He stole you from our house after making a desperate bargain with our father. He forced you to marry him. He doesn't love you—he probably isn't capable of such an emotion."

A servant appeared and after making arrangements for their refreshments, Gemma quietly but firmly shut the door. She took a deep breath before she turned back to her sister.

"There are a great many wrong things about what you just said," she said, trying to keep her tone from being sharp. "So many, in fact, that I scarcely know where to begin. First off, you already know that it wasn't Crispin who came to our house like a villain with a plan. Father took advantage of *both* of us with his schemes."

"The difference is that you were an innocent in that plot and *Crispin* gambled with every knowledge of who he was sitting down with. He says he was an innocent party, but how do we know the truth. He could have been in league with Father all along."

Gemma gritted her teeth. Mary seemed so very young right now and so very set in her ideas. "I promise you, I am no fool. I believe that Crispin didn't have any idea as to Father's machinations."

"And yet you're still married," her sister said softly.

Gemma folded her arms. "Which, if you must know, was my doing. Crispin wanted to get the thing annulled and was willing to go to court to argue a fraudulent marriage. But he asked me what I wanted, Mary."

Mary's eyes went wide and Gemma nodded.

"Yes, a man who asked my opinion on my own life, isn't that a thought?"

"So you are saying staying wedded to this man was *your* idea?" Mary burst out in what seemed to be pure shock.

"Because the alternative is not very pleasant, my dear. Think about ruin. Think about destruction. Think about you never being able to wed well. If that had come to pass, Father would have simply sold you to the highest bidder." Her sister went very pale. "When Crispin heard my plea for you and thought about the consequences of such a decision for his own family, we agreed together to stay married and make the best of this very bad situation."

At that moment, there was a knock at the door behind them and it opened to reveal one of the maids and her tray of tea and food. She set it out for Gemma to serve and bobbed out a nod before she left the sisters alone again.

Gemma poured Mary a cup of tea and flavored it to her liking. When she looked up to hand the drink over, she found Mary staring at her clenched hands in her lap, her lip quivering.

"What is it?"

"You stayed married for me," her sister whispered. "You gave up any chance you have at true happiness for me."

Gemma set the teacup down and shifted to sit on the chaise next to Mary. She wrapped an arm around her and hugged her gently.

"You misunderstand. Yes, Crispin and I made a decision to remain in this union partly to reduce the scandal for those around us. But..." She hesitated for she was about to admit something out loud that she didn't know if she was ready to say.

"But?"

"Crispin is not what you have made him out to be," Gemma whispered. "He is far from a monster. He is also far from perfect, but so are all of us. He can be very kind, he can be very attentive, he can be..."

She trailed off, uncertain how to proceed. She and Crispin had been together for less than a week, but yet she felt she had known him for far longer.

"What can he be?" Mary asked, swiping at the tears that had sparkled in her eyes a moment before.

"He can be a good husband," Gemma offered since she could say no more without revealing too much, even to herself. "And...and you may be right that he does not love me, you may be right that he will *never* love me. But that does mean that we could not have a good life together. I accept him and he accepts me. Sometimes that is the best one can hope for."

But as she said the words, she realized how hollow they sounded. She had not often thought of another marriage after Theodore died. But when she had, she'd hoped she might get a chance to choose her mate for love.

She pushed the thoughts away.

"At any rate," she continued, forcing Mary to meet her eyes. "I urge you to give him a chance. And since this is his house and he is kindly allowing you to stay here, I order you to at least give him the respect he deserves."

"Because if I don't, he might turn on us?" Mary asked, a twinge of fear in her voice, even as she reached for the forgotten cup that had been prepared for her.

Gemma shook her head. "No, he isn't like Father. You do it because he deserves that respect, if nothing more."

Mary took a sip of tea as she pondered Gemma's words. When she set the cup down, she sighed. "I will do as you ask of me, Gemma. I will try to get to know the man, at least a little. For you."

Gemma relaxed a little. "Good. It means a great deal to me."

Mary sent her a side-glance. "Is that because Crispin means a great deal to you?"

Gemma caught her breath. Her cheeky sister had just shot an arrow at her without even knowing what she did. There was truth in the question. Even after such a short acquaintance, she did think of Crispin as an important person in her life. In fact, she thought of him all the time.

She shrugged, the motion entirely dismissive of the confusion in her chest. "He is my husband, Mary. I don't think it is such a foolish thing to view him as a significant part of my new life."

Her sister pondered that. "I suppose not." Mary let out a long sigh. "Well, why don't you tell me about this duke and duchess, then? Will they be very hard on me as chaperones? I don't want to make a fool of myself with my country manners."

Gemma leaned forward and began to reassure Mary of all the kindness she would find in Rafe and Serafina, but even as she did so, her errant mind kept coming back to Crispin and the realization that her sister was right. He was terribly important to her.

And that would not, *could* not end well.

Although it was only late afternoon, Crispin's curtains were drawn and he sat in the dark, a drink in his hand, staring at the fading embers of his fire.

How long had he stood in the hallway, listening to Gemma and Mary whisper? Giggle?

"Too long," he muttered to himself.

He took a sip of his drink, though he didn't know how many this one made. He'd stopped counting at three. All he knew was that for the first time since he married Gemma there was a blessed sense of calm over him. A cloudiness to his mind that made it hard to think about things he didn't want to consider. So many, many things.

The door to the office opened and in the light from the hallway, he recognized the perfect form of his wife as she stepped inside into his darkness. She hesitated in the light for a moment and then pulled the door shut behind herself.

He could no longer see her face, but he heard the disapproval in her voice as she said, "There you are. I have been looking for you."

He had been slouching in his chair and forced himself to slide up, straighten up, as he watched her shadow stride across the room. She stopped at the fire, where she threw a log or two in and stoked the flames back to life, lighting up the room again.

The firelight hit her face and Crispin took a long breath. She looked like an angel. A flame-haired angel, one that had battled and lost but kept going.

She stared at the drink in his hand and she frowned slightly. He felt the strangest urge to set the drink aside, hide it. After all, he had been trying to improve himself since they wed. Trying to prove to her…and to himself…that he could be better. But maybe he couldn't.

"Is your sister settled?" he asked.

She remained at the fireside, watching him. "Yes," she said softly. "I put her in the guest wing room closest to our side of the house, but still far enough away that she will not, er…hear anything that would shock her."

Crispin chuckled as he drank again. "Yes, we wouldn't want to do that to the poor girl."

Gemma didn't laugh with him. "Are you sorry she's here?"

He jolted at the question. His mind might be addled, but he didn't recall being sorry that Miss Mary Quinn was here. Hadn't he arranged the whole thing in order to gain some of his wife's approval?

Or perhaps that was what his *brother* had done. He scowled.

"Crispin?" she pressed.

He blinked. He hadn't answered her question. "No, of course not. I wanted Mary here as you did. I'm pleased to have her."

She took a step toward him. "Then why didn't you stay with us when she arrived or join us for our luncheon? And why are you sitting in the dark half-drunk?"

He arched a brow. "You don't like my drinking."

She folded her arms. He couldn't help but notice how the action lifted her breasts ever so slightly. Breasts he suddenly wanted to see, to lick, to fondle until she stopped frowning at him.

"Your drinking tends to get you into trouble, Crispin," she

said softly.

He got to his feet, drink still dangling from his fingers, and took another step toward her. "Am I in trouble?"

Her lips pursed and she explored his face. There was true concern in her eyes, worry that he had seen too many times and on too many faces of those who loved him. Of course, she didn't love him. And yet she was still concerned for him. Somehow.

"I don't know, you don't want to tell me," she whispered. She shook her head and auburn curls danced against her pale cheeks. "In truth, I sometimes feel I don't know you at all."

Crispin tensed. "You know enough. If you get too deep—"

He cut himself off, and she stepped closer. "What will happen if I get too deep?"

"One of us will get lost. One of us will drown," he whispered.

She held steady on his gaze for a long moment before she finally let out a small sigh. Then she closed the remaining gap of space between them and cupped his cheeks. She drew him down and surprised him by pressing her lips to his. She was very gentle with the caress, but insistent as she pressed her tongue to his lips. He parted them willingly and groaned as she pushed inside, tasting him. Tasting the evidence of his drinking, though she didn't recoil from it.

What she did do was glide a hand down his arm and take his glass away. She parted from their kiss only long enough to set the glass aside on the table, then returned to him to wind her arms around his neck.

"Mary is upstairs, settling in and then having a nap. She has not slept well in the days since you and I wed and she was left alone with my father."

Crispin smiled. "That is excellent, both for your sister's health and so that we have enough time to do more of this."

He cupped the back of her head, tilting her face up and claiming her lips in one smooth, gentle motion. She let out another sigh, but this one was not one of frustration or resignation or upset, but of surrender, and it was like music to his ears. He guided them toward the settee, never breaking the kiss and sat down. He drew her into his lap where she settled in, stroking his hair as they kissed.

His arms tightened around her and he reveled in how it felt to have her there. It felt so right, so perfect, so utterly wonderful.

His eyes came open and he drew back to look at her. When he was with her, he didn't think of the past, he didn't torture himself about the future. He was just *here*, in this moment.

And though his addled mind knew that was a betrayal, a lie, a bitter forgetting of what he had lost…he still drowned in it, losing himself in her smile as she shifted to straddle him.

She kissed him again, deeply, and his mind emptied of his strange, drink-induced thoughts. He simply enjoyed the way she undulated above him, grinding down against him in the rhythm they would soon take together. He found the buttons along the back of her gown and began to unfasten them, and she shivered.

"This morning when you did that, it took everything in me not simply bend over and let you have me in the dressing room."

Crispin's cock throbbed at that unexpected and highly erotic admission. "I would have very much enjoyed that."

She looked at him a moment, then got to her feet. She shrugged out of the now-unfastened dress and slowly turned to face the desk where they had already made love once before, with her bruises as a result.

She leaned over it, lifting her backside so that he could see the hint of her pink pussy through the slit in her drawers.

"You can enjoy it now," she murmured. She blushed as she said it, her boldness still new to her, and he actually liked that all the more. She was every inch the lady, even when she was bent over in offering like the most talented bawd in town.

"I think I will," he murmured, getting to his feet and unfastening the flap on his trousers. As the fabric fell to dangle between his legs, his cock popped free and he hissed as the warm air brushed over his sensitive skin.

He positioned himself behind her and reached his fingers through the opening in her drawers to stroke over her entrance. To his surprise, she was dripping wet, so very ready for him. He groaned at the heated response of her and the way she pushed back against his fingers as she sought relief. How had he been so lucky to be tricked into marriage with someone so well-matched to him physically?

He ignored the other ways they seemed to be well-matched and instead focused on aligning his hardness to her softness. She let out a low, keening sound as he slipped into her body, stretching her and claiming her.

"Hard," she grunted as she gripped the edge of the desk. "Please."

Those two words hit him in the already tight and tingling balls, and he began to pound against her, thrusting wildly even as the tiny part of him that wasn't drunk reminded him about her pleasure.

But her pleasure didn't seem to be an issue. Leaving one hand on the desk edge to steady herself, she snaked the other between her legs and began to stroke herself in time to his thrusts. Soon she bucked, her cries growing louder and her body milking him with her release. His control was gone thanks to drink and high emotion, and he clasped her hips as he thrust a few more times, then came deep inside of her clenching body.

Without a word, he withdrew and swept her into his arms. He returned to the settee where they had begun and perched her in his lap. With a sigh, she rested her head on his shoulder. They were quiet for a long time before she lifted her head and studied him.

"Thank you," she said softly.

He blinked, his mind still reeling from both the drink and the power of their joining. "For what?"

She blushed again, despite what they had just shared. "For

not making me feel…damaged. Or unwanted." She turned her face. "That sounds silly."

He caught her chin and kept her looking at him. "You are not damaged, Gemma Flynn. And you are most definitely wanted."

She smiled at him and he caught his breath. This was not a smile he had seen before. This expression was just for him. And it hit him in the gut like a punch before she settled her head back on his shoulder with another little, satisfied sigh.

Later, when he was sober, he knew he would lament his increasingly tangled feelings for his new wife. He knew he would punish himself for allowing her to pierce even a tiny fraction of the armor he had carefully built around himself over more than a year.

But for now, he merely held her close and enjoyed the pound of her heartbeat which so closely matched his own.

CHAPTER EIGHTEEN

Gemma kept reminding herself that she shouldn't be upset. She told herself that it was better this way. But as she stared at the empty seat her husband should be sitting in, sharing a luncheon with her and Mary, her heart still sank.

It had been this way for four days. Since her sister's arrival, Crispin had been more and more scarce around their home. During the day he left, telling her muddled stories about potential investments and financial meetings that she found herself praying were the truth. And he came home after supper many a night, only to join her and Mary for after-dinner drinks.

He never missed the after-dinner drink.

Of course, he never missed joining her in their bed, either. His lovemaking was as ardent and pleasurable as ever. But she still felt him pulling away, peeling himself from her day-to-day life.

What surprised her most was how much she missed him.

"Are you even listening?" Mary's laughing tone interrupted her reverie and Gemma jerked to pay attention.

"I'm sorry, darling," she said with a shake of her head. "Woolgathering."

"Mooning, you mean." Mary smiled and Gemma couldn't help but join her. One very positive development in those same four days had been that when Crispin was around, he had worked very hard at earning Mary's regard.

And it was working. Of course it was. When he made even the barest attempt, he could be devastatingly charming.

"Will your Notorious Flynn be joining us today?" Mary teased.

Gemma pursed her lips. "Oh, don't call him that, Mary. It isn't respectful."

"He laughs when I do it," Mary insisted. "And I would never outside these walls. But *is* he coming?"

Gemma bent her head. "I-I don't know. He didn't exactly inform me about his plans."

Mary's smile fell, and after the servant had taken her empty plate and left the room, she leaned forward to touch her sister's arm. "He cares about you, Gemma."

She pursed her lips, embarrassed by the statement. "Does he now?"

Mary nodded. "He does, indeed. It's obvious."

Gemma laughed, though she felt anything but amused. "Obvious how?"

Mary shrugged. "The way he talks about you when you aren't in the room says it all."

Leaning back, Gemma stared at her sister. "What do you mean he talks about me when I'm not in the room? When?"

"I don't know. Oh, like last night. You left the parlor to deal with some question from the kitchen. The moment you were gone, Crispin was going on and on about you."

Gemma lifted her eyebrows. "This comes as a surprise to me." She hesitated, for she should simply let it stand, but her curiosity was raised and she found herself whispering, "What does he say about me?"

The moment she asked the question, she heard how desperate—even pathetic—it sounded. After all, Crispin was likely only telling Mary nice things to get in her sister's good graces and convince Mary he wasn't the monster she had built up.

"He said you were a fine woman," Mary said.

Gemma's frown drew deeper. He would likely say the same about the cook.

"He said he was lucky to have you placed in his lap."

Gemma jerked her gaze to her sister. Certainly that was not something Crispin would say about the cook. And in some small, sad, lonely part of her, she ached.

"Well, I think we are both lucky," she managed to say, her throat suddenly dry. "Either of us could have done much worse in a forced union."

"But you think more highly of him that that," Mary said, making a face. "I know you do."

Gemma took a breath, uncertain how to explain her complicated thoughts to her still-innocent sister, but she was saved when the door to the dining room opened and Crispin himself stepped inside.

She pushed to her feet. "Good afternoon."

"Hello," he said with a quick smile for them both.

"Would you like lunch?" Gemma asked. "We have just finished, but I'm certain—"

"No, no," he said with a wave of his hand. "I ate at Annabelle and Marcus's."

She flinched. So that was where he had been. Calling on his family. Without her. "I hope they are well."

He nodded. "Yes, very well. And I bumped into Rafe there as well. He said he had something to discuss with all of us, including you, Mary. So he is on my very heels."

Mary tensed. "So I shall finally meet this duke."

Gemma turned her attention away from her husband and to her sister. "Don't fret, he is not a scary duke. He's the most unduke-like duke I've ever met."

"Tell him that, he'll love it," Crispin said, smiling, but she could see his distraction. That same distraction that had stood like a wall between them for days.

"Well, we needn't have this discussion of his in the dining room," Gemma said. "Why don't we go to the blue parlor? It's my favorite in the house and has comfortable seating for us all."

Crispin nodded and offered her his arm. She hesitated a moment before she took it and his eyes darkened at that fact. But he said nothing as he led her from the room, her sister a few steps behind them.

"Is everything all right?" she dared to ask.

He glanced down at her as they entered the blue parlor, and he released her. "Of course," he said with a nonchalant shrug. He moved to the side bar and stared at the liquor, but to her surprise, he took nothing. He merely leaned back against the edge.

Within a moment, Fletcher appeared in the doorway with Rafe at his side. "The Duke of Hartholm," he intoned, as seriously as if he were announcing him at a formal ball.

Out of the corner of her eye, Gemma caught Crispin flinch at the use of his brother's title. But then he smiled. "Hello, Rafe. Fletcher, can you get some refreshments for everyone?"

The butler bowed out and Crispin stepped forward. "Your Grace, may I present Miss Mary Quinn, Gemma's sister."

Mary blushed, rubbing her hands on her skirts before she held one out to Rafe. She bobbed a curtsey as he took it. "A pleasure to make your acquaintance, Your Grace."

Rafe laughed and shot a look at his brother. "You told her I'm a fop, didn't you?"

Mary looked to Gemma with confusion. "I-I'm sorry, Your Grace?"

Rafe shook his head and placed his second hand over Mary's. "My dear, I have only been duke for a blink of an eye and I never wanted the job in the first place. You are family now so you must call me Rafe, at least when the world isn't watching. I do hate being Your Graced."

Mary smiled, as everyone did when faced with Rafe's charm, and nodded. "Very well, Rafe. I do appreciate what you and your wife are offering to do for me. I hope it will not put you out."

He released her hand. "Not at all. Serafina looks forward

to it especially."

Gemma stepped forward and Rafe leaned in to kiss her cheek. "Hello, Rafe. How is Serafina?"

"So very well." His eyes lit up at the subject and Gemma barely resisted the urge to look away. "She is almost fully healed from the birth of the baby and is looking forward to resuming normalcy. Or as close as she gets to it with me in the house."

They all laughed at his self-deprecating humor as a maid entered the room with a tray of refreshments. Gemma sat on the settee, her sister beside her, and poured the tea. "Crispin tells us you have something to discuss with us all."

Rafe took the cup she offered and settled into as chair. Crispin pressed his lips together when she lifted the pot in his direction, but nodded slowly and came to sit on the chair across from his brother.

"There is a ball tomorrow night that is being hosted by Lord and Lady Elsworth," Rafe began. "And Serafina has ensured that you and Crispin are invited to it."

Gemma blinked. "Mary and Crispin?"

Rafe shook his head. "No, not Mary. Not yet. Serafina has plans for you, Mary, and I will get to them in a moment. For tomorrow's gathering, it is Gemma and Crispin who have been invited."

Crispin clenched his fists. "I don't want to go to some bloody earl's soiree."

"He's a marquis, actually," Rafe said with a glare in his brother's direction. "And if you let me finish, I shall explain why this has been arranged."

Crispin rolled his eyes. "*Fine.*"

"You know there is much talk about the union between you," Rafe said. "Thanks to your father bragging in an attempt to force you to stay together, the *ton* has tongues a wagging. Serafina believes if you come to this event, show that you are truly together, perhaps even play up that you have some affection for each other…"

Gemma looked at Crispin when his brother said those words, but her husband remained focused on Rafe. She frowned.

"...then you could quiet some of it," Rafe finished. "And we can also set the stage for Mary with a few comments from me and some hints about the second event that will happen this week."

"Second event?" Gemma asked.

Rafe smiled at Mary. "My wife thinks that by Saturday she will be well enough to play hostess, and so we will be having a ball at our home. To celebrate the birth of Little Crispin, the marriage of Big Crispin and you, and also to announce our support for Miss Mary Quinn."

Mary's eyes were wide. "A fresh coming out?"

Rafe nodded. "Yes. And of course we will pay for a beautiful new gown for you, Mary. You can come tomorrow while Crispin and Gemma are at the ball and be fitted with Serafina at your side—if that is amenable to you, Gemma."

Gemma was about to agree when Crispin pushed to his feet. "I will pay for Mary's new gowns, Rafe."

Gemma froze at the look on her husband's face. He was infuriated, but also humiliated as he glared down at the brother he loved so much and yet had such a complicated relationship with.

Rafe hesitated, but then inclined his head. "Of course, Crispin. I did not mean to tread into your responsibilities. I will have the dressmaker bill you if that is your preference."

"It is," Crispin said, his tone icy as he stomped once more to the sideboard and the liquor there.

Rafe swallowed, and for a moment he looked at Gemma. She saw he was as concerned as she was about Crispin's drinking. And that struck even deeper fear in her. They both looked at her husband, but Crispin was only holding a bottle in his hands. He had not yet poured himself a drink.

"Is this arrangement to your liking otherwise?" Rafe asked softly.

Crispin turned, setting the bottle back in its place as he moved. "Do I want to go to a stuffy ball, either yours or this Elsworth's? No. Will I in order to repair any damage I've done and to help ease Mary's transition back into Society? Of course."

Gemma let out a sigh of relief and she thought she saw Rafe do the same as he stood.

"Then it is settled. Serafina will send you all the details for both balls, Gemma, and arrangements for Mary to join her tomorrow for her first fitting. And I am off."

"Actually," Crispin said, stepping forward. "I have something else to discuss with you. In private."

Gemma tensed as she pushed to her feet. "Well, Mary and I can go up to my room. It seems I must choose a gown of my own for the ball tomorrow and I could use her assistance."

Rafe nodded. "Then I'll see you tomorrow night, Gemma. And it was a pleasure to meet you, Mary."

Mary said something appropriate and all but skipped from the room. Gemma moved slower, watching Crispin as she crossed to him. She touched his arm and he looked at her. His expression felt so very empty, so very blank that her heart hurt. What had she done?

"Crispin," she said softly. "He is on your side."

His mouth thinned and he nodded. "Of course he is."

She wanted to say more, but could see he was not open to her at this moment. So she merely squeezed his arm gently and left him alone with his brother, hoping that the two wouldn't come to blows and wondering how she could get back the intimacy she had once begun to build with Crispin outside of their bed.

***

Crispin watched Gemma walk out of the room with an ache in his heart. He knew he was hurting her by withdrawing, but after that drunken afternoon a few days ago, he had no other choice but to do so. He did not want feelings for his bride. He didn't want feelings at all.

"She is a good woman," Rafe said softly, dragging Crispin's attention from Gemma.

Crispin stepped forward and closed the door before he faced his brother again. "She is."

"You ought to—"

Crispin raised a hand to stop him. "I'm not going to talk about her with you."

Rafe frowned. "Then why did you want to talk to me?"

Crispin moved forward, the anger that he had been keeping in check bubbling to the surface. "Who the fuck do you think you are, paying off Gemma's father without consulting me?"

Rafe took a step back, surprise clear on his face. "This is about the money?"

Crispin ground his teeth. "How much did you give him for that 'generous settlement' he threw up in my face?"

Rafe shifted, and Crispin's heart sank. "A thousand pounds."

Crispin's stomach turned. He didn't have a thousand pounds to spare at present, especially if he had to pay for Gemma and Mary's gowns.

"So much," he said softly.

Rafe watched him for a moment, and Crispin could feel his brother's caution, his search for delicacy. "I know you have lost a great deal of money in the past year or so."

Crispin jolted. "It's none of your damned business."

Rafe's nod was his unexpected response to Crispin's outburst. "I agree. It is not my business what you do with your funds. Although I think the reason I found you today at Marcus and Annabelle's with Paul Abbot is because you are trying to amend whatever damage you did."

Crispin clenched and unclenched his hands in frustration. "Yes," he finally admitted. "Abbot is helping me look into some investments in order to..." He trailed off and Rafe nodded in understanding.

"And what is his thought about your chances at regaining some of the wealth you lost?"

"It will take time," Crispin replied. "A few years at least. Some of the investments might be faster, others are more long term and steady."

"And you went there in order to keep this from Gemma?" Rafe pressed. "How much does she know?"

"Some of it."

Crispin bent his head and turned back to the alcohol he wanted so fucking badly that he had begun to sweat. He'd only been having one after-supper drink with his wife and sister-in-law every night, and by the time he had that, he was shaking. The only thing that made the pain end was going to bed with Gemma. Her touch saved him every time.

It shouldn't. But it did.

"She knows some but you still hide?" Rafe asked.

Crispin faced his brother again. "I know when she looks at me, she sometimes sees the life she led at her father's, always wondering if it would be all right. Always trying to fix what he destroyed. I don't want her to see that with me. I will fix this without involving her, troubling her."

Rafe moved toward him and slowly lifted his hands to close them over Crispin's shoulders. "Allow her to be your partner, Crispin, in your troubles as well as your triumphs. Show her that you are not her father by allowing her to see the actions you take. The girl cares for you, the way she tracked your every move in the parlor today told me that."

Crispin flinched. These things Rafe said were exactly what he could not do, did not want. "You don't understand."

Rafe released him. "No," he said, his tone laced with bitterness. "You are right. I don't understand. Because you have shut me out as neatly as you attempt to do with her. I hear whispers, I see glimpses, but I have no idea what happened to change you into the man who stands before me today. But I'm your brother, your blood, and I love you enough to keep trying. I hope you don't destroy Gemma's desire to keep trying before you realize how valuable it is."

"Are you finished?" Crispin asked, hating how harsh he sounded. But Rafe couldn't help. No one could help.

Rafe sighed. "Yes. I'll see you at Elsworth's tomorrow, then. And we can pretend this, as so many other conversations, did not happen, I suppose. Good day."

His brother said nothing else, but left the room and left Crispin alone. And once he was alone, he muttered, "I know how valuable she is. What she offers in those eyes. It doesn't mean I can have it."

CHAPTER NINETEEN

The sounds of music and talking people pressed around Gemma, making her throat as tight as if it was in a noose. She forced her smile broader and looked around the room at all the Society lords and ladies and saw so many faces looking back. Judging back.

As it had been for so very long.

She knew why they stared. They stared because of her father's reputation. They stared because they liked to call her a killer. They stared because of her scandalous forced marriage to Crispin.

"It looks like you could use this."

She turned to find Crispin approaching her, a tumbler of some kind of spirits in his hand. "Normally I do not approve of drowning one's troubles in drink."

"Yes." He chuckled. "I had guessed that."

She shot him a look and took the glass. "In this case, perhaps I will make an exception."

As she lifted the glass, he placed a hand on the small of her back and before any spirit touched her lips, a sense of calm began to fill her. She glanced up at him, amazed by how this gentle touch could be so soothing. He returned the look, his eyes locked with hers.

"I see your anxiety on every line and flutter of your face.

You don't have to worry about their thoughts regarding you," he said softly.

"But I do. For Mary."

He pursed his lips. "You spend so much time worrying and fretting over everyone else."

The burning heat of a blush filled her cheeks and she looked away from him at last. "It is all I can do," she whispered, then cleared her throat. "At any rate, if my feelings are so obvious, then I am in trouble regardless."

He shook his head. "I do not think they would be obvious to anyone else."

She jolted. "Then how can you see them so clearly?"

He was quiet long enough that she forced herself to look up at him again. He was suddenly grim. "I know you," he finally retorted, but the admission seemed to give him no pleasure and hit her like both a stab to the heart and a warm embrace.

Such discordant feelings only fueled her tangled state of mind.

A state of mind that was not helped when she looked over his shoulder and saw the approach of one of her least favorite people in London.

"Oh, damn," she said, downing the drink in one slug.

Crispin stared at her, eyes wide. "What brought that on?"

"Lady Winterhaven is approaching."

"Who?"

She almost laughed at his refreshingly out of touch confusion. It would not help Mary, but it was a happy change from her father, who only cared about rank and rule.

"The Countess of Winterhaven came out the same year I did, and for whatever reason, she decided we were rivals."

Crispin cast a glance over his shoulder at the still-approaching lady. "Perhaps because you are a dozen times more lovely than she?"

She smiled despite her increasing nervousness. "I have no idea, but she would malign me whenever she got the chance.

And I know she was one of the people who spread the rumors that I killed Theodore. Her maid and one of my footmen were...involved in some way, and I think she wheedled some of the story from them and embellished greatly."

To her surprise, Crispin's face, which had been amused and relaxed, not tightened with anger on her behalf. "That bitch."

Gemma flinched. "Well, I wouldn't start the conversation that way because she is... Hello, Lady Winterhaven."

Crispin set his jaw before he turned to greet the intruder with a stiff nod.

"Gemma," the countess said, dismissing any rank Gemma had or had ever had.

Gemma pursed her lips as she looked the other woman up and down. Lady Winterhaven...Lady *Margaret* as she had been known when they came out the same year looked as fresh as she had during her diamond debut. Her blonde hair was perfect, her elegant curves were perfect. Her green gown was stitched with jewels throughout the fabric and made Gemma very aware that her own ball gown was two seasons out of fashion. As usual she felt dowdy and plain next to this woman.

"I did not know you were in attendance, my lady," Gemma said, forcing her tone to remain light, unaffected.

Lady Winterhaven smiled, her teeth all but glinting in the light from the chandeliers in a most predatory way. "Unlike some people, I am invited to *all* events."

Gemma flinched. She had opened a door wide open for that barb. She shook her head. "Forgive my manners, I have not yet introduced you to my new husband. May I present Mr. Crispin Flynn?"

"The brother of the Duke of Hartholm, I know." Lady Winterhaven let her eyes drift over Crispin. They held a strange combination of both disdain and what could only be called sensual interest.

Without thinking, Gemma slipped her hand into the crook of Crispin's elbow and squeezed gently, as if that action could somehow stake a claim on a man she held so little claim upon. It was an empty action, but then none of her weapons against Margaret had ever had much edge to them.

Women like Lady Winterhaven always won.

"My lady," Crispin said coolly.

"You are quite a pair," Lady Winterhaven chuckled. "The killer and the cad. And the way you wed, it was priceless. I think my sewing circle and I must have laughed for a full five minutes when we heard. You do always entertain, Gemma."

Gemma swallowed hard, wishing she could stop her heart from pounding. She always came up with retorts for this woman, but they came too late. They woke her in the middle of the night rather than springing to her mind in the midst of an attack.

"Why would you laugh?" Crispin asked, his tone blank as if he truly didn't understand. Gemma groaned. He would only make it worse.

"Because it was a bet you *lost* that forced you to marry her." Lady Winterhaven was speaking louder now, clearly drawing attention to them purposefully. And it was working for those around them were edging closer, listening while trying to look like they weren't.

Gemma's cheeks burned. This would damage Mary so much. She wanted to sink into the floor or die on the spot just to escape the humiliation and disappointment.

But Crispin seemed less affected. He tilted his head back and laughed. "Is that what you heard?"

At his laughter, Margaret's green eyes narrowed. "It is what is true."

"For one who has so much guile, you are surprisingly gullible. The story you have heard is pure, ridiculous poppycock. Gemma and I married because I fell wildly in love with her and I convinced her father to allow us to marry. When he said yes, I could not wait another moment to call her my wife."

"What?" Lady Winterhaven asked, her mouth agape. Not

that Gemma could blame her. It was rather her own reaction to this tale. "That is not the story I heard."

Crispin shrugged. "Well, 'tis true, I assure you. I met Gemma's father in a gaming hell, that is correct. And we did play a few friendly card games together. When I was invited to his home to pay him what he'd won, I caught a glimpse of the beautiful Gemma in the hallway and I was…"

He looked down at her, his eyes shining with something that looked like truth even though Gemma knew it wasn't. But it was so convincing and…and tempting to see it here.

"Crispin…" she began.

He tapped her nose gently with the tip of his finger. "Let me tell the story. You know how I love to do it." He shifted his attention back to Lady Winterhaven. "Well, I was awestruck. Gemma is the most beautiful woman I have ever known. And although everyone knows I am a committed rake, in that second, I realized I no longer wished to be. So I wooed and won her and here we are, as happy as two people have ever been."

He took Gemma's hand and raised it to his lips, and Gemma could have sworn she heard a few sighs from the crowd that was now not even trying to pretend they weren't listening in.

Lady Winterhaven glared at her, but then shrugged. "Well, many felicitations to you. You deserve each other."

She turned to go, but to Gemma's surprise, Crispin stepped forward to stop her. "You know, Lady Winterhaven, I have been trying to place where I know you since you approached, but I have finally determined it."

Gemma watched as her husband leaned in close to Margaret. Her heart pounded as he whispered something in the other lady's ear. But it obviously wasn't something sweet, for Margaret's cheeks went deathly pale and she jerked away from Crispin.

"I declare, I do not know what you are talking about," she snapped, her angry tone breaking before she skittered away with only a panicky glance over her shoulder at Crispin.

He turned back to Gemma and his smile was broad and proud and so delectable that she wanted to kiss him right then and there, despite the impropriety of the action. He held out a hand to her, looking every inch the fairytale prince as he said, "May I have this dance, Mrs. Flynn?"

And though her mind was buzzing with questions about what had just transpired, she could do nothing but take his offering and follow his lead.

Crispin couldn't take his eyes off his wife as they spun into the first steps of the waltz. She looked dazzlingly beautiful under the soft lights of the ballroom, and it was almost an irresistible temptation to have her in his arms.

She smiled up at him as they slowly made their turns. "What did you say to Lady Winterhaven to make her look that way?"

He grinned. Turning that bitch's tail beneath her legs and sending her running in fear had been the highlight of his month, not just his night. After the way she had treated Gemma, she deserved far worse.

"Do you really want to know?" he asked.

She nodded. "I do. When you first leaned toward her, I thought you might be flirting with her and my stomach lurched."

He almost faltered in his steps at that admission. "Gemma, I would not betray you like that, but certainly never with someone who had been so abjectly cruel to you. Your enemies are my enemies."

"I hardly know what to do with such loyalty," she murmured, her cheeks growing pink.

"You deserve it," he reassured her. "And what I said to *Lady* Winterhaven was that I recognized her from Marcus's club and I wondered if her husband and her sewing circle would get as much of a laugh out of that fact as they had about you."

Gemma blinked. "Margaret has been to an undergrounding gaming hell?"

He smiled. "It's a bit more than just that, I assure you." He watched her for a moment, thinking of her unrestrained passion and trying not to get hard as steel at the memories. "Actually, you would like it. I will take you some night. When Marcus is *not* working."

Oh, the things he could do with her there…share with her there. It was almost too perfect.

She obviously still didn't understand, for she shrugged delicately, as to not interrupt the dance. "Well, I appreciate your putting her in her place. And for the other things you said."

He looked into her eyes and saw the pain there. The rejection she had suffered, the loneliness she had endured. He had known her story about her first husband and guessed how terrible her life with her father had been through both her stories and the bastard's actions.

But he had never put those things together with how abandoned that must have made Gemma feel. To never be good enough, to never be cared for just because she was her own wonderful self.

"Why did you tell the lie to her about how we met and married?" she asked, her voice dropping to a whisper.

"Not all of it was a lie," he said, just as soft.

The moment he said it, he wished he could take it back. He didn't want her to know how enamored he had been of her since the moment he woke to find her in his bed. It felt wrong to do so.

She tilted her head. "Which parts were true?"

He swallowed. He could dismiss what he said entirely, but he knew that would cut her down. So he settled for a compromise.

"I have thought you incredibly beautiful from almost the first moment we met. I would have thought it from the first moment, but I don't recall that moment, of course."

She shook her head with a low laugh just for him that hit him in the gut like a punch. It faded and she tilted her head. "If I accept your tale that the moment you were sober enough to recognize I was another human and female that you found me attractive in some way, the rest of the lie you spun still stands."

He motioned around the room as the music came to an end. "They were watching, weren't they? And to make your sister's life easier…to make your life more bearable, I thought it was better to leave them believing that we fell suddenly and irretrievably in love. Even if it is…" He found himself hesitating, though he didn't know why. "…not true."

"So you said it for her benefit." Her tone was very neutral, as was her expression. "And theirs."

He nodded. "But here is what is not for their benefit. I want you, Gemma. So much that I'm not sure I will be able to wait the entire carriage ride home to have you. Will you leave with me now?"

She nodded without hesitation, but then her logic seemed to intrude upon her desires. "But it is still early—"

"After the story I just told, us sneaking out together will only cement the tale of our passionate love," he said, hoping he would strike on something that would make her agree once and for all.

It seemed he had, for she nodded again. "If it is for the good of the lie, how can I say no?"

She took his hand and let him lead her from the dance floor, from the ballroom and eventually to their carriage. He felt eyes follow them and didn't care. All he cared about was having her alone. Having her at all.

The moment the vehicle door closed and they were moving, he launched himself to her side of the carriage and covered her mouth with his. She lifted to him hungrily, answering his need with one of her own, as sweet and hot as anything he had ever experienced with any woman.

Any woman.

He pushed that thought from his mind and focused on Gemma. Gemma's little moans as he tucked his arms around her hips and pulled her against him. Gemma's arching back as he thrust against her and let her feel the hardness of his cock through all the frustrating layers of clothing.

"There's…too much separating us," she said, her tone filled with desperation.

"Not any more than the last time we did this," he teased, loving how her cheeks darkened at the reminder that they had surrendered to pleasures in their carriage before. He certainly hoped they would do so again. Over and over.

She met his gaze, and there was a sudden, unexpected wickedness. "Well, my ball gown is more intricate, but you…" She found the length of him through his trousers. "You could be easily freed, couldn't you?"

His eyes went wide as he watched her caress him, her fingers light and teasing. "Gemma," he breathed, a word that begged as well as warned.

She unfastened the flap on his trouser front with a slowness that could only be deliberate and lowered the bib to reveal him, naked and proud, thrusting to greet her.

"Mmmm," she murmured. "Do you know how much I like it when you put your mouth on me?"

He jolted as she took him in her fist and stroked him with confidence. Once, twice, until a droplet of moisture pooled on the tip of him.

"I can do that," he said, though at that moment he would have told her he could procure the crown jewels if it meant she would continue to touch him.

"Perhaps later," she purred, watching his face as she stroked him. "I am actually wondering if you would like the same."

He jerked in her hand. He had not asked her for that pleasure. Not because he didn't want it, not because her full lips, her hot mouth wasn't made for it. But because not all ladies liked it and pushing her didn't seem fair.

But now she offered him heaven without so much as a hesitation.

"I would very much like it," he growled. "I have dreamt of it since the first time I felt your mouth on mine."

"Denying you this dream would be very uncaring of your wife," she teased as she shifted on the carriage seat so that she could bend over him. "For your pleasure, Mr. Flynn, and mine."

Her lips brushed him and he grunted out a sound of surrender. She glided them over the head, chaste, closed mouth caresses of exploration. Down his shaft, she kissed, over his tight, full balls. He wanted to bark at her to open her mouth, to lick him, suck him, but he didn't. He let her take her time, find her way.

And she did. As she made her way back up his shaft, those closed-mouth caresses became wanton licks, her hot tongue stroking his every inch, swirling around his girth until she returned to the head.

She lifted her face, looked up at him with a smile of possessive, female power and then took him into her mouth. Slowly she lowered over him, taking inch by inch, lower and lower until he just touched her throat. The sight of her red head descending over his swollen one was enough to make him spend, but he held back, leaning against the carriage seat with a guttural groan of pure pleasure.

She began to thrust over him in earnest, mimicking the way she would ride him if she was astride, sucking him on the descent and swirling her tongue around his girth as she withdrew. It was a wild, animal rhythm she set, and he placed his hand on her back to feel her hips undulate in time, as if this act gave her pleasure.

He felt his seed galloping to be freed, the pressure in his balls mounting until he could no longer control it.

"Gemma, I'm going to spend," he managed to croak out,

gripping the seat edge with enough force that he feared he would tear the leather in pieces. "You must stop—"

She ignored him, lifting just her eyes to watch him, wicked pleasure in their gray depths as she took him to the edge and then sucked him over.

He roared out his pleasure and felt his seed pump free into her mouth. She took every drop, continuing the onslaught of her tongue until he went soft inside of her and she gently removed him with a pop.

He stared at her, this wild woman who had overtaken his passionate, but always proper wife. Her hair was tangled now, her face flushed with pleasure and triumph.

"That was incredible," he gasped, trying to find enough air to refill his empty lungs.

She smiled. "I am learning, I think, how to make you quake."

He laughed as he watched her tuck him back in place and fasten his trousers. "Learning? If you are not already an expert, I fear I may expire."

She tensed at the words and he turned his face with a curse. "I'm sorry, Gemma, that was a foolish thing to say."

She shook her head, though she did not look at him. "You didn't mean anything by it. I know you were only teasing."

Still, he saw the pain on her face. The embarrassment and the guilt. He placed a finger beneath her chin and forced her to look at him.

"No one should blame you for what happened to Laurelcross," he said. "I think I've proven that I will go to battle with anyone who dares. And that includes you, wife."

"You would go to battle with me?" she asked, a wavering smile returning to her face.

The carriage slowed as they reached their home, and he nodded slowly. "I will torture you, with pleasure, until you admit you have done no wrong."

Her eyes lit up and desire washed away the other feelings that had been placed there. "Then I think we should go to war," she said, trying to pretend seriousness even as a smile trembling at her lips. "And I shall not surrender easily."

He drew her closer and grinned. "I certainly hope not."

CHAPTER TWENTY

Gemma lifted an arm as the seamstress had told her and held very still as the woman pinned a few places here and there. The final fitting of her gown for Serafina and Rafe's ball had been going on for half an hour, but it felt like an eternity. Still, as the woman turned her so Serafina could look at her, Gemma couldn't help but smile. The duchess held Little Crispin in her arms, a beautiful Madonna who almost shone with the love for her child, her husband...her life.

But it hadn't always been that way, had it? Gemma had slowly begun to realize how very different things had been for Serafina and Rafe just a little over a year before.

"You look beautiful," her sister-in-law reassured her. "Except for that pensive look on your face."

Gemma laughed, though the comment made her uncomfortable. "Am I pensive? I shall have to be certain not to make this particular face at the ball. There I shall only be happiness and comfort, I assure you."

Serafina shrugged. "But not here. Here you can be you. Is there something troubling you?"

Gemma hesitated, shooting a look toward the stranger in their midst. In the mirror, the woman caught her look and straightened up.

"You know, I forgot a few rolls of fabric I wanted to show

you, Mrs. Flynn. Would you mind waiting in the ball gown while I fetch them? It will be no longer than..." She glanced between the two women, as if making a judgment. "Shall we say half an hour?"

Serafina smiled as she rose to her feet. "You are an angel, Madame. Thank you."

With a swift nod for them both, the seamstress departed, and Serafina shut the door behind her. When she turned back, her eyebrows were lifted in question. "Does that make you more comfortable?"

Gemma only stared at the door. "She just swept out of here to give us privacy?"

"I'm a very good customer," Serafina laughed. "Or at least Rafe insists I be. Madame knows she will be paid for her time one way or another. Now, why don't you tell me what is on your mind?"

Gemma ducked her head. "I don't know."

"I'm your best option. God love Annabelle, but she is Rafe and Crispin's sister. She doesn't want to hear details of anything intimate about their marriages. And she has a tendency to be a bit defensive of the two of them. The same goes for Mama Flynn. So you and I must be little islands for each other if we can be."

Gemma looked at her hands, clenched before her. Serafina made a great deal of sense, of course. But it was still difficult to just flat-out ask about Crispin, especially when he was so obviously reticent to have her know any secret he kept.

"How are *you* feeling, Serafina?" Gemma asked instead.

Her sister-in-law sighed. "Much better, thank you. There's still some soreness since the birth of the baby, but I had a far easier time than some women. I shall be very ready to host and celebrate you and your sister at Saturday's fete."

Gemma nodded as she examined the sleeping face of Little Crispin. "He is a handsome boy already," she sighed. "He doesn't look much like Annabelle and Mama Flynn, though, does he?"

"No, he favors his father and uncle," Serafina said, her voice gentle. "From all I have heard and the portraits I've seen, they look like their father, Reginald. Hence our son's middle name."

Gemma stepped down from the little dais where the seamstress had been making her alterations and paced to the window. "Did you ever meet Mr. Flynn?"

Serafina shook her head. "No. He died several years ago, long before I came into the picture. Why all the questions about Crispin's father?"

"He was wild, wasn't he?" she pressed. "Was he...was he cruel?"

Serafina's eyes went wide. "Gracious, no. I have never heard a story about Reggie Flynn from any source except that he was exuberant and filled with life and love, especially for his children. Questionable in judgment at times, but the boys adored him, as did Annabelle and Mama Flynn. He is still missed by them all, I think."

Gemma's lips pressed together, and now Serafina gently placed the baby in the basket next to the settee and marched toward her. "What are you trying to determine, my dear? I function much better if you ask me what you want to know directly."

Gemma sighed. Serafina had offered to be a confidante and it seemed she needed one. Desperately.

"I suppose I had hoped to understand why Crispin has been so...so unhappy in the last eighteen months. Why he was driven to drink and bargain away his fortune and trade away his freedom with a bet with my father. I know there are some men who are tormented by pasts with their family, so..."

She trailed off, and Serafina nodded. "I understand. Have you tried talking to him about it?"

Gemma felt her cheeks darken. "We are not like you and Rafe. We don't have the kind of marriage where he opens up to me. He says everyone has their secrets."

Serafina bent her head, and there was an air of defeat to

her that frightened Gemma. "Crispin certainly has those," she said softly. "But I'm afraid he has kept them from us all. You know that until he married you, he had not seen his brother or his sister for months. And he had not been actively part of this family for even longer."

Gemma took a deep breath and forced herself to say the one word she was so uncomfortable to voice. "Why?"

"When Rafe inherited his title from their cousin…inherited *me*…it wasn't a future anyone in his family desired for him. Rafe didn't desire it either, but we all quickly realized that there wasn't a choice in the matter. We came to accept it. But Crispin fought it more than anyone."

"Yes, there is still a certain tone he takes when he talks about the duke, although it has softened considerably since he began spending time with his brother again." Gemma thought of the flinches and the faces he sometimes pulled.

"I hope he is beginning to see that his brother is not changed by this transformation in his life." Serafina sighed. "Because when it first happened, it was as if Crispin thought his brother was being murdered, replaced by someone new. They had several rows about it."

Gemma moved toward her. "You know he is never anything but positive when he speaks of you."

Serafina took Gemma's hand, her face softened by a gentle expression. "Well, I thank you for that, but he's always been kind to me. In fact, he even helped his brother realize that he cared for me when we were at our darkest hour."

Gemma pursed her lips. "So my husband went wild all because of this change in his brother's life."

Serafina released her hands and caught her breath, as if she were considering what to say next. Finally, she murmured, "I think it is far more than that."

Gemma's stomach turned at the look on her sister-in-law's face. Serafina was uncomfortable. And she knew something. Something she feared Gemma wouldn't like.

"Serafina, I must know," Gemma whispered. "Even if it is

difficult, even if it hurts me to hear it. I need to know the truth because this man is, in whatever way we come to work it out, my future."

"You deserve to know," Serafina murmured. "A-a few months ago Annabelle began going to Marcus's club and spying on Crispin. She thought somehow she could save him from himself in some way. She didn't find out much, but she said that one night when he was deep in his cups, he muttered something about…about…"

Gemma could scarcely breathe. "About?"

"About *her*."

Her. The word hit Gemma in the stomach like a bullet and she stepped back. "A woman."

Serafina nodded. "Apparently so."

"Who was she?" Gemma asked. "What did he say about her?"

Serafina shrugged. "I don't know and neither does Annabelle. He was muttering, half-crazed with drink. He never gave any further details."

"Have they looked into it?" she pressed, shocked that she could form any kind of words with her head spinning as it was.

"Rafe, Annabelle and Marcus? Annabelle asked them to do so, and I think Marcus did a bit of snooping, but there wasn't anything to find. We are as in the dark as you are. I believe Rafe was simply trying to get his brother to come back into the fold in any way at all and then he would press him. But if he's talked to Crispin about it since your marriage, I don't know."

Gemma turned away, her cheeks flaming as she moved to look out the picture window to the garden below. Crispin's fall had been partly because of a woman. She would have to be quite something to inspire him to such depths.

Had he loved her? Did he love her still? Those questions swirled in her head and made her entire body ache with what she recognized as hateful, horrible jealousy. Crispin wouldn't give her a part of himself because that part belonged to someone else.

"You are very quiet," Serafina said softly from behind her.

Gemma squeezed her eyes shut. Tears pricked and she refused to let them fall and open herself up to questions about her own feelings. It was foolish to even have them about a man she'd known so short a time. Foolish to have them for a man who had never promised her anything except to be kind to her.

And he had kept that promise.

"Have I hurt you by sharing this?" Serafina asked.

She turned to face her friend, her sister-in-law, with the most false smile she had ever exhibited. "Of course not. I asked the question and you provided me with an honest answer. I appreciate knowing even some small details about Crispin. They will help me as I move into the future with him."

"But you and he—"

"Have not even a marriage of convenience," she finished. "We were forced into this situation and are making the best of it. But no one is in love with anyone, no one has any cause for hurt. He has not declared that I am his love, nor would I...nor would I desire such a silly thing. So you couldn't hurt me by telling me that the man loves someone else enough that something about her would spiral him into the depths of despair."

Serafina's face was filled with empathy and she moved on Gemma swiftly. "You must know that I have never seen him as happy as he has been recently with you. You bring out something good in him, Gemma. Something Rafe says he hasn't seen in a long time. You are good for him. And there is nothing that says that he couldn't feel—"

There was a light knock at the door, likely signaling the return of the seamstress, and Gemma was relieved when Serafina moved to the door and let the lady in.

"Welcome back, Madame," Gemma said. "Oh, those fabrics are lovely."

She followed the woman to the nearby table where she began to spread gorgeous lengths of silk, satin and muslin across the surface. And though they were all beautiful, Gemma could hardly see them, hardly think about them.

Because all she could think about was Crispin, in love with some other spectacular woman. A woman who one day might very well steal all Gemma had built.

CHAPTER TWENTY-ONE

Crispin hated a ball—always had. But even he could admit, albeit grudgingly, that the one Serafina and Rafe were hosting was a smashing success. Their ballroom overflowed with the very best of Society, along with a spattering of far more interesting people from the world of art, politics and even the underground. Everyone seemed to be having a wonderful time.

Everyone except for the one person he actually gave a damn about. Everyone but the woman standing next to him in an ocean-blue gown that highlighted the red fire of her hair and the gray depths of her eyes. Everyone but Gemma.

She stood at his side, stiff and uncomfortable. But then she had been acting in a peculiar fashion since yesterday after her fitting. Yes, she still talked to him, she made love with him, but he saw a fresh pain in her eyes that he did not understand.

Strangely, he wanted to.

He shook the thought away and looked across the room to where Mary stood with Rafe and Serafina and a few eligible men. His new sister-in-law looked enchanting with her dark hair—so unlike Gemma's—bound prettily at her neck and her orange gown bringing out the porcelain quality of her skin. She laughed and the others joined in.

"Mary is doing very well," he said, certain that would

draw Gemma to a subject she wished to discuss.

To his surprise, she jolted as if she hadn't been looking at her sister. Apparently, her mind had been elsewhere. "Yes," she said, now focusing on the same group he had been observing. "She has a lovely personality. With Serafina and Rafe's help, I'm certain she will do very well."

"It must take some weight off your shoulders," he pressed.

She glanced at him from the corner of her eye and her mouth drew down slightly. "Of course. Nothing would make me happier than to see her settled and free of our father."

Her words had no weight. He could see that in her eyes, hear it in the pain in her tone. But he could do nothing. The walls he had to erect kept him from offering or receiving true comfort.

He turned toward her. "Shall we dance?"

She hesitated, her gaze flitting to the dance floor where the waltz was just ending. "I—"

"They will expect it at a ball celebrating, in part, our marriage," he urged her.

She nodded. "Well, if they expect it."

As they approached the dance floor, the couples began to line up for the allemande. Crispin pursed his lips. Although they would remain together for the duration of such a dance, it wouldn't exactly provide any intimacy with its intricate steps and turns.

Still, he took his place beside her as the music swelled. For a few turns, he was quiet, watching her as she made the delicate twists and curves that made up the dance. If he had thought her elegant in the waltz, she was more so here. She moved her body naturally, her rhythm precise.

It strangely put him to mind of the way she moved when they made love, and the longer he watched, the more enamored he became of her grace. Why did she have to be so damned perfect in so many ways?

"You are quiet tonight," she finally said, breaking the silence as they touched hands and then broke apart once more.

He smiled. "I could say the same about you."

"Am I?" she asked, all innocence, though her deep blush told him that she had been caught.

"Indeed. You have been since you were fitted for that gloriously beautiful gown yesterday afternoon. Tell me, did Serafina say something to hurt your feelings?"

Her eyes went wide. "You know she would never do such a thing!"

They twirled away from each other briefly, circling around another couple before they returned to touch hands once more. God, it was electric every time.

"Well, it cannot be because you don't like the gown," he continued. "Because it is most fetching. I don't think you've ever been so beautiful."

She stumbled in one of her steps and looked around to be certain she hadn't trod on any toes. When they touched this time, he saw her face flicker with the same awareness as his own. He pulled her a touch too close and her breath hitched.

"Crispin," she whispered.

He didn't allow her to say more, for they spun away, hands in and then out. For the rest of the song, she said nothing, but focused intently on every movement she made.

He frowned. Whatever was troubling her was deep, indeed. Worse, he was beginning to suspect it had nothing to do with gowns or even Mary and her future.

He feared that Gemma was so distant because of *him*. But didn't he deserve it? For the past week, since the afternoon her sister had come to stay with them, he had been more and more withdrawn.

How could he explain to her that it was because he wanted her too much, he liked her too much? How could he say that he was forced to push her away? There was no way to say those words and make them sound anything but foolish and cruel. They would open him up to explanations he did not want to make to her…to anyone.

The song ended and she curtseyed to his bow, then slowly

reached out to take his hand. He led her from the dance floor and on the edge, he stopped.

"How can I make you smile again?" he asked.

She blinked. "I am smiling."

With a shake of his head, he murmured, "Not with your eyes."

Those same eyes went wide, dilated as she opened her mouth and shut it again, as if she struggled to speak. Sadly, she was not allowed to do it, for over her shoulder Crispin spotted two women coming toward him. All thoughts of Gemma faded as his world shrank. His life shrank. He everything shrank.

And in that moment he needed a drink more than anything.

Gemma struggled for words, but could find none, especially when Crispin's gaze moved away from her and settled behind her. His cheeks paled and his eyes went wide. Heart pounding, she turned to find what had stolen his interest.

Approaching were two women, twin images of each other, with blonde hair and icy blue eyes. They were beauties, to be sure, and Gemma's heart stuttered. Was one of them *her?* The *her* that had been built up in Gemma's mind so much in less than twenty-four hours that it seemed everything in the world was about the stranger her husband apparently cared for?

The women lived up to her imagination.

"Crispin Flynn," one of them hissed, her face a twisted mask of unadulterated rage. "How dare you?"

Crispin swallowed. "Imogen, Isadora, how lovely it is to see you. I did not realize you had been invited."

"Of course you didn't," the second woman hissed, just as angry. "You would have hidden like a coward if you had."

Gemma jolted. There was so much vitriol from these two that she had to believe one was his love.

"And you," said the one who had spoken first, her

attention on Gemma now. "*You* must be the fool who tricked him into your bed."

Crispin stepped forward and insinuated himself between her and the women. "Have a care—this is my wife."

Gemma touched his arm and then slipped from behind him. "We have not been introduced," she managed to say, her voice shaking just as her hand shook when she held it out. "I am Gemma Flynn."

Crispin made a pained sound in his throat. "These are Miss Imogen and Miss Isadora Brookfield."

Neither woman took her hand, but both looked her up and down like she was trash.

"Was this what you were doing when you were ripping our sister into shreds?" the second twin asked.

Gemma's gaze darted to Crispin's face. So neither of them was *her*. Their sister was *her*. So where was she? Here lurking? Watching her sisters confront the man she loved and the wife she had to hate? Or was she home mourning her loss?

Gemma's stomach churned, but she forced herself to watch Crispin. His face was filled with so much pain that she wished she could comfort him. But that would be very wrong right now.

"Enough," he said softly. "That is not how it was."

"Wasn't it? You told people at the ball a few days ago that you loved this woman, that it was all a fairytale," the first twin sneered. "I know, let's ask Alice ourselves how it was. Oh no, we can't. She isn't here."

Relief flooded Gemma for a moment. So the lady, *her*, was not watching. That was something. But she could not stand by while these beautiful harpies attacked Crispin.

"I do not know what your quarrel with my husband is," she said, and now it was she who stepped between Crispin and the women. "But to address him in this fashion in his brother's hall is not appropriate, whatever your anger stems from."

The first twin looked her up and down and then laughed, though the sound had no pleasure to it. "You have found a champion, Flynn. Once again, far better than you deserve." She turned her attention to Gemma, and the hate in her blue eyes was staggering. "You may convince yourself that you love him, *Gemma Flynn*, but he is incapable of loving anyone but himself."

Gemma's eyes narrowed. "This is not my home, but I am going to ask you to leave."

The sisters exchanged a glance and then flounced away toward the ballroom exit. Gemma exhaled a long breath and turned toward Crispin. He stood staring after them, his lips pressed so hard together that they were white. His shoulders were shaking.

"Crispin," she whispered.

He jerked his head in an indication of the negative. "Don't, Gemma. Please."

He said nothing more, but went in the same direction the ladies had just departed. She watched him for a moment before her body seemed to make a decision all on its own and she followed.

He trailed through the ballroom, ignoring those around him, and out into the foyer. But he did not follow the departing ladies, as she had feared he might. Instead, he stumbled down the hallway and threw himself into a parlor, slamming the door behind him.

She stopped at the barrier, thrown up to keep her out likely more than anyone else. But she could not allow it. She would not. She reached out and opened the door, stepping into a dimly lit room and shutting it behind her.

He stood at a table beside the fire, his hands shaking as he uncorked a bottle. He didn't wait to pour himself a drink, but tilted the bottle back to drink directly from it.

She let out a cry and rushed toward him. "Stop, Crispin! Stop!"

He lowered the bottle, swallowing before he set it down. "Go away, Gemma."

She flinched, for there was no doubt he meant that order.

And a part of her wanted to follow it. To depart the room and leave him to his drink and his loss and his feelings. Delving into them only opened her to what she knew was going to be a great deal of pain.

But as she stood there, staring at this man who was so utterly lost, she realized how deeply she cared for him. And if their future was together, she had no choice but to help him overcome his past. Or at least make herself aware of what she faced if this woman was still a part of his heart.

"Who is she?" she asked.

"Leave it alone," he said, turning away from her.

She squeezed her eyes shut and tried to measure her erratic breathing. "Crispin," she said, gentling her tone. "You said everyone has their secrets and that is true. But this secret seems to have consequences for me and I feel I have a right to know at least some facts."

He turned on her. "How does any of this have consequences for you?"

She arched a brow. "Those two women...*her* sisters...just attacked you at a party meant to celebrate our supposedly loving marriage. If they are willing to do that within earshot of dozens of people, I'm certain they are saying worse elsewhere. Who is she? Who is this woman who meant so much to you that you spiraled into despair?"

"Who said *she* made me spiral into despair?" he asked, his tone suddenly sharp and his gaze focused.

"Annabelle heard you talk about her when she was watching you at Marcus's club a few months ago. Serafina told me yesterday afternoon at my final fitting."

He scrubbed a hand over his face and a stream of curses left his lips that made Gemma blush to the tips of her ears. When he finally uncovered his face, he looked her in the eye. "That explains why you have been so odd over the last day. What did she say?"

"Not much," she said, honest because she required the same of him. "No one knows much, if that is what worries you.

Just that there might have been a woman who caused part of your...your breakdown over the past year. That coupled with Rafe's situation took you over the edge."

He let out his breath in something that resembled a chuckle, but there was nothing of light or humor on his handsome face. Just pain. So much pain.

"That is an apt description," he murmured.

"And yes, hearing about this woman troubled me," she continued. Her heart began to pound. "I-I was surprised to know that someone had so recently held your heart, and I fear—"

She broke off, the confession too close, too raw for her to say easily.

"What do you fear?" he asked in that same flat, awful tone that had come into his voice the moment he entered this room.

She swallowed hard. "I fear that she still holds it, Crispin. And I know we agreed that love would not come into our union, but the idea of a lady who holds something so close and dear to you roaming in our circles can't help but make me anxious. Will she come to me at some point, as her sisters came to you, accusing me of stealing you? Will I bump into her at charity events and be forced to make polite conversations about the weather when we both know I have your bed and your name and she has your heart and your soul?"

"Please stop," Crispin whispered.

It was the tone of his voice that made her obey. He sounded so broken, so lost, so filled with pain. She shut her mouth and waited, waited for him to be ready to respond to her questions and fears.

He leaned both hands on the back of the closest chair and took a few long breaths, as if he had to settle himself before he could speak. Think.

"You do not have to worry about seeing Alice," he finally said, his voice low. "Alice is dead."

CHAPTER TWENTY-TWO

Crispin was so on edge that Gemma's gasp sounded like a gunshot. He wished it was, aimed straight at his heart so that he wouldn't have to tell her this story. Wouldn't have to say all the words that buzzed in his mind. But she was right.

She deserved to know the truth. No matter how much he hated it. No matter how it would make her see him for the bastard he was when he was finished. No matter how it tore him…and them…apart.

"I met Alice Brookfield at a country gathering eighteen months ago," he began. "She was very pretty and she made me laugh."

Gemma's flinch was so slight that someone else might not have seen it, but he was so focused on her that he did. It was all about to get so much worse, he shuddered to think what she would do in a moment.

"I wasn't looking for someone to take my heart," he continued, turning his face so he wouldn't see Gemma's every inhalation, every blush. "But Alice pursued me in a way no lady ever had. There was this innocence to her, this sweetness that had never felt real with other women. After a few weeks, I was smitten, and it was then she revealed to me that she was supposed to marry in a fortnight."

"She hadn't known that before?" Gemma asked softly. "A

forced union like ours?"

"No," he admitted. "She had known about the marriage for months. He was a marquis. Woodley. With all the advantages of the title and the money to go along with it. Even more money than I had at the time."

She tilted her head. "Woodley. Why do I know that name?"

"Just wait," he managed to rasp past his suddenly dry lips. Damn, but he wanted that fucking bottle he had started. He wanted that one and another and another until the past went away. It was the only way he knew how to make that oblivion come.

But Gemma wouldn't let him. He wasn't certain whether to love or hate her for it.

"Alice told me that while she had once been pleased to marry, she now loved me and she couldn't go through with it. I told her I would speak to her father, I would try to make him see reason. But something always kept me from him. I went to Alice's room the night before the wedding. I asked her to run away with me. We would go to Gretna Green, we would marry. But she refused."

Both Gemma's eyebrows lifted. "Why? If she loved you, why would she refuse such an offer?"

"She said she owed it to Woodley to keep her promise. She had far more integrity than I. She said that we could be lovers. That we could meet in secret after her marriage."

"So you did."

"No," he said. "No, I didn't want that. I told her if she loved me as I loved her, she couldn't accept that either. I asked her again to run away and she refused. So I left. And she married him. She wrote to me several times, but I didn't answer her letters."

Gemma moved a step closer. "You said she died. What happened?" His breath shook as he exhaled, and to his surprise, Gemma reached out and took his hand. She lifted it to her chest, holding tight. "I'm here."

"She threw herself down the stairs," he said, his voice strangled. "At their London home. She left a note that mentioned me, though I never was allowed to see it. It was my fault."

He expected her to pull back, to recoil from the fact that he had all but murdered someone he had loved and who loved him. But instead, her expression softened. Her fingers lifted and splayed across his cheek, and she whispered, "It is not your fault."

"Yes, it is." He tried to pull away, but she held fast.

"Have you ever spoken about this to anyone before?" she asked.

"No," he choked out. "No one. About the time she married, my brother was elevated to duke and everything started happening with Serafina. After she died, I wrapped in around myself."

She filled in the space his story left. "You drank to punish yourself. To forget."

He nodded. "And I told no one. I suppose I was a coward not to want more censure than I heaped on myself, than her family and husband heaped on me."

"And they didn't tell anyone either," she said.

"To protect her reputation, of course not."

Her lips pursed and she hesitated a moment before she spoke. "Would you like an outsider opinion about this?"

"I would scarcely call you an outsider," he whispered.

"The opinion of someone who wasn't there, then," she offered.

He shrugged. "If you have one."

"Of course she must have wanted you, I don't know how any woman could look at you and not want you. But she knew she was meant to marry when she met you, but she withheld that information. When you offered to sweep her away and marry her, she refused. Crispin, it sounds to me as if she was playing a game that perhaps went far out of hand."

His lips parted in shock at that assessment. "You don't

know her."

He pulled away, and she let him go. "Of course I don't. And I'm certain there were nuances there that I cannot see. But you must at least acknowledge that she was duplicitous in some way."

He turned his back on her. She was saying words that made Alice seem like a villain in some way. And they were words he had occasionally thought himself, but never allowed to stay in his mind. Words he had punished himself for.

"Gemma, you don't know what you're talking about," he whispered. "Alice was…it was complicated. But I cared for her. And she loved me. She deserved better than her end."

"An end that was her choice," Gemma insisted. "One that was not your fault, not her husband's fault. I am sad that she had troubles that led to her choices, but they *were* her choices."

"They were her choices that I didn't stop. If I had done as she asked, become her lover, perhaps it wouldn't have become too much for her. Perhaps she would have survived."

"And the two of you would have been tangled in a prison together forever," Gemma said. "It was unfair to ask it of someone she claimed to love."

He wanted to deny that, but her words were certainly reasonable.

She edged even closer. "Crispin, whatever you believe about the past and her motives, Alice's death is not your fault. You cannot punish yourself forever because of it. Not by drinking. Not by locking yourself away from the people in your life who love you. Not by…" She took a deep breath. "Not by pushing me away."

He froze. Her face was unturned, filled with hope, hope for him, hope for them. She was so utterly beautiful and yet when he felt this draw toward her that went beyond physical desire it sparked such guilt in him.

"Gemma," he said, his voice breaking. "I *must* push you away. When I look at you and see you as the most beautiful woman I have ever known, I betray her. When I ache not just for your touch but for your very presence, I betray her. When I think of you and forget her, I betray her. And I cannot do that. I'm sorry."

Pain flared on her face as if the words were written there. Pain he caused and hated himself even more for. Pain he couldn't face.

So he turned and left the room without another word or explanation. Because he knew that if he ran, if he hid, if he drank, the pain might be avoidable for just a little while longer.

Although she had done nothing more that evening than dance and smile and pretend everything was all right, as Gemma exited the carriage with Mary at her heels, her entire body hurt as if she had been in a physical altercation.

"Poor Crispin and his headache," Mary said as they entered the house. "I hope he is well."

Gemma flinched. That was the excuse she had given as to why Crispin had disappeared from the party. The excuse her sweet sister believed, but Crispin's family did not. All of them had taken their turns trying to find out the truth, but she had repeated her lie over and over.

What was she to say? That Crispin loved a dead woman who had possibly been using him and he had all but told her he would never care for her out of respect? That he had left her standing in the parlor like a fool? That truth was too awful and humiliating.

Fletcher came to them in the foyer, smiling as he took their wraps. "I hope the evening was a success," he said, looking first to Gemma and then to Mary.

"Very much so," Mary all but bubbled. "Though we did worry over Mr. Flynn. Is he abed? Has his headache subsided at all?"

Fletcher blinked and Gemma's heart sank. "Mr. Flynn

isn't..." He stopped, met Gemma's eyes for a moment, then he nodded. "Miss Quinn, I believe he is a little better. I wouldn't disturb him, though."

Mary smiled and then turned to squeeze Gemma's hand. "Thank you again, for everything you did tonight. It was the first time since my original coming out that I could breathe. But I'm exhausted and I think I will turn in."

Gemma nodded. "Of course, love. Good night."

Her sister pressed a quick kiss to her cheek then flitted up the stairs as if the music from the ball still played in her head. When she was out of earshot, Gemma turned to the servant.

"He did not come home?" she asked.

The butler's gaze fluttered away. "No, ma'am. I thought perhaps it was better not to say that to Miss Quinn."

"A good instinct," Gemma said with a sigh. "I did not truly think he would be here." Fletcher shifted in discomfort and Gemma shook her head. "I'm sorry. I'm thinking out loud. I will retire, as well, Fletcher. Thank you."

The butler let her take a step before he called out, "Mrs. Flynn?"

She faced him. "Yes?"

His kind expression softened further. "Is there—is there anything I can do?"

She shook her head. "No. I'm afraid there is nothing to be done. Except wait. Thank you, truly, for your kindnesses. They have not been overlooked since my arrival."

"The household is very pleased to have you," he reassured her. "And...and I have known Mr. Flynn a good many years, and I can tell you that he has not been so happy in all that time as he has been these few weeks with you."

Gemma clenched her fist at her side. Did those words make her feel better or worse? She wasn't certain in this moment.

"Thank you. Good night."

She moved up the stairs at what felt like a snail's pace. When she entered the chamber she shared with Crispin, though, all the emotion she had been fighting to keep in check burst free.

The room looked of him, with his book on his end table, the towel he had used to dry his face draped on the basin. It smelled of him. That rich, spicy maleness that made her thighs clench and her heart beat faster.

She loved him.

The words flitted through her, but they were not a surprise even though she had never allowed herself to form her burgeoning feelings into words. It had happened little by little since that first morning he woke and told her he did not recall making her his wife. Every moment since then had been a surrender, a slow fall into something he had already told her he would not ever share.

Tonight he had *shown* her how serious he was.

She was a fool to love him and she knew it. But her heart didn't allow her to deny it. It didn't allow her to pretend. So what could she do now?

She sighed as she sank down on the edge of their bed, remaining fully clothed as she turned on her side and grasped Crispin's pillow. She hugged it against her chest, breathing in his scent.

He cared for her, that much she knew. His parting words had told her, and couldn't that give her hope?

"When I think of you and forget her…" she mused out loud, saying those words he had said, letting them roll on her tongue.

Was it possible she could make him forget *her*, Alice, more and more? That she could slowly heal his wounds not by demanding he forget them, but by simply spreading the balm of her feelings across them?

"You would have to risk yourself," she said as she rolled onto her back and stared at the ornate ceiling. "You would give without ever being certain that he would return your affection. He might not ever let himself."

Those words stung as she said them. But they also gave

her strength. They gave her a plan. They gave her a tiny thread of hope.

She rose to her feet and pulled the bell for Kate. When her maid arrived, she said, "Was the other item I ordered from Madame Clout delivered today?"

Kate nodded and slipped into the dressing room only to return with a large white box, tied with a scarlet ribbon. The seamstress's insignia was embossed on the top. "Shall I open it?"

Gemma blushed, but steeled herself. She had to remember she was in a war. With a dead woman, of all people, someone it would be hard to compete with. So she could not be missish now.

"Yes," she said. "Open it."

Kate untied the ribbon and opened the box lid. She pushed aside the filmy tissue paper within and revealed a frothy pile of black lace and red ribbon. Her maid blushed as she lifted the item.

It was small, it was nearly see-through and it was scandalous.

"It's perfect," Gemma breathed. "Help me undress and then draw me a bath. Afterward, I'll be putting it on. I will also want extra candles and scent the pillows. Be sure the fire is high and that we have extra kindling so I can keep it so."

Kate's eyes went wide at the swift directions Gemma threw out, one after the other.

"Of course." Her maid smiled. "You seem to have plans for quite a night."

But as Kate went to ring for the bathwater, Gemma shook her head. "No," she whispered, only to herself. "Not a night. A battle. The first of many to come. The first of many I intend to win."

CHAPTER TWENTY-THREE

Crispin stepped into the foyer and winced as he saw old Fletcher waiting there for him despite the ridiculously late hour.

"Good evening, Mr. Flynn," he said as he took Crispin's coat.

"Good morning is more like it," Crispin said, glancing at the clock. Nearly three.

"Will you require your usual remedy?" Fletcher asked.

Crispin shook his head. "I am not drunk."

The answer was as shocking to him as it seemed to be to his servant. After his horrible moment of confession to Gemma, he had left his brother's party with every intention of finding the worst hell he could and drowning himself in cheap liquor. And he had tried.

But every time he went to lift a glass to his lips, he saw Gemma's face. He saw the disappointment and pain in her fathomless gray eyes. And he couldn't do it.

How he wished he could be angry with her and how she had disrupted his routine of wallowing and self-loathing. Her sunshine, her sweetness, her *everything* was changing him. When he had spent such a long time trying to punish himself rather than change.

"Go to sleep, Fletcher," he said, waving the butler off.

"God knows you're too old for these hours."

The butler made a sound that was somewhat like a laugh and shuffled down the hall. At the bottom of the stairs, Crispin let out a long sigh. After his performance tonight, he didn't expect to find Gemma in his bed. She had likely locked herself in the attached quarters, locked *him* out.

He would deserve no less.

He trudged up the stairs one by one and stopped at his door. With another deep breath, he opened it and came to a sudden stop.

A cold, dark chamber was what he had expected. Instead, he found candles on every surface, the fire burning high, and standing beside his bed was Gemma.

Gemma in the most scandalous and sensual scrap of nothingness that he'd ever seen a lady wear. It was black and made her skin look like fine bone or ivory in the firelight. And it was lace, so her skin peeked out from beneath the fabric, including the pale pink hint of her hard nipples that he wanted to suck until she screamed his name.

Instead, he closed the door behind him and leaned against it. "What are you doing?"

She blushed. "Waiting for you. Is that not obvious?"

"There's a great deal obvious when you wear that…that…"

"I bought it with my pin money when I ordered the ball gown. Do you like it?"

He could still hardly breathe. "It is beautiful. You are beautiful." He stepped closer, unable to resist her siren song. "But what are you doing, Gemma?"

Her eyes fluttered shut, and for a moment he thought she might cry. Instead, when she looked at him, she met his gaze evenly, confidently.

"I'm waiting up to make love to my husband," she said softly.

"Even after tonight?" he asked. "Even after what I told you, even after I ran and left you in what I assume was an awkward situation?"

She shrugged one shoulder, and her breasts strained against the lace. God, he could tear it open with his teeth and get to her.

"You don't have to love me, Crispin," she whispered, and now it was she who moved closer.

She reached for his hand, lifted it to press his palm against her cheek. She leaned into him, impossibly soft, impossibly beautiful. Improbably his.

"Gemma," he murmured, almost lost even though there was a voice in him telling him how unfair this was.

She shook her head. "Just don't shut me out." Now she glided his hand lower, until he touched her breast and she shivered. "*That* would break my heart."

He might have retorted or resisted, even though his cock swelled with need. She didn't allow it. She lifted up on her tiptoes and cupped his neck, drawing him down for her kiss that was headier and more drugging than any spirit. And in that moment, he did exactly what he had been trying to do all night.

He forgot.

He forgot Alice. He forgot Gemma's accusations that Alice wasn't true. He forgot that he refused to let Gemma close. He forgot that he was a failure and a disappointment to everyone, including himself.

All that there was, all there ever would or could be, was Gemma. And her arms coming around him, and her body molding to him and the way she gently sucked his tongue and sent heated desire to his willing and ready cock.

She broke the kiss before he was fully swept away and stepped back. "Undress," she whispered.

He did as she said, as swiftly as his shaking hands would allow, and smiled as her gaze dragged over him, her eyes still wide with wonder at his form.

"Thank you, Father," she muttered as she pressed a hand to his chest and pushed him toward their bed, "for tricking such a well-formed man into becoming my husband."

His eyes grew wide at her half-smile. Was she actually teasing him about the circumstances of their union? Playing with him in such a comfortable and erotic way?

He rather liked that, actually. This light that was suddenly in her eyes was something very special. And he never wanted to lose it. Never wanted to see it go out, even though he feared it would.

He fell back across the bed and shifted to half-sit by leaning on the pillows that had been fluffed against the headboard. She smiled down at him.

"Are you comfortable?" she asked.

He nodded. "Yes."

"Are you ready?"

Her voice was so seductive he could have spent just by listening to her. Instead, he swallowed. "Oh, more than ready, Gemma."

She crawled up beside him, sitting up on her knees as she took another long, heavy look at him. She licked her lips and his cock twitched in memory of when she had taken him in the carriage, drank him down, claimed him.

Her hand snaked out, tracing his thigh with her fingertips. Gliding higher to swirl over his hip. She met his gaze as she fisted him, stroking him once, then twice.

"Very ready," she murmured. "I approve."

"When did you become such a wanton?" he groaned as she stroked him again. He reached out to trace her cheek with his fingers and she looked up.

"When you told me it was safe to do so with you," she whispered. "When you made my desires something not to fear, but to celebrate." She leaned up, her mouth close to his. "Thank you, Crispin Flynn."

Her lips descended and she claimed his mouth once more, her tongue dueling with his, her lips tasting like honey. He shut his eyes and surrendered to the sensation, giving over, at least for a while, his thoughts and troubles. They would be there in the morning.

As if she sensed his surrender, her ardor ratcheted higher and her hands slid up to steady herself on his shoulders. She moved. He didn't open his eyes or break their kiss, but he felt her move to straddle him. The lace of her gown tangled around them, soft, but not as soft as her thighs as she positioned herself.

He felt her humid heat teasing him, but she didn't slide down just yet. Instead she arched higher, continuing to kiss him as she moved her hands to massage his chest.

"Mmmm." The sound came deep from her throat. Her lips barely moved far enough from his so she could whisper, "I meant to seduce you far better than this."

"I'm hard as steel, Gemma. I don't think you could do more," he chuckled, still keeping his eyes closed. "I'm yours do with as you please."

She tensed, and now he did look at her. Her expression was suddenly very tight and her lips thin and pale. She gave him a smile.

"I may take you up on that," she said, her voice shaking a little before she maneuvered herself a bit.

His mind emptied as her slit stroked over him and then he was inside of her, filling her in slow inches until he was fully seated inside her hungry body. She draped her arms around his shoulders again and held perfectly still with a sigh of pleasure.

He tucked a lock of red hair behind her ear and smoothed the back of his hand down her cheek. "Are you all right?"

She nodded and met his eyes, and what he saw there shocked him. Such softness in her expression, such deep connection that he felt from her, from himself. It was almost as if she...cared for him. More than cared for him. Felt for him something he had vowed never to feel again.

But she couldn't love him. That was a crazy notion.

One she swept away when she began to rock over him. Her hips rolled, her breath became gasps and he could do nothing but grunt in pleasure as her body gripped him, slid over him, building his release with every thrust.

Her breasts bounced, practically in his face, and he chuckled as he reached up to tug the lace down and reveal one perfect globe. He leaned in and sucked her nipple into his mouth.

With a cry of pleasure, her thrusts increased. Her body tightened over him, bringing him an answering pleasure that was greater than any he'd ever known with any woman. He watched her face as he swirled his tongue over her, watched the pure bliss their joining created. Felt it echoed in his own aching body. He suckled her harder, harder and with a scream she came. Her hips jerked over him, her moans and sighs louder and more musical than ever.

"You make that seem easy," she panted as she went limp over him.

He removed his mouth from her breast and laughed. "Then let me do it again."

She watched as his hand slid across her chest to tug away the lace a second time. "Crispin," she whispered, a needy plea for his pleasure.

He was more than willing to grant it. He brushed a thumb over her opposite nipple, teasing the hard tip as her breath became shorter once more. "Tonight, with you in that ball gown, there were times I pictured doing just this. Pulling the bodice down and suckling you."

Her hips began to flex, this time the movements slower as she rode over him in smooth, steady waves. "Right in front of everyone?" she asked.

He heard the shock, but also the excitement in her voice. Interesting. He truly might have to take her Marcus's club one night. Let her see. Be seen. Be had in one of the club's naughtiest rooms.

He thrust up hard with the thought, and she cried out. Good, she was close.

"With everyone watching," he murmured, then ducked his head to trace just the tip of his tongue over her nipple.

She sighed, tilting her head back and arching her back to

give him more access to her. He took it greedily, sucking her hard, swirling his tongue around her, loving how her thrusts became erratic, her cries louder and stronger. Finally, she began to buck again, coming, and he could no longer hold back. With his own guttural cry, his seed burst free, merging with her juices, granting them both release as she collapsed over him.

He lowered her to his side, separating their bodies with a moan they mutually shared. Then he tucked her against him and held her, smoothing her hair as their breath slowed and finally matched in cadence.

He looked down at her. Her eyes were droopy, sleep was eminent, but she smiled up at him regardless. That open smile he had come to like so much, come to look for to sooth his mind.

But after the ball, after the confrontation, he knew how unfair this all was. He might have brought Gemma pleasure tonight, but only after he had hurt her deeply.

Only after he hurt himself, too.

And that couldn't go on, even if he wanted to live in this fantasy world where only they existed.

CHAPTER TWENTY-FOUR

Alone.

That was how Gemma had woken up. That was how she had taken a mostly uneaten breakfast. And that was what she was as she rode in her carriage across what felt like a very long few miles to her destination.

Oh, her maid was in the vehicle with her, of course, but even Kate's company couldn't make her shake the feeling that she was all alone in the world in some way. That she had lost something.

Crispin had said nothing, not even waken her, when he rose and left her in their bed. He hadn't left her a message with the servants to tell her his whereabouts. He had merely disappeared. She'd almost expected to find money on the bed stand, like she was a lightskirt. Hadn't he once thought that was what she was, the first morning he found her in that same bed?

And here she thought so much had changed.

"Are you well, Mrs. Flynn?" Kate asked, her tone wary and low.

Gemma jerked her gaze to her maid. "Of course, why?"

"You just have a look about you and you've been very quiet all morning."

Gemma shrugged, hoping she seemed more blasé about

what she was doing than she felt. "I have a lot on my mind."

"Do you mind if I ask, ma'am, where we're going? This isn't the way to your father's or to any of the homes of Mr. Flynn's relations. Nor to the seamstress or the milliner or anyplace else I can think of. And you refused to allow Miss Mary to join us when she asked."

Gemma lifted her chin. "We are making a call to a stranger, Kate," she said. "No one either of us has called on before."

Her maid looked confused. "Ah, I see," she said slowly. "And…and what kind of business do you have with her?"

"Him," Gemma corrected softly. "And it is very personal business, indeed."

She'd spent hours contemplating what she was about to do, how badly it could go wrong. She and Crispin were just overcoming a scandal and this moment she was in, this decision she could still undo, could destroy that.

And yet she was still here. Because Crispin's peace meant more to her than her own reputation. Than her sister's.

That was how much she had come to love him. She could only hope it wouldn't come to the worst.

The carriage stopped, and after a moment, a finely liveried footman opened the door and helped her out. With Kate trailing behind her, she made her way up the stairs and knocked on the great wooden door.

A butler met her, taking her card. She thought his eyes widened a bit before he said, "How can I help you, Mrs. Flynn?"

"I am here to see Lord Woodley," she said, wishing her voice didn't tremble. "I realize I do not have an appointment and this is very irregular, but it about a matter of great import."

The butler ushered her in and showed them to a parlor that was finer than anything she'd ever seen. Every stick of furniture, every drop of paint, every portrait and landscape had been chosen with the clear desire to show off the importance and wealth of the inhabitants of this hall. Her heart began to beat faster at the thought of what kind of man she was about to meet.

"I will ascertain if the marquis is in residence," the butler said, beginning to close the door behind himself.

She rushed forward. "Tell him I am here to discuss his late wife. And my husband."

Now the butler blanched. Gemma's cheeks flamed, but she somehow managed to keep her gaze even on the servant as he backed away. When he had shut the door, Kate stepped forward.

"Miss Gemma!" Kate gasped, so shocked, apparently, that she reverted back to her very first address. "What are you doing?"

Gemma straightened her spine and turned on her maid. "I appreciate your attempt to help, to protect me, but I know exactly what I am doing. You will say nothing more. And when the marquis comes...*if* he comes, you will step into the hallway."

"I cannot—"

"Kate!" she burst out, raising her hands to her hot cheeks. "Please."

The maid observed her, then she nodded. "Very well. I will do so, against my better judgment." They stood in silence for a few moments before Kate added, "You must love Mr. Flynn very much."

Saying it to herself was one thing, but Gemma nearly buckled at hearing it stated out loud. She forced herself to remain calm and merely said, "Enough to do this."

The door to the parlor opened and this time it was not the butler who greeted them. It was a tall, wiry, very handsome and very young man, dressed in the very best but not in any way resembling a fop.

"Mrs. Flynn," he said as he entered the room. His cheeks were pale. "I am Lord Woodley. I've heard you have come to discuss something with me."

Gemma took a step back. *This* was the marquis? She had

pictured him older, perhaps even decrepit, rather like her own late husband. She'd thought of the kind of man who would inspire a woman to want a younger lover like Crispin. But this man was...well, he was no Crispin Flynn, but he certainly would turn heads at any ball.

"Kate," she said, and her maid stepped from the room with a deep frown, leaving them alone. The marquis watched her go with wide eyes, but said nothing. She cleared her throat. "My lord, I realize this is an abnormal visit."

He arched a brow. "I would say so, considering the message my butler conveyed to me." He looked her up and down. "I heard *he* had married. You look nothing like Alice. I thought you might, but I'm glad you do not."

Gemma caught her breath. That was something she had never considered, that perhaps she looked like a dead woman Crispin had loved. But then, he hadn't chosen her. If he had, maybe he would have looked for an Alice replacement.

"I am here, my lord, because I have only just learned about the existence of your late wife. And the important role she played in my husband's life in the past year and a half."

"It seems like longer," the marquis mused, almost more to himself than to her. "Come, why don't we sit? I do not think I can take this conversation while standing."

She drew back. There was a great deal of kindness in this man's eyes, even when she spoke of Crispin. And he had not yet put her out when he had every right to do so. Instead, he motioned to the settee and then moved to the sideboard.

"I could have tea made, or if you'd like to join me in something stronger, you can take your pick." He poured himself what looked like sherry and lifted the bottle in her direction.

She found herself nodding as she sat down. "I think I could use one, despite the early hour."

He smiled as he poured a second drink and brought it to her. He settled on the chair that faced her and took a sip. "So you have been told about Alice and Flynn," he said. "It was long before he met you, if gossip is accurate about the whirlwind nature of your courtship."

She drew back. Was he trying to comfort her? That was an odd thing, considering what Crispin had done behind his back with his wife.

"I wasn't worried about that, actually," she said. "Let me explain. Crispin was verbally attacked last night by your late wife's sisters."

Woodley pulled a face. "Ah yes, Isadora and Imogen. The twin visions of beauty and vitriol. If they attacked him, please tell him he is not alone in their blame. They show up here regularly to harangue me about causing Alice's suicide."

"They do?" Gemma breathed. "I am sorry, my lord. That must only add insult to significant injury."

"What did Flynn tell you?" he asked, setting his drink down and steepling his fingers.

She shifted. Crispin hadn't wanted to tell her this story, she was certain he would be angry that she had gone behind his back to tell another person, especially his lover's husband. But she needed something from Woodley and this was likely the only way to get it.

"He told me that they met at a country gathering and Alice flirted with him. That by the time he found out she was to marry you, he was already smitten." She hesitated, but Woodley waved her on and his face revealed no pain in the telling, so she pressed forward. "He said she told him she did not want to wed, but when he offered to take her away, she refused and went forward with the marriage. She asked him to be her lover in secret and when he said he could not. Ultimately, she—she killed herself."

"He offered to run away with her on the eve of our wedding," Woodley said, his voice very soft but not pained or angry. "If only…"

She shook her head at his words. "My lord, I don't mean to hurt you with this story."

He laughed. "Hurt me? Oh no, my dear, you couldn't hurt

me with this. It is everything I already knew or had guessed. What do *you* think of it? You must have an opinion since you came here to my door so brazenly."

Gemma caught her breath in surprise. She had been taught not to speak ill of the dead, especially the dead's bereaved loved ones. But what choice did she have?

"When Crispin told me the truth after the twins' attack on him, I was taken aback. It seemed to me that your late wife—"

"Alice," he corrected, his voice barely carrying. "Please don't call her my wife."

Gemma blinked. "A-Alice…it seemed to me that she was playing a bit of a game with Crispin. She lied by omission about her engagement and even when she was offered what she claimed to desire, she refused him. It seemed…"

"Unfair," he said.

She nodded. "I recognize that you likely don't see it that way. After all, she was your fiancée and later your bride, and I'm certain you don't want to think—"

"That she led Flynn on?" He laughed again. "Oh, but I do. Let me tell you the story from my point of view. Alice was a beauty, a diamond of the first water, and she set her sights on me the moment she stepped out in her first Season. I tripped over myself falling in love with her. But after I asked her to marry me, I began to realize she was not what she seemed. She could be cruel when it suited her. She took pleasure in hurting those with less power. She was spoiled beyond measure. And her desires and expectations for me grew exponentially."

He got up, his face darkening with what she realized was not upset or grief, but anger. She swallowed. "How so?"

"The diamonds weren't big enough, the proposal wasn't romantic enough, the gestures weren't grand enough…" He turned away. "It went on and on, I shall not bore you. She left for that country party angry at me for some petty grievance, and she shouted at me, 'If you do not give me what I want, someone else will.' I admit I almost hoped she would find a new suitor."

"She left threatening to overthrow you, despite your engagement?"

"With the wedding of the year planned in just two months' time," he said with a nod as he faced her again. "And when she came back, her wicked little smile told me she had found some prey. She wasn't very secretive about it, not to me. And when confronted, she bragged that she could have the most notorious man in Society wrapped around her finger."

Gemma clenched her fists at that statement. Alice had been using Crispin, far worse than she had ever imagined.

"There was no way out of the marriage," he said, his tone very flat now. "She made it clear she had not bedded Flynn, and I had no recourse to break the agreements that had been made. So I married her. And she toyed with him, toyed with me for months. She became pregnant."

Gemma gasped, and the marquis held up a hand. "With my child. She was going to do nothing that would give me cause to end the union, I assure you. Poor Flynn who could have anyone likely never got what he wanted from her."

Gemma blinked, trying to picture any woman withholding her physical affections from Crispin, especially if she cared for him. But she was beginning to see that Alice hadn't.

"I hoped the child might settle her," Woodley continued. "That she would be satisfied, but she wailed about her figure. She wept about how much she hated me. Finally, one night we had a row and I told her how much I despised her. That all I wanted was my heir. It was a dreadful mistake."

Gemma's lips parted. "She killed herself."

He nodded. "In truth, I don't think she meant to do it. She wrote the note, of course, she threw herself from the staircase in the most dramatic fashion. But based on her diary, it is clear she hoped to injure herself, lose the baby and put me in my place where I deserved to be. Only she miscalculated how hard and steep those stairs are. She broke her neck and died before she even stopped falling. *That* is the true story."

Gemma covered her mouth, her stomach turning with the

tale. "I am so very sorry, my lord."

His face softened with surprise. "Thank you. I know Flynn has wrecked himself since her death. I suppose I tried to tell myself there was more to it. But if he has blamed himself, he should know that Alice's actions were almost entirely to hurt me. She did mention him in her note, but I saw it for the ploy it was."

Gemma drew her breath, trying to calm herself, trying to keep from casting up her accounts on the fine Persian rug that graced his beautiful hall.

"You may have seen it as it was truly meant, but Crispin does not, I fear." She squeezed her eyes shut to control the tears of anger and heartbreak that threatened to flood them. "My lord, he has punished himself for his part in Alice's death. He continues to do so. I have come here in the hopes that you could offer me some proof to give him that he was not the cause of any of it."

The marquis shook his head. "Such as? Do you wish me to speak to him? Because I admit that would be difficult."

"No, I doubt he is any more ready for such a confrontation than you are. But I wonder...I wonder if you still have the note your wife wrote before her suicide."

His eyes went wide. "Yes, I do."

"Could I—could I take it to Crispin?" When he drew back, she hastened to add, "I know it is asking a great deal, too much, but it seems to me that your late wife was very content to destroy as many lives as she could. I don't want Crispin to be her permanent victim. Because, you see, I am in love with him, my lord."

His lips pinched. "I can see that. And I know the feeling of wanting to do anything for the one you love. It ended badly for me, but...but perhaps your fate will be different." He let out a long sigh. "I do have the note. Give me a moment and I will retrieve it."

She was glad to be sitting, for she felt she would have collapsed if she hadn't been. "Thank you, thank you so much,

Lord Woodley."

He smiled, a tight and pained expression, and quietly left the room. When he was gone, she jumped up and began to pace the chamber. Her plan had only gone so far as to come here and hopefully retrieve the note so Crispin would see the truth and not just the horrible things he had built up in his head. Monsters created by guilt and heartbreak.

She hadn't actually believed the marquis would indulge her, so now she had to come up with a second part to her plan. Crispin had left her this morning without a word and she had no idea where he had gone or when or if he would return.

"Where could he be?" she muttered as she stalked back and forth across the floor. Then she recalled another night when he had also disappeared. He had been at Annabelle and Marcus's home that day. Was it possible that was where he was now?

She would have to find out.

"Mrs. Flynn?"

She turned to find the marquis was back. He had a much folded and unfolded letter in one hand. In the other, he held a slim, leather-bound book.

"Here is the note." He hesitated before he held the letter out. "Perhaps you would be so kind as to burn it when Mr. Flynn has finished with it."

Her eyes went wide. "You do not want me to return it?"

"You are correct that her poison has had its effect for far too long. Destroy it. Reading it again will bring me no peace." He held out the other item. "This is her diary for the time just before she met Flynn to the night she killed herself. I think there are more answers there than anywhere else. And it will give her note more context."

She stared at the journal. "I could not—"

"Violate her privacy?" Woodley asked, his tone bitter. "For your husband's sake, I hope you will. Take it."

She did as he asked and he wiped his hand on his trouser leg, almost as if he were wiping away the residue of something dirty. His face was such a twisted mess of pain, so similar to Crispin's when he spoke of this dead woman, that she wished she could somehow help him as well.

But *he* was not her problem. Crispin's heart was the one she yearned to heal.

"Thank you," she said softly. "This is a kindness you most definitely didn't have to offer. And I will not forget it."

He nodded. "I never blamed Flynn. He was her pawn, sent out in a war with me. And if this helps you, then I am happy to do it. And perhaps it is best to get rid of these things at last. They have held too much power over me as it is. Destroy the diary when you are finished as well."

"I will if that is your wish. And I have taken enough of your time as it is. Thank you again."

"Goodbye, Mrs. Flynn," he said with a small bow. "I hope you don't mind if I allow you to show yourself out."

She nodded, understanding completely. "Not at all. Goodbye, my lord."

She left the room, motioning to Kate as she reached the foyer. As she took her reticule and placed the letter and the diary inside, her stomach began to churn.

"Where are we going now?" Kate asked, wary as the carriage returned to receive them.

"Annabelle's house," Gemma said, nodding to the driver until he acknowledged her request. "I have a husband to find."

CHAPTER TWENTY-FIVE

Gemma could hardly breathe as she entered Annabelle and Marcus's foyer a half an hour later. Their butler, Green, smiled at her as he took her wrap.

"Have you come to join Mr. Flynn, Mrs. Flynn?"

Her heart jumped. "So he is here?" she asked, unable to keep the relief and the fear from her voice.

Green took a step back, but quickly regained his composure. "Indeed, he is, Mrs. Flynn. He has been working away in Mr. Rivers' study with Mr. Abbot for hours. But Mr. and Mrs. Rivers just joined them, so their business must be concluded."

"Show me," Gemma managed, her voice trembling.

She followed the servant down a long and twisting hall until he stopped at a door and knocked. He opened it and she stood just behind him, out of view, as he announced, "Mrs. Flynn is here."

She moved around him and stepped into the room. Crispin slowly rose from behind Marcus's desk, his gaze locked on her as she walked inside. The others in the room also rose and greeted her, but she was too driven by her need to talk to Crispin to be polite.

"I need to speak to you," she said to him. Annabelle and Marcus exchanged a glance from the corner of her eye, but she refused to acknowledge that humiliating fact. "Now."

Crispin did look at the others. "Would you excuse us for a moment?"

Abbot nodded. "I need to get back to the club anyway."

"Thank you, Abbot," Crispin said, shooting the man a very genuine expression. "Truly."

Annabelle stepped forward as Abbot left the room. "Is everything well?"

Gemma forced herself to look at her sister-in-law. "I just need a moment with my husband. I am sorry, this is your house and your study, but—"

"There is no need to apologize," Marcus said as he stepped forward and took Annabelle's hand. He began to move her toward the door. "We'll be in the parlor when you have finished. Join us for tea."

As they exited, Gemma thought she heard Annabelle say, "The hell we will be. I'm going to list—"

But she was cut off by the shutting of the door.

So they could very well have an audience outside. There was nothing to be done about it. This was the moment Gemma had to face, one way or another.

"You are pale," Crispin said, though he stayed behind the desk, as if it offered him protection from her. "Will you sit?"

"No," she whispered. "You left this morning without a word."

He flinched, as if caught in a lie. "Yes. I had an appointment with Abbot."

"You said nothing, you left no indication. I wasn't even certain you would come home again." Her voice broke and she turned her face so he wouldn't see how hurt she was.

But she obviously didn't hide it well, for he came around the desk in three long strides. "Of course I was coming home. I wouldn't just disappear, Gemma. You must know that by now."

"I don't know. After all, so much has changed in less than twenty-four hours."

He shook his head. "Nothing has changed."

"*Everything* has changed," she argued, her voice elevating a little even as she desperately tried to rein in the emotions that had begun to bubble over the weeks they were married, had boiled at the ball and were now threatening to overflow. "There has been a wall between us from the beginning, but for the first time I know why. Now I know there was an Alice. And that you blame yourself for her death. And that you feel any tenderness between us is proof of a betrayal."

"But we never wanted love, Gemma, either of us. Why does it make a difference?"

"It does," she said, unready to tell him the truth that was in her heart. Not until he could separate himself from the past and hear her without Alice's voice, her lies, in his head. She cleared her throat. "I also went out today."

He shifted at her change of subject. "You did?" he asked with an uncertain tone. "Where did you go?"

"I visited a man," she admitted, her hands beginning to shake.

"A man?" he repeated, his expression growing guarded. "I don't understand. Your father?"

"No." She focused on remaining calm as she said, "I called on Lord Woodley."

His face drained of all color and when he staggered back he hit the desk with his legs and sent the items on it tumbling. He didn't seem to care, didn't even notice the ink that splashed across the wood behind him.

"Lord Woodley," he repeated, his voice raw with pain. "You did not."

"I did. He received me. And then he told me his side of the story of Alice and you and her death."

He moved on her, his expression wild. She expected him to grab her, but he never touched her. He just stood in front of her, face twisted in betrayal and anger. "Why would you do that?"

"Because I think that you are caught up in a fairytale,

Crispin. You were designed to believe yourself her savior and to blame yourself for her death. But I knew that couldn't be true. That there was more. And there was, Crispin. So much more."

"What more?" he barked as he all but shoved past her and walked to the other side of the room. As if he couldn't get far enough away. "You want to believe she was a liar, but you didn't know her."

"But *he* did," she insisted. "More than you, even. Woodley told me that her pursuit of you was as a revenge on him. He knew about it, she bragged about it, Crispin. It was leverage for her to control him. And she threw herself down the stairs for the same reason."

"How could you know that? How could anyone know her heart?"

She dug into her reticule and pulled out the items Woodley had shared with her. "I read several entries of her diary on the way here and I examined her note to Woodley on the night she died." She winced, her stomach turning as she remembered the woman's poisonous, hateful words. "She is not what she seemed, what she made you believe she was."

He stared at the objects in her hands and slowly reached out to take them. He said nothing.

"Crispin," she whispered, meeting his stare, hating the pain and the anger she saw there. "I care for you. I more than care for you. But your beliefs about this woman and the situation you shared with her are what drove you to the edge. And they are what keeps you there now, balancing between an attempt to better yourself and a desire to remain in a pit of despair that is endless and destructive. Read what she wrote. Hear the truth of it as it rings in your head. Please. Please don't throw yourself away, throw whatever life we could share away, for nothing."

He stayed motionless, still empty in every way but his flashing, emotion-filled eyes. Then he turned away and crossed the room. At the door, he stopped.

"I can't believe you would do this behind my back." His tone was filled with betrayal.

She winced. "I did it because—because I love you."

He didn't recoil from the declaration. But he did turn away, open the door and leave.

The moment he was gone, Gemma's legs went out. She collapsed onto her knees, shaking, unable to cry, unable to move. She just stared at where he had been. Where he had left.

Annabelle rushed in, and she stopped at the sight of Gemma's form on the floor. Gemma looked up at her and at the kindness in her sister-in-law's face, her tears began to flow.

Annabelle didn't hesitate, she didn't speak. She just sank down on the floor next to her and held her as she wept.

"What did you hear?" Gemma asked between sobs.

"Enough," Annabelle whispered. "Marcus went after him, but he will not be able to stop him. When Crispin runs, he *runs*."

Gemma's heart hurt. Like someone was inside her chest, squeezing with all their might, trying to steal all her blood and her love and her life.

She looked up at Annabelle. "Did I do the right thing?"

Annabelle cupped her cheeks. "You tried to set him free," she said. "And if he can manage to see that, if he can truly believe it, that is the best chance you have at doing what we've all been trying to do for months."

"What's that?" Gemma asked, beginning to regain the composure that had been destroyed by the confusing hours that had passed since the ball.

Annabelle looked toward the door, looked toward where Crispin had gone. "Save him."

It was dark by the time Crispin turned his horse up the drive to Rafe's home, but he had no idea of hour. He also couldn't have reasonably told someone how he came to be here. All he knew was that he'd looked up and there was his brother's house, bright and filled with light, waiting for him like a beacon.

And here he was, swinging off his horse, hoping he would find Rafe home. Hoping he would be the only one there since he didn't want anyone else to see him as he was.

He'd sat in the park to read Alice's letter. He'd sworn he wouldn't read the diary, wouldn't invade her personal thoughts. But the poison she had spilled in her letter to her husband forced him to do the thing he had promised not to do.

And now he knew the truth. And everything in his life had been blown apart like he was a battlefield causality.

The door opened before he could knock and he was shocked to find it was Rafe himself who greeted him.

"What are you doing?" Crispin asked.

Rafe's smile was very small. "I've been waiting for you." He stepped aside and motioned for the foyer. "Come in."

Crispin staggered through the door and Rafe caught his arm, supporting him even as he shut the door. "Are you drunk?"

"No," Crispin said, his voice cracking.

Rafe steadied him, then released him to lead him to the study where he grabbed a bottle of whisky and handed it over silently before the brother's took the chairs beside the roaring fire.

"I thought you believe I drink too much," Crispin said, eyeing the bottle with both desire and disdain.

"You do. But I think you've earned it."

Crispin swallowed hard, struggling with the urge to drink coupled with the urge to be set free from his past. Slowly, he set the bottle down. His brother knew something. Which meant Gemma must have been here. Was she still?

"Where is Serafina?" he asked. "The baby?"

Rafe took a long breath. "They went to your home with Annabelle and Mama. To comfort Gemma." Rafe arched a brow, as if daring him to respond.

Crispin draped his arms over his legs and put his head in his hands. Thoughts of Gemma had been confusing to him since he left her that afternoon. Since she told him she loved him.

Hadn't she? Or was that a falsehood his mind told him? Kind of like the ones he had believed about Alice.

"Is Gemma well?" he finally asked, looking up from his hands at his brother.

Rafe leaned back in his chair. "She is upset. Very upset. She wanted to go look for you, but we managed to convince her to stay where she was. And I came back here because I hoped that you would come to me, as you once did, to discuss your pains."

Crispin nodded. "I found myself here. I don't know how. But it sounds as if you already know my pains."

"I know a little," Rafe said. "But why don't you tell me the whole story?"

Crispin's breath eased out of him in a shuddering burst and he struggled to find words.

"Just start at the beginning," Rafe said, his tone kind.

Crispin struggled, but somehow he found the words. He spoke for nearly forty-five minutes, spilling his heart about every secret he'd kept from Rafe. About meeting Alice, believing he loved her and she him, her marriage, her death and the violent, destructive thoughts that had plagued him in the months since. When he finally stopped speaking, his brother leaned forward and took the bottle Crispin had left untouched. Rafe uncorked the bottle before he took a long drink.

"It is quite a story," Rafe said. "Worse than what Gemma told. She obviously tried to protect you...and us."

He thought of Gemma's giving spirit. Her need to save everyone else around her. "That would be like her."

Rafe smiled, but it wavered almost immediately. "Why didn't you talk to me before this, Cris?"

Crispin got to his feet and paced to the fire. He stared into the flames as he tried to find the answer. "At first, I couldn't believe I was being seduced by the charms of a lady, of all things. Once I discovered she was engaged, I think I didn't tell you to protect her reputation. By the time she had married, you were knee-deep in your inheritance of your dukedom, in your own situation with Serafina. I didn't want to lay it at your feet."

"And?" Rafe asked softly.

Crispin turned, smiling even though his heart hurt. His brother knew him too well. "And a part of me hated you, even as I tried to help you win Serafina, for having what I believed had been stolen from me. Once Alice was dead…well, I was no use to anyone. I wanted to punish myself."

"You certainly did that," Rafe said with a shake of his head. "Almost to your own death."

"And yet it now turns out that everything I built my love and guilt around was nothing more than a lie." Crispin faced the fire again and the anger in his chest burned even hotter than the logs before him. "And perhaps part of me knew that. Maybe I reacted so strongly to Gemma pointing out the unfairness of Alice's behavior because I already knew she was untrue. But to admit that meant admitting I was…wrong. So wrong."

His brother was silent for a few moments, allowing Crispin his reflection on the past. Then he cleared his throat. "Do you love Gemma?"

Crispin stiffened. That was the question he had been trying not to answer for weeks. To have it asked now, in this moment, was like a kick to the gut. He faced Rafe with a frown.

"We're talking about Alice," he said.

"No. We *were* talking about your past. Now let's talk about your future. Do you love her?"

Crispin stared at Rafe. Despite their difficult beginning, he knew Rafe adored Serafina with a dedication and passion he never would have thought his brother capable of. And she felt as strongly about him. Their love was obvious. But his…he didn't know what it was. Especially now when he feared he couldn't trust himself to know his own heart.

"How do you know?" he asked.

Rafe stood. "When you want her happiness more than your own. When you would *die* to give it to her. And before you died, you would only want to see her face. But you also want to *live* for her. To create a future. A life. A family. A home. To see her through her darkest times and celebrate her best. And she's the only one who you want by your side at your own darkest and best times. *That* is love, Crispin."

He shut his eyes. Rafe was describing exactly how he felt about Gemma. In so short a time, she had so fully inserted herself in everything that mattered to him and he wanted her there. Forever.

"I love her," he managed to choke out, the words seeming thick and heavy on his lips.

"Of course you do," Rafe said with a laugh. "But if you don't say it and *show it* soon, you will lose her. And I think you have lost more than enough already." His brother moved on him. "Go home. To your *wife*."

Crispin nodded as he reached out to clap Rafe's shoulder. "Thank you."

CHAPTER TWENTY-SIX

Gemma sat on the bed she had shared with Crispin for such a short time, yet it felt like home being here in the space. Still, she was watching the dismantling of this home as she watched Kate slowly pack her things. The maid would look up at her from time to time, questions in her eyes.

But they weren't questions Gemma could answer. Not to her servant. Not to herself.

The door behind them opened and Gemma slid from the bed to her shaking feet as Crispin stepped inside. He looked disheveled, tired, raw in a way she'd never seen before. He stared at her for a long, charged moment, before his attention was caught by her trunks and Kate's presence in the room.

"What are you doing?" he asked.

She took a step toward him and immediately regretted it. It was silly, but she felt like she could feel his body heat, even from so far away.

"I-I—" she began, trying to find the words.

He turned to her maid. "Kate, please leave." Kate looked at Gemma, but he raised a hand and pointed to the door. "Don't look at her, just step out. Go downstairs and eat something. Please."

Kate ducked her head and all but ran from the room, leaving Gemma alone with her fate. Crispin looked at her another moment before he stepped back and closed and locked the door in one smooth motion. He dropped the key in his pocket and turned toward her once more.

"Where is everyone else?" he asked, changing the subject. "My sister and mother and Serafina?"

She shook her head. He must have gone to Rafe's home, for he was the only one who knew the entire family had come to sit and wait with her, offering their comforting platitudes about love. Except Crispin didn't love her. And the more she thought of it, the more oppressive their company had become.

"I managed to convince them that I could be left on my own," she whispered. "And finally got Mary to believe I didn't need her to stay with me."

"And then you came up to our bedroom. And what are you doing?" He repeated his first question, and there was a strain to his voice that she had never heard before.

She turned away. There was no hiding now, but at least she wouldn't have to look at him when she said the next thing. "I-I went too far." Her voice broke and she swiped at the tear that tried to wend its way down her already tear-streaked cheeks. "I went too far. I pushed you and—"

"I want to be pushed," he interrupted her.

She spun around and found that he had taken two steps toward her. He wasn't yet touching her, but if he reached out his hand, he could. And now she truly *could* feel his body heat.

"What?"

"I *needed* to be pushed," he said. "And I don't want you to go."

That sentence was like a gunshot to her chest, and Gemma staggered. Everything in her told her to launch herself into his arms and make love to him. If she touched him, she knew he would let her. And they could pretend this hadn't happened, perhaps. Go back to how it was.

But there was one thing she'd learned in the past few hours while she waited for him. The way it was…wasn't enough.

"You told me that when Alice offered to be your lover,

you told her you couldn't."

He jolted. "This isn't about her."

"But I can't do the same with you," she finished.

He shook his head. "What do you mean?"

"I can't be your lover, Crispin."

He reached for her and she shivered as his fingers brushed her cheek. "You are my wife," he reminded her.

"I am not your wife because you chose me," she said. "We were forced into this circumstance, and the most you have been able to do is make me your mistress. I am your mistress with your name, Crispin. And I can't be that."

"Then don't."

She tilted her head, uncertain if he meant that she could be more or that she was right to end things between them. But before she could ask, he shocked her by falling to his knees.

"Let me love you, Gemma Flynn. Let me start over."

Her lips parted and she could hardly breathe as he reached to take her hand and drew her closer. She stared down at him. "What?"

"I love you," he said, his voice shaking with emotion. "I have tried to pretend it wasn't happening, out of guilt and self-loathing. But you broke the lock I've tried to keep around myself, Gemma. *You* were the key. And not just today when you gave me my freedom from my guilt over Alice. But before that. Since I found you in my bed and discovered you were my wife, you have been setting me free bit by bit. I *love* you."

She was dreaming. That was all there was to it. She'd fallen asleep and now this very vivid dream was offering her everything she'd ever wanted.

"You are shaking your head," he said, still not rising from his place before her. "Does that mean you don't love me anymore? Did I wait too long?"

She made a pained sound from the very pit of her soul and clasped his hand with both of hers. "I do, I do love you," she said.

His face lit up with happiness. True happiness. Real

happiness. Something she'd never seen in his eyes before. And he looked younger and even more handsome than he had ever been. So handsome she nearly dropped down to the floor with him to kiss him.

"Please be my wife," he asked.

She blinked. "I am your wife," she said with a laugh.

He shook his head. "No, you misunderstand. *Be* my wife. Let me *be* your husband. In truth. By choice. In every way. For now and for always. Please, please, Gemma. Say that you'll stay with me."

She stared at him. "You—you mean it," she whispered.

He nodded. "I mean it, Gemma. I truly do."

She slid down to her knees with him and cupped his face. Here was this man. This beautiful, complicated, everything man. And he loved her. Wanted her. Despite their beginning, despite all that had kept them apart since it. He loved her. And she so desperately loved him.

"Yes," she whispered as she stroked a tear from his cheek with a smile. "Yes, I'll stay with you. And build our life with you. And I will love you until the day I die."

He let out a cry of happiness and dragged her against him, joining their lips with the same hunger that every kiss contained. But this one was different. This one connected them as they had never allowed themselves to be connected before. And as he lowered her back on the carpet, his kisses growing deeper and more purposeful, she knew for the first time that her future was going to be everything she'd ever dreamed of.

EPILOGUE

"Little Crispin is already picking up bad habits from Big Crispin," Serafina teased as she entered the room, and Crispin stopped kissing his wife.

All heads swiveled to the baby, who was now sitting up by himself at the table. As if on cue, Little Crispin laughed and the table erupted with more of the same.

"I think it's a good thing if he sees such love in his midst," Rafe said, catching his wife and dragging her into his lap before he dipped her back and kissed her just as passionately as Crispin had kissed Gemma.

Marcus and Annabelle looked at each other, shrugged and also joined in before their mother waved her napkin at them all. "Stop it now! Not only are you embarrassing poor Mary, but the food is getting cold."

Once again the table filled with laughter and talking as the rest fell into raucous conversation. Gemma leaned forward to join in the talk, but Crispin caught her arm before she could and drew her attention back where he liked it best. On him. Her gray eyes lit up with love, just as they had been for three months.

"Do you know my secret?"

She smiled. "I know all your secrets, don't I?"

He shook his head. "Mama would say not. So would Rafe.

Though you know most. But this is a *new* secret."

She was laughing now and leaned in, her soft scent filling his nostrils, her warm touch tangling through every cold part of him. "What is your new secret?"

"I love you more each and every day," he whispered, close to her ear.

She swatted his leg gently. "It is a secret we share, then," she murmured. "For I feel the same way. But I have one of my own."

He tilted his head. "Do you? And what is that?"

She leaned closer and said, "The baby is coming in May of next year."

He drew back, his heart leaping. "Baby? What baby?"

She didn't answer, but just smiled and drew a hand across her belly. He stared into the eyes of this woman, his wife. He had never expected to find her, certainly never expected to want her and love her as deeply as he now did. What was equally shocking was how much he wanted the baby she had just revealed was coming. A child created from their love. A child who would carry his name and perhaps her eyes.

"Crispin?" she asked, her tone filled with concern. "Are you happy about this?"

"Happy?" he repeated on a laugh. Then he let out a bark of joy that shocked the entire table into silence. It was an amazing thing to realize his heart had never been so full. "I have never been so excited to meet another person in my life."

Other Books by Jess Michaels

THE NOTORIOUS FLYNNS
The Other Duke (Book 1)
The Scoundrel's Lover (Book 2)

THE LADIES BOOK OF PLEASURES
A Matter of Sin
A Moment of Passion
A Measure of Deceit

THE PLEASURE WARS SERIES
Taken By the Duke
Pleasuring The Lady
Beauty and the Earl
Beautiful Distraction

MISTRESS MATCHMAKER SERIES
An Introduction to Pleasure
For Desire Alone
Her Perfect Match

ALBRIGHT SISTERS SERIES
Everything Forbidden
Something Reckless
Taboo
Nothing Denied

Jess Michaels raffles a FREE Kindle or Amazon gift certificate EVERY month to members of her newsletter, so sign up on her website: http://www.authorjessmichaels.com/join-the-jess-michaels-newsletter/

**Take a Sneak Peek at *No Gentleman for Georgina*
Book 4 of the Notorious Flynns:**

CHAPTER ONE

Paul Abbot had no idea why the Duke and Duchess of Hartholm continually insisted on inviting him to their balls and soirees. He had no title, little fortune and he was nothing more than the manager at their brother-in-law's notorious club.

But perhaps that was the answer. His employer's new family, the Flynns, were welcoming to all comers and for some reason he had been swept up in their wake. But he knew his place even if they pretended not to do the same.

And so he stood as far to the back of the ballroom as he could, watching the attendees to the ball swirl by in their foppery and finery. He sipped his one and only drink for the evening and all but forced himself not to look at the pocket watch tucked in his jacket.

"Counting the moments until you can flee is not good manners," he murmured to himself as he stifled a yawn. There was nothing here to tempt him.

Nothing but…

The moment his mind began that errant thought, his gaze slid across the room and landed squarely on the one and only temptation London Society had ever held for him.

Miss Georgina Hickson stood on the other side of the room. And she was beautiful, just as she was always beautiful. Her dark blonde hair was fixed just so that it framed her oval face perfectly, accentuating high cheekbones and full, rosy lips. He had wondered, more than once, how those lips would taste.

Her bright blue eyes were expressive as she chatted with her companions.

Companions who were all men.

His heart sank. Georgina never seemed to be short of partners when he was invited to events they mutually attended. Paul held his breath every day when he looked at the notices in the Times, waiting to see an announcement of her impending nuptials to the Earl of Very Important Things or the Duke of So Far Above Paul Abbot.

As if she sensed his stare on her, she suddenly looked across the room. Her gaze locked on him and her smile broadened. His heart stuttered and he forced himself to smile back, to lift a hand in a polite wave.

She returned it, then spoke to her companions once more before she began to come across the room toward him.

Paul held his breath as he watched her approach. He had less than thirty seconds to give himself the same talk he always did when Georgina came near. The talk that reminded him that when they had been introduced at a party to celebrate the shocking marriage of his employer, Marcus Rivers and Georgina's good friend, Annabelle Flynn, two years ago, that Georgina had only been polite to talk to him. That it was her continued politeness which drove her to carry on their odd friendship all these years later.

She was a nice girl and she had to recognize just how out of place he was at these gatherings. Beyond that, her interest in him was less than nothing.

"Mr. Abbot," she said, that beautifully melodious voice washing over him like a soothing rain after a too-hot day. "I did not know you were in attendance or I would have sought out your company sooner."

He swallowed hard and found his voice. "You seemed quite enthralled, I would not have pulled you away from your companions."

She glanced over her shoulder at her circle of men. "Them? Not enthralled, I assure you, nor they in me. We were discussing the weather, of all things." She rolled her eyes and laughed. "I cannot tell you how utterly uninterested I am in the Almanac's predictions for this year's rainfall."

He laughed. "That does sound rather dull."

"So in a way, you saved me," she said with another of those dazzling smiles. "I am most obliged."

"At your service," he said with a stiff bow that brought a twinge of pain to his shoulder. Pain he had been ignoring for well over a decade and intended to continue ignoring now.

"How are you, then?" she asked. "I feel like I have not seen you in an age. I always look forward to your company when I visit Annabelle and Marcus's home."

Paul shifted. He wished he could say the same to her, but from his lips those words would be a desperate confession versus her polite over statement.

"With Rivers spending more time at home, we *do* often conduct our business there." He smiled.

"It must be rather thrilling, running such a successful establishment."

His smile slowly faded. Being an innocent, Georgina had no idea the truth about the club he managed. The Donville Masquerade, Rivers' den of sex and gambling, would horrify her if she ever did discover the reality of it.

"Sometimes I think I should sneak a visit there, perhaps convince Annabelle to allow it," she said with a light laugh.

Paul stiffened at the idea of Georgina there. Of watching her watch the debauched acts. Despite himself, his cock began to swell at the thought and he fought for the control he always held over himself before he said, "I doubt your father would approve of such a plan, Miss Hickson."

She shrugged, but the light in her eyes dimmed a little. "My father approves of so little I do anymore, Mr. Abbot. It makes me wonder if I should not try to please myself for a little while since he will not be pleased by *any* action I do or do not take."

About the Author

Jess Michaels writes erotic historical romance from her home in Tucson, AZ. She has three assistants: One cat that blocks the screen, one that is very judgmental and her husband that does all the heavy lifting. She has written over 50 books, enjoys long walks in the desert and once wrestled a bear over a piece of pie. One of these things is a lie.

Jess loves to hear from fans! So please feel free to contact her in any of the following ways (or carrier pigeon):
www.AuthorJessMichaels.com
PO Box 814, Cortaro, AZ 85652-0814

Email: Jess@AuthorJessMichaels.com
Twitter www.twitter.com/JessMichaelsbks
Facebook: www.facebook.com/JessMichaelsBks

Jess Michaels raffles a FREE Kindle or Amazon gift certificate EVERY month to members of her newsletter, so sign up on her website:
http://www.authorjessmichaels.com/join-the-jess-michaels-newsletter/

Printed in Great Britain
by Amazon.co.uk, Ltd.,
Marston Gate.